The Leopard of Fernandina

The Leopard of Fernandina

By
David Tuttle

Library of Congress Control Number: 2005907887

Tuttle, David 1941-
The Leopard of Fernandina

ISBN 13: 978-0-9677419-7-0
ISBN 10: 0-9677419-7-1

Published by Lexington Ventures, Inc.
107 Centre Street
Fernandina Beach, FL 32034

Printed in the United States of America
Delta Printing Solutions
28210 N. Avenue Stanford
Valencia, CA 91355

Cover Design by Thomas R. Johannes Graphics.

Acknowledgements

Research adds realism to any story. Many people helped as I struggled to achieve realism in *The Leopard of Fernandina.*

I spent time with Lt. Willie Scott of the Fernandina Beach Fire/Rescue. He led me through the flow of events that occur when they get a call to save a life.

Sheree Williams at the Nassau Baptist Hospital's Emergency Room helped a great deal. Sheree is the charge nurse, and her insight on what happens from when a patient is brought in until the patient is taken by TraumaOne helicopter to Jacksonville, was impressive. Thanks to Debbie Dunman and Mimi Stewart for arranging my meeting with Sheree. Thanks to the Nassau Baptist Hospital staff.

Andrew Curtin, Viet Nam veteran and TraumaOne helicopter pilot, assisted in sorting out what happens when he is called on to transfer critically injured people to hospitals. Andy and his fellow pilots do it every day and receive too little credit.

Dr. William Birdsong, an old dear friend, guided me through the telling of the story and prevented me from making some medical blunders. With his help, I discovered how the average person, such as myself, could get a sequence of medical events all wrong. His suggestions made the scenes more real to me.

Not only is it essential to get facts straight, but also getting a foreign language correct is most important. Leslie Zambrano did the Spanish translations for me.

Lt. Jim Coe, of the Fernandina Beach Police Department, is a valuable source of information and guidance into investigative procedures. Jim is the Supervisor of Investigation at the department, the same position as Wilson holds, the main character in both *The Leopard of Fernandina* and *Murder In Fernandina*. Jim also wrote a few chapters for *Murder In Fernandina*.

My friend of great patience is Cara Curtin. Cara read the first draft and ran out of red ink while making corrections to punctuation and grammar. I love her line, "David is a good storyteller." The other side of the page that I read is, and I do this with a smile, "...but he can't get his 10th grade English to kick in."

Editors, I have found out, have no qualms about stepping on egos. Thank goodness for that quality. Emily Carmain did excellent work with *Murder In Fernandina* and I went to her again to edit *The Leopard of Fernandina*. Writers over-write and editors bring them back to earth.

None of the above could have happened without the encouragement and help of my publisher, Don Shaw. On several occasions, his infectious enthusiasm was what I needed to continue this project. Thanks to Don. Jan Johannes is a master of layout and graphic design. The end result of this project, included the graphic talents of his son, Tom Johannes, who designed the cover.

Above all, thanks to my wife, Barbara, for missing me while I hid away in the computer room day after day.

Foreword

The *Leopard of Fernandina* sprang out of the darkness. Perhaps I had been unconsciously thinking about the sequel and it decided to make its appearance at this terrible hour of 3 a.m. I got up, went to the computer and started writing. After many cups of coffee, I stopped around noon and slept for a couple of hours, then went back at it.

So began the further adventures of Wilson, the Supervisor of Investigations of the Fernandina Beach Police Department. Readers kept asking questions: why was Dianne's car at the Ritz, do Wilson and Dianne get married, who was the man in green at LaFontaine's funeral and does Wilson actually have a first name?

Wilson is now teamed with a tactless detective from the past, learns Dianne has a fondness for Pre-Columbian art, moves in social circles he's uncomfortable in, and briefly finds out that there are ghosts haunting some Amelia Island residents. His search for the Leopard has him chasing a potential murder suspect on jet skis down the Amelia River and to a startling revelation.

Over the next four and a half months, I spent most waking hours writing the rest of the story. Yes, some of those waking hours were at 3 a.m.

This time around, it was my "voice," thus my style of writing and not the gathering of ten different authors, as in *Murder In Fernandina*. You will find some of the characters again, the main ones, of course, and a few new ones drop in to add flavor and diversion to Wilson's investigation.

When word got around that I was working on a sequel, many people said they were looking forward to it and asked would I keep Wilson alive. I said I wasn't sure; we'd have to see. We'll see.

Chapter 1

April 2004

Alfred, right now, that's not my concern. Your job is to see things like this don't happen, yet it did. What are you going to do about it?" The cold voice snapped out the words.

The answer came quickly, "I'll see to it that whoever took the shipment will be dealt with and we'll get it back."

"This is the third time it's happened. The others weren't too bad and I overlooked it, but this one is worth several million. You know this can't go on."

"I know, and it won't. Believe me."

There was a pause. "Do you know who might be behind the theft of the shipment?"

"One of my men said he recognized somebody he worked with in Texas. That's all I know now. It could either be Houston or Dallas people." The reply was apologetic, but it didn't go down well.

"I'll make a call out there. In the meantime, I want to see you up here. Bring whatever you have left. The people up here need some reserves. Use the *Well Behind* and make it look like a pleasure cruise up the Intracoastal Waterway. I don't want any suspicions aroused, so don't screw this up.

Can you do that?"

"Yes, Leopard. It will be there safely."

"It better be." The Leopard hung up the phone, pausing only to glance at the guest before striding across the imported Italian marble floor. The expensive leather slippers didn't make a sound. Once through the french doors, a cigarette was lit and gray eyes looked over the sand dunes to the calm Atlantic Ocean. The ever-present wind blew the cigarette smoke back toward the multi-million-dollar house. The fountain's water danced in the wind, spilling over fine marble into the pool below. A jungle-like array of strategically placed shrubs and flowering plants framed the view to the ocean.

A tall man wearing a green shirt and shorts followed the Leopard into the golden sunlight that flooded Amelia Island. He sipped smooth bourbon from a Waterford glass while the host again stared at the ocean, thinking of which option would best suit the situation. Finally, the Leopard spoke, "Board the boat in St. Augustine, and after the drop here, kill him and drop the body in the ocean. You can gather sharks by tossing raw meat out for chum." The voice was expressionless. "No one will ever find the body."

The man in green nodded silently, his sandy hair tossed by the breeze.

The eyes narrowed as the words came, "I'll call the boat's captain later and tell him to follow your orders. You knew Alfred in Miami?"

"Only in a business way, never face to face. He didn't work that way. You might say we…aren't on the same plane. He has his friends and I have mine." The man took another sip of his drink. "I know that he's smart and he'll have people with him who are dedicated to his welfare."

"Loyalty can be bought and sold easily enough." With a wave of the hand the Leopard added, "I've heard rumors that in the Miami trade…" the cigarette was lifted slowly

"…loyalty follows the winds." A gust of wind blew the smoke toward the ocean and then back.

The guest swirled the remaining bourbon in his glass, looked at it, then finished the drink. "One has to protect one's interests and obligations."

"Precisely." The piercing gray eyes searched for a reaction.

"I'm out of Miami now. My services aren't…let's say…ah, needed there at this time."

"I have you here to do one thing only. I've mulled this over for some time and he's getting greedy. I don't believe this Texas crap he's telling me." The Leopard paused. "And I know he's stealing from me. I have contacts in many places and if *you* decide to take the money and walk… well, a person in your line of work is easy to track down, and I'll make your life uncomfortable."

"Oh, come on. Let's not start with the veiled threats. You know the story of the three monkeys and evil." He smiled broadly to show the Leopard he wasn't rattled.

"You have the brass balls of a monkey, too; I like that." The host walked back into the house, but stopped at the doors and turned. "The captain will call me ship-to-shore when Alfred swims. The boat will return to the Fernandina docks. Your money will be waiting for you. It will be in a plain package and I'll leave it in the Harbor Master's office under the name of Simms." The host stayed in the doorway, indicating that the underling wasn't to go in. "That's it. I don't want any connection between us. Come here again — you're dead."

The assassin knew his not-so-gracious host meant what was said. He adjusted his sunglasses. "It's been real and it's been fun, but it ain't been real fun."

The Leopard watched him saunter along the side of the house, and then called after him, "By the way, don't worry about Alfred's people. They know where their paychecks come from."

Chapter 2

Spring days replaced the mild winter, and the Fernandina Beach Police Department challenged the Nassau County Sheriff's Department to a benefit softball game. The proceeds were going to the Police Athletic League's new building under construction near the Peck Community Center. Both departments hoped the game would be an annual event and the next year's proceeds would go to the Sheriff's outreach program.

In the dazzling blue sky, wisps of cirrus clouds lazily floated. The Saturday morning game was loose and good-natured insults were tossed about. Players on both sides jostled the umpire, the City Manager of Fernandina Beach. No one missed an opportunity to give him a hard time.

Toward the end of the game, Chief Charles Evans, a lean, muscular African-American in his fifties came over and sat next to Detective Lieutenant Wilson. Evans' easygoing ways with his men won his department's endorsement when he was selected as the Chief of Police of Fernandina Beach three years ago. The former chief had been convicted of murdering two people; one a prominent wealthy citizen and the other, well known but not so well off.

"Why didn't Dianne play? Afraid she might outdo you?" He nudged Wilson.

"She said it's a testosterone thing that the male animal has to go through this ritual every so often. Something like that. You know, sometimes college screws your brain up." They both laughed. "Actually, Dianne is getting ready for tonight."

Evans looked at his Supervisor of Investigations and raised an eyebrow.

He quickly explained as he tossed back a foul ball, "Tonight's our third anniversary."

"Has it been three years? Doesn't seem like it, does it?"

"No, it doesn't." Wilson recalled the wedding day, especially the shoes that were a half size too small. Dianne had looked radiant, as all brides must. The beautiful auburn-haired secretary he'd met at the police station captured the hearts of all the guests. During their courtship, she had attended the Jacksonville Police Academy and become a patrol officer in the Fernandina Beach Police Department.

Wilson, a widower, had been nervous among the crowd of wedding guests. As a former Army Ranger and now a police detective, he was trained to be cool under unusual circumstances, but he had let his guard down. Dianne had put her arm through his and whispered to him as the photographer took picture after picture, "Turn more to the right, honey" or "This photo is just for us girls, honey."

His two daughters were the flower girls and fidgeted next to Wilson during the ceremony. He and the girls, Priscilla, then eight years old, and Lisa, five, had long talks about the new life that his remarriage was going to bring. He explained his love for their mother would never diminish, but they all needed someone in their lives.

At the wedding reception, Priscilla announced to her family that she now wanted to be called by her middle name, Michelle, since her Grandma Wilson was Priscilla, and she didn't want any confusion when they were together. Wilson agreed, since she had already refused to be called "Prissy" any longer.

Dianne had insisted the honeymoon be a Disney cruise with all four of them going.

Wilson was brought back to reality when he heard the chief yell, "Incoming!" and another errant foul ball kicked dirt on Wilson and hit the lawn chair next to him. Evans laughed as he said, "Yes, sir, you were really on top of that one."

Wilson retrieved the ball and tossed it back. "Just remembering the wedding day."

"You better pay attention to this game, boy, we're about to lose." Evans nudged him again.

"Right."

"Win or lose, I'd like you and Dianne to come to my office on Monday morning."

"Both of us, huh?"

"Yes, it's something I can't discuss here, but I need both of you in there."

Jacqueline Evans strolled over to offer cold bottles of water to the two. "You aren't talking police business again, are you, Charles?"

He looked at his wife, took the water and gave one to Wilson. "Not me – you, Wilson?"

"No, ma'am."

She looked at them for no more than a second. "Right. Leave it at the office, okay?"

"Yessum," they said in unison.

Chapter 3

S omewhere in the Caribbean, a United States Navy E2C Hawkeye Command and Control aircraft taxied onto a runway. "Seeker Two Four, cleared for take-off." The tower operator clipped his words into the microphone.

"Roger. Seeker Two Four on the roll." The aircraft commander eased two throttles forward. The turbine powered plane leaped down the runway, accelerated on the long concrete strip and lifted off into the setting sun.

Climb-out was routine, and, reaching cruising altitude, the pilots settled in for a boring night working on this drug interdiction mission. They would be the airborne Command and Control for intercepts that might occur in their area of responsibility.

Night after night, they or one of the four other crews assigned to the Southern Region Air Defense took to the skies in a craft with a huge saucer on top of the frame that housed long-range surveillance radar. Inside the tiny fuselage, four officers readied themselves for the night of watching radar screens. They would monitor the world in a three-hundred-mile radius. Anything that moved at a speed over fifty miles an hour would be picked up and tracked.

The lieutenant commander in charge sat back in his padded chair while he watched and waited for a target to appear.

Three weeks earlier, a continent away, a reconnaissance satellite had revealed to photo interpreters a narrow strip of freshly cleared ground in the dense vegetation nestled in an Andes Mountain valley. A pre-dawn flight by a U-2 plane confirmed the new ground was a four-thousand-foot runway carved onto a flat spot in the hills below towering snow-capped mountains.

Now a black private jet sat there in the fading sunlight while men swiftly loaded kilo bricks of cocaine in silence. The aircraft's nose was pointed down the sloping dirt grade. The pilot hoped this would ease the task of gaining enough speed to get his heavy-laden airplane in the air, and not be splattered on the hills beyond. John Mason sat in the cockpit while the boxes were stacked against the shut door, sealing him in the tiny space.

Mason felt the weight of his 9-millimeter pistol against his chest and saw armed guards standing at the jungle's edge. More guards stood around the plane. The one directly in front of the left wing, who seemed to be in charge, watched both the loading and the pilot, while keeping the AK-47 propped on his hip. Mason finally heard and felt the cargo door slam shut. The dark figure looked at the pilot and spun the rifle barrel in little circles to tell him to start the engines and take off. There was no expression on the guard's face as he and the others melted into the trees. The whine of the turbines rose higher in pitch as they spun up to speed. Mason realized he had to urinate. He held the brakes and pushed the throttles forward, hoping his bladder pressure would ease in the five-hour flight. He knew from experience not to drink anything several hours before flying but the tense situation caused his body to react.

The engines were at 100 percent; he released the brakes and guided the sleek black craft down the runway, blasting dust into the air. He lifted off into the dark valley that lay beneath mountains where snow glistened, tinted rose by the setting sun. Watching from the trees, the leader of the band of camouflaged uniformed men stared up at freshly painted numbers on the jet flashing past him.

———— •■• ————

"Attention please, PanAir Flight 1032, non-stop from Bogota to Miami is now boarding at Gate 21. This is the final call for first-class passengers. Thank you."

Sean O'Brien followed his wife toward the door while watching for the woman who owned the silky voice that made the announcement. Not spotting her, he entered the jet-way and headed into the 747's first-class section. Connie O'Brien was barely aware of her husband's movements behind her. She carefully found the three-seat row she had requested and placed the package she cradled on the middle seat. She had bought a ticket for this package, a one-foot cube, and was taking her time to see that it was properly cared for. The O'Briens sat, separated by the package. Before long, the PanAir Flight 1032 with its human cargo and one precious package was lifting off for its flight to Miami.

———— •■• ————

At Caracas International Airport, three men sat in a private jet waiting on the taxiway for their turn to take off. It was an exact copy of the jet John Mason was flying. The sun had just set, painting the sky in brilliant coral and gold streaks.

Finally, the jet taxied into position. "Sierra Two One Seven November, cleared for take off," the control tower radioed the black jet. The pilot looked over at his copilot and pushed the throttle forward. Easily, with several thousands of pounds of thrust, the engines pushed the jet up to join the moonless night.

While the call sign broadcast to the tower had been

correct, quick drying paint had been sprayed on the plane to give it new numbers before it left the ramp.

--- • ● • ---

"I don't see why you couldn't have checked that jug in with the luggage," Sean said to his wife.

She didn't fully turn to him. "I don't want some baggage handler tossing my ten-thousand-dollar piece of Pre-Columbian work around in the belly of an airplane. And it's not a *jug*, it is an incense urn for the dead."

Sean was not interested in the artifact. "Probably fake," he said, looking out the window.

"If it is, I'll come back and wring Pablo's neck."

On into the sky the 747 airliner climbed while, far away, the two private business jets sped toward a point in the Caribbean that would intersect the airliner's path.

--- • ● • ---

Mason set the Colombian jet's autopilot course to zero three zero and altitude to a thousand feet, then wiped the sweat from his forehead. This path would take him over the Windward Passage between Cuba and Haiti; then he'd turn to head almost north to Florida. He wanted to stay low to avoid any radar that might be out there. The altimeter stayed at a thousand feet. He didn't like flying this low, especially at four hundred and fifty knots, and at night.

He took the headset off and leaned back against the padded headrest, closing his eyes for a minute. Mason thought of this last flight and the money he would make. He could pay off his debts and get his wife and three daughters out of the hole where they were living. He hoped to move to a new part of the States where he could start over and not have to risk the danger of going to prison for decades if caught.

He opened his eyes to look at his watch; the rendezvous

would be in one hour and fifteen minutes. He spun the small black knobs on the radio's control box; setting the numbers to the contact frequency he was told to monitor. The radar screen displayed several targets, but none concerned him at the moment. He laid his head back and blew air out, puffing up his cheeks. He wanted this flight to be over.

———————— • ■ • ————————

Inside the Navy E2C, the radar screen's glow cast dim images of the men who hunkered over them. Each dot on the screen, representing aircraft, had markers on it identifying it by type and flight number. All aircraft that entered their radar range were supposed to file flight plans to avoid being intercepted by U.S. drug interdiction program enforcers. The regular flights out of South American countries were well known to the crew of Seeker Two Four. so when an unknown showed up they could tell with fair certainty that it was an aircraft loaded with contraband.

The lieutenant at the third console pressed his microphone button. "Skip, we've got a bogie in Sector Seven Easy. Speed...four hundred fifty knots. Looks like a biz jet. Heading zero three zero. No transponder code or altitude info but he looks low...less than two thousand, I'd guess."

The lieutenant commander leaned over and took a look. After several seconds he said, "Okay, I'll send it in to Southern Region. Let them worry about it. We just find 'em, they kill 'em," he joked and turned to push a few buttons on his console. He soon had the information relayed by way of the satellite system orbiting 23,000 miles overhead. He turned back to the screens. A circle was around the unknown target now moving swiftly from the coast of Colombia.

———————— • ■ • ————————

Over a thousand miles away, at the American armed

forces Southern Region Command Center, radar information was silently streaming to a bank of operators. A chain-link fence surrounded the nondescript building in Dade County, Florida. It fit in the industrialized neighborhood, and this one, too, had a guard at the gate. What made this guard different from most in the neighborhood was the M16 he carried, loaded with thirty rounds, and he was proficient at using it.

The data from Seeker Two Four instantly appeared on a large computer-driven screen. The supervisor looked at the information and pressed the radio mike switch attached to his belt. "Scramble two. Initial heading two seven zero."

On a small island in the Lesser Antilles, three Florida Air National Guard F-15 pilots ran from their Alert Shack to waiting jets. Four airmen scurried after them. One airman hurriedly snatched the *Remove Before Flight* tags, ground wires and other connections, while the others helped strap the pilots in their seats. One plane had two pilots in tandem; the other was a single seater. Tonight their call signs were FANG 12 and FANG 13.

In less than five minutes, their hours of training paid off as the night sky lit up with the fire from four high-powered jet engines. The blue flame traced the path taken by the advance jet fighters into the dark Caribbean sky. The tower controller was reminded of a welder's torch as the F-15s rotated for flight, then shot up at a forty-five-degree angle. He turned control of the fast moving jets over to the Southern Command's vast network. Their intercept would be controlled by Seeker Two Four.

———————— • ■ • ————————

In the black biz jet from Caracas, Sierra Two One Seven November, the copilot held the plane's encoding altimeter in his hand. While the pilot remained at the controls, a third man moved to the rear of the plane, opened the lavatory door, stepped in, then nodded to the copilot.

"Ready," the copilot told the pilot.

Looking at his radar screen, the pilot saw PanAir flight 1032 ahead by fifteen miles. On the left of the screen was another soft green dot, the Colombian jet.

The pilot keyed the microphone, "Mayday, mayday. Sierra Two One Seven November. Mayday, mayday." He paused, waiting for an answer.

There were several overlapping responses. Weak, yet the strongest of those answers was a controller saying, "Sierra Two One Seven November, Kingston Departure. How do you read and nature of emergency?"

"Kingston Departure, Two One Seven, One engine out and the other losing power. Squawking sevens on the transponder. Over."

"Roger, you are too far out. No radar contact. Your position please." The controller motioned for his supervisor to listen in, who in turn, notified several military units. They knew that the United States military had surveillance planes in the area south of them.

The pilot of the jet nodded to the copilot, who began to turn screws extending from the back of the encoding altimeter to send false altitude information over the transponder.

"We are approximately two hundred miles north-northeast of Maracaibo," the pilot responded.

"Stand by. We'll see who's in the area to assist." The Kingston controller came back. "Do you have an HF radio?"

"Negative," the pilot lied as the copilot listened to the HF long distance radio.

The copilot knew the emergency frequency of the HF radio and listened to the Kingston controller. "Seeker Two Four, Kingston Departure."

"Kingston, Seeker Two Four, go ahead."

The controller told them of the situation and asked if

they could rendezvous with the crippled jet. "We have three targets in that area and should be there in...fifteen minutes."

"Roger, Two Four. I'll relay. Thanks, Kingston Departure."

The sophisticated Seeker Two Four was able to receive and decode commercial aircraft transponder information, so the crew had the jet's flight plan annotated on the screens. The altitude information they were receiving was getting lower and lower. Seeker Two Four's copilot dialed in the civilian emergency frequency.

"Sierra Two One Seven November, Seeker Two Four. Do you copy?"

"Roger. Stand by for a second. It's a little busy here."

"Roger. Standing by. We'll be with you in fifteen minutes."

There was no response from Sierra Two One Seven November. The Caracas jet flashed its landing lights twice and in the near distance, one flash appeared in response. John Mason was right on the intercept course. Both jets saw PanAir Flight 1032 just a half mile ahead. The copilot of the "disabled" aircraft nodded back to the man in the lavatory. He lifted the lid of the toilet and slid a canister the size of a coffee can into a specially designed chute leading to the underside of the plane. He sealed the lid and pushed a release button. He heard a *whoosh*, then pushed the button again and the noise stopped.

By now the copilot had the false altimeter readings down to one hundred feet.

"Sierra Two One Seven ditching." The pilot radioed over the emergency frequency. The spiraling canister sped earthward and, when it reached an altitude of five hundred feet, exploded with vivid pyrotechnics.

John Mason maneuvered his plane just yards from the tail of the big PanAir plane. Tucked under here, he would not appear on any radar screen as long as he stayed less than one hundred feet from the giant 747.

Immediately the Caracas jet took the old heading of Mason's jet. Anyone tracking John's plane would think that the path had merely crossed that of Flight 1032. The kicker was the substitute plane had nothing on board that would qualify as contraband.

"Sierra Two One Seven, Seeker Two Four." Over and over again, the Navy plane's pilot tried to communicate with what he thought was a downed aircraft. After a few minutes he radioed, "Kingston Departure, Seeker Two Four. We saw a bright flash on the horizon — about twelve miles ahead. We just missed them."

The two scrambled F-15s were quickly approaching and the Seeker Two Four alerted them to the new problem.

They responded, "Seeker Two Four, FANG 12 flight. We saw the flash also. We're twenty out. What about the other target?"

The Seeker Two Four voice radioed back, "Roger, continue on the intercept and identify. Turn to heading three six zero and intercept."

The FANG 12 flight of F-15 Eagles banked and rolled out on the new heading. Seeker Two Four turned to the heading where the flash had appeared and the last radio contact had come from the biz jet. The pilot throttled back the engines and began a slow spiral to have a look at the black ocean below.

Mason's skill in flying kept his jet safely tucked under PanAir Flight 1032 and on its way to a landing spot near Florida's Everglades.

———————— • ■ • ————————

"Ladies and gentlemen, please raise your seats to the upright position. Our flight attendants will be serving dinner shortly. Thank you." The soft voice came over the overhead speakers. Connie had her eyes closed but did not sleep. Sean finished his second scotch and water. His wife opened her eyes to check on the treasure beside her, and Sean slowly shook his head in wonderment at her affinity for these "pots of grungy dirt," as he called them. He couldn't wait to get back. It was Friday night and the college football game reruns were on Saturday. He spent most of his weekends watching the games on TV or rounds of golf.

Connie, on the other hand, was an active woman. She lived life to its fullest, whatever whim struck her at the moment. At sixty-five, she had done everything from scuba diving to skydiving and taking flying lessons. She still kept her high school dress size, with the help of tennis and morning power walks on Amelia Island's beaches.

Sean, retired from a large food company, wanted to retain the feeling of power. He had had his own special reason for going to Colombia.

The flight attendant handed the couple their trays of better-than-average airline food, an assortment of dishes tagged with French names.

———————— •●• ————————

In the darkness, with no horizon to gauge level flight, the two F-15s headed toward their target. The lead pilot wiggled the wings slightly, indicating to the wingman to start his climb to be eight hundred feet higher and slightly behind the lead. He was in position to take any action to protect the lead plane. Two nights earlier this same crew had been fired upon from the opened copilot's window of a piston-powered twin-engine airplane. The machine gun's flame spat out of the barrel, missing the F-15. A two-second burst from the high-cap F-15's Gatlin gun sent the drug runners spinning into the sea below.

Now, the pilot in the rear seat of the lead F-15 switched off his instrument panel lights. He turned on the highly sensitive night-vision goggles, and then he clearly saw the target a quarter of a mile ahead and to the left.

Even on the darkest nights, the green amplified light gave a clear picture of the area. Starlight was enough to activate the sensors this night and the copilot hit his mike button.

"Seeker Two Four, FANG 12. We have target in visual and there are no markings on the jet. It's a Valiant, Model Fifty."

"Roger, FANG 12. Break it off, we'll contact INS and Border Patrol."

"Roger." The two F-15s banked right and, unseen by the crew of the dark jet, headed back to their tiny island base.

Seeker Two Four made a slow turn to the left and resumed its racetrack course in the sky.

PanAir Flight 1032 resembled a huge shark soaring along with a suckerfish attached to its belly. The crew and passengers were unaware of the drama surrounding them. The cocaine-laden Valiant Fifty, with Mason in the cockpit, matched every move of Flight 1032 and listened in on all of its radio contacts.

Seeker Two Four's controllers watched a green dot representing Flight 1032 on their screen head toward the east side of Cuba and on a course to Miami. They also tracked the Caracas Valiant Fifty, with three men inside but no cargo, as it made a slight turn on a more easterly heading, indicating perhaps it was headed to an island in the Bahamian chain.

Meanwhile, Flight 1032 turned for its final approach to Miami International Airport. This flight path took them over the Everglades National Park, where Mason saw the dim lights of his destination and left his decoy. He dropped quickly to land at a grass strip, into the waiting hands of a drug dealer's squad. Silent men hastily loaded bricks of cocaine from the plane onto trucks, and one passed a briefcase to Mason. It contained twenty-five thousand dollars in small bills.

"What about the plane and a car for me to get out of here?" Mason wanted to know.

"Don't know, man. We just were told to load and go; the plane's yours." The reply came as the pickup's engine started.

Mason started to move toward one truck. "Let me catch a ride into somewhere where I can get a car."

From almost nowhere a shiny pistol appeared, pointed directly at the pilot. "Listen, man, I could pop you right here and take your money and no one would find you for weeks, you know, after the buzzards got finished. So, you don't want to fly out of here? Start hiking." The pickup truck moved out, leaving Mason in the dark with a briefcase full of money, to watch the rapidly disappearing taillights.

In Miami, the O'Briens went through Customs with unusual ease and boarded a jet for Jacksonville to be met by a sleepy-eyed friend. The 3 a.m. arrival at Jacksonville International Airport meant not much more than nods of greeting and brief small talk while waiting for the one suitcase to appear at the luggage claim area. Connie held the Pre-Columbian treasure close to her the whole time.

The E2C, Seeker Two Four, followed the Caracas jet until it reached the edge of their control space, then another surveillance plane took over. The second surveillance plane followed it on radar to its landing at St. Eustatius, the small leeward island owned by the Netherlands. There, armed police surrounded it. The crew explained they were delivering the plane to a client in Bermuda. All the identification and paperwork verified their story.

The police inspected the plane and found no contraband, but fined the crew for lacking landing permission. The three men were told to refuel and proceed.

On Amelia Island, the O'Briens thanked the neighbor who had driven them from the airport and then retired for a long overdue sleep.

Chapter 4

At 8:01 a.m. a knock sounded on Chief Evans' door. "Come in." Evans unfolded his six-foot-two frame from his chair and moved around his desk to greet the Wilsons. "Dianne, you didn't have to be in uniform." He motioned them to chairs around the small conference table.

"I came on duty at 7, Chief." Dianne's appearance had undergone a radical change with the switch from secretarial attire to her police uniform, and she'd tamed her wavy auburn hair into a businesslike bun.

"Oh, okay." Evans said. "Here's what's happening. We've been asked by other agencies to participate in a drug bust on the island. It isn't a typical deal. They have good reason to believe that someone big in the operation is going to be in on this, and the deal will go down soon." He paused, giving them a moment to absorb the situation. "Since it's going to be on our turf, they want someone familiar with the area to be in on the bust, but it will be dangerous."

Wilson looked at Dianne. "And who is that *someone*?"

"Dianne, you've been here all your life and know every place along the Amelia River."

She nodded.

"A single person will coordinate people from INS, Border Patrol, and FDLE. It seemed like everyone wanted in on the bust, but we can't let too many people know about it; too much danger of leaks. There's a procedure we have to follow here. You, Wilson, will be the person I send."

Dianne started to speak but held back. The Chief looked at her and said, "The reason I called you both in is, now that you are on the force, Dianne, you realize what jeopardy he will be in. I feel that both of you have to agree that Wilson will take this case."

She interjected, "Was I considered?"

"Not really." Evans opened his hands. "I could throw all the old excuses at you. but it comes down to Wilson's experience."

"Yes, sir," she agreed with little enthusiasm.

"For the next few days, I want you two to go out on fishing trips together. Do you have a boat?"

They shook their heads. "Take mine. Dianne, you show him the places where a boat could be out of sight of the river traffic and still be able to unload a lot of cocaine. He'll need to tell the rest of the team about all of these nooks and crannies."

"Can I ask some questions?" Wilson spoke for the first time.

"Shoot, but FDLE will have most of the answers." Evans leaned back in his chair.

"Who from the FDLE is in charge? How many law enforcement people will be involved? Any from Miami? I know a few of the INS troops there."

"Jack Brandon is in charge." Wilson nodded and Evans continued, "I'm not privy to the rest of the information. Brandon is at the Best Western on Sadler Road. Here's his room number." He slid a sheet of paper to Wilson. "Do you want to do this?"

Wilson and Dianne looked at each other and she gave a slight nod, knowing the danger that he was going to face.

"Sure," Wilson said. "Brandon will be able to tell me who, what, when and where?"

"You better be sure, because there'll probably will be fireworks." Evans sighed heavily. "And we want to keep it low profile *and* away from town as much as possible. Brandon is expecting you at 10 this morning. Do you know him?"

Wilson nodded. "Yes, we rode together in Miami. He pushes the envelope sometimes to get a job done, but who hasn't?"

"Good. I'll call him in a few minutes. That's it…and thanks. I know you are the best one to do this."

Wilson and Dianne walked to the end of the hall and into the lobby. "Will I see you at lunch?" she asked.

"I don't know. I need to see what Brandon is up to. He sometimes can be a loose cannon and…well, we'll talk about it later." In the courtyard of the new Police Headquarters, he kissed his wife with a "See ya later," and she went to her patrol car parked at the curb.

The Police Department had moved to its new headquarters on Lime Street a year earlier. Leaving the old building in the downtown Historic District had been a wrench in some ways but had given the department much needed space and new facilities and furniture. Wilson had been glad to get rid of his old, squeaky chair. *Never did remember to bring in the WD-40.* He had almost kept it as an antique piece.

The old police station on Ash Street had long since been the victim of the wrecking ball, and someone had planted flowers along the sidewalk's edge, while the grounds had been cleared and smoothed.

Wilson punched the code into the key lock and entered his office. He glanced at the status board to see today's schedule and where the rest of the detectives were. The clock above the board displayed 8:30. He went to the coffee pot and poured the hot brew into the cup that had a big heart on it and "Number 1 Dad" on its side.

Leaning back, he looked at the family pictures on his desk. Lisa was a cute, innocent eight years old now, and Michelle at eleven was into pop music and pre-teen fashions that girls that age find new and fascinating. The girls flanked him and Dianne in the family portrait that his new wife had wanted. Lisa had a big, sincere smile with two missing baby teeth, while Michelle was clearly forcing a grin. Wilson was dismayed that his older daughter still hadn't fully accepted Dianne. It had been five years since their mother had died. He had toyed with the idea of looking into counseling about Michelle's attitude but Dianne was reluctant.

The door banged shut and Wilson looked up to see his new detective, Albert Newman, come in. When he nodded a good morning, Wilson greeted him with, "Al, do you go fishing much?"

"Uh...not as much as I'd like to." Newman raised his eyebrows.

"I'd like to get to know where some of the good deep spots are along the river." He motioned for Newman to sit down.

"Well, let's see. There are several spots I like, mostly where one creek flows into the river. That's where you can catch the red bass, when they're running. What are you trying to catch?"

Wilson grinned. "Crooks."

"Crooks? I'm not familiar with that fish."

"Just a bad joke. Drug runners might use a place along the river to dispose of their product. Just thinking out loud, really."

"Umm...that could be any place along the river. They wouldn't even have to stop. Just pass from one boat to another and continue on their way." Newman stood. "That's what I'd do. Do it down towards the south end of the island."

"Thanks, that helps…if I were after smugglers, that is."

Newman shrugged, turned to leave, and paused at the door to say, "Wilbur called in while you were in the Chief's office. He's stopped by on the way in to check a little more on the B&E yesterday morning."

"Okay. Thanks."

Wilson reached for his ringing telephone. "Investigations, Wilson."

"Honey, I've got just a second." His mother was on the other end of the line. "Nell is coming over to get me. You remember her?" She didn't wait for an answer. "We're going to the Senior Bingo at church, so if you call, that's where I am."

"Okay, Mom, I thought that was tomorrow. Thanks for letting me know." He was happy she was getting around some. "I have to run, too. Love you. And win a lot."

"I'll try. Goodbye, dear."

He sat back, shifted gears, and recalled the Jack Brandon he knew and how their paths had crossed. Jack had grown up in a tough neighborhood on the east side of Jacksonville, near the old Gator Bowl complex. Wilson recalled Jack saying that in his neighborhood you had to make one of two decisions: Get out and make something of your life or die with needle tracks for souvenirs. Jack's idea of getting out was to be a police officer.

This contrasted with Wilson's younger days when Charleston's middle-class neighborhood had given him the opportunity to do the normal teenage things. He'd tried marijuana and had gotten so sick he'd thought his guts were going to come up. That ended his drug experiments. He had weathered his father's tirades when he got the speeding tickets.

But Jack had always been on the fringes of the law and learned that working both sides had its benefits, as well as its pitfalls. He was smart enough to see that being on the side of the law generally added years to your life—especially after he buried his brother George. George had thought that being a drug dealer was the only way to make it, until a deal didn't go down as planned; an eight-inch hunting knife had cut short his path to riches.

Brandon finally had joined the Jacksonville Sheriff's Office. He always felt that busting a few heads while getting information was the way to work. Although generally succeeding, he had a higher than average number of police brutality complaints against him. Supervisors up and down the line had warned Jack many times that they wouldn't put up with his strong-arm methods. All the way from the Police Academy to his final disciplinary hearing, Jack had been warned about his tough hand. Jack resigned the day after that last hearing, thereby leaving him the option of being hired by another city.

Wilson remembered when he heard that the Miami police had hired a tough guy from Jacksonville. Patrolman Wilson had been assigned to ride in a neighborhood where the dealers and hookers stood at the street corners and were gutsy enough to approach you at traffic lights. He had been assigned in the zone for three months while waiting for his move into the Homicide Division. Then Jack Brandon was assigned to ride with him.

Brandon had seen the game in Jacksonville, and it wasn't any different in Miami: you arrest the hooker or dealer and they are back on the street before you finish your shift. The frustration factor rose when you'd go back and arrest them a week later on the same street corner. Jack had had to learn the Miami way of doing things, and it was touch and go for a while. Wilson tried to show him, but Jack's nature would surface. Busted heads got immediate results, but there were long-term consequences. Jack had been shot at from dark alleyways; his car had been followed. Wilson had told him that these were warnings to back off, but somehow Brandon survived the tough streets of Miami's drug culture.

On a patrol early one evening, Wilson had tried to explain, "You can bust the little people here and do it again the next week and the next week and the next. But you start moving up the line as to who's doing what, and you'll get nailed. You have to play by the rules."

"Screw the rules when you're dealing with these people. All they understand is fear. Not fear of you, or me, but fear of dying, because it's a fact they face every waking minute. You have to have been there to understand." Brandon paused, then said just above a whisper, "They're caged animals." Wilson remembered how Brandon's hands had been shaking.

"You're right, I don't understand from their perspective. I only know that we face dying, too, every time we come out here in a uniform. Any information you get, you pass on to Vice or Narcotics. Let them deal with the big people; we deal with the little people. That's the game."

The dispatcher sending them to a disturbance at a convenience store interrupted their conversation. When they arrived they had to part the crowd surrounding a person slumped against the side of the building. In the receding sunlight they could see a trail of smeared blood down the side of the building. They found a girl, maybe eighteen years old, with congealed blood trailing from the corner of her mouth. It had dripped on the dirty T-shirt before she died. Her eyes were still open. There was a triangle of blood starting where the small caliber bullet entered her chest, at the heart, and fanned out and down to the top of the shorts she wore. Her legs were splayed out in a last effort to stop herself from falling to the pavement. The two officers recognized her from having arrested her several times for drugs and prostitution. Wilson thought of the tragedy of a young life, while Brandon barked orders for the people to get back and went for the yellow crime scene tape. As he passed Wilson, he said, "That's the last time she'll spread her legs."

Wilson just looked at him and thought, *You're a real son-of-a-bitch.*

Chapter 5

W ilson entered the motel room, noting the smell of cigarettes in spite of the "non-smoking" placard on the door. He looked at the men sitting around the bed and recognized Brandon sitting cross-legged at the head of the bed.

"Wilson, come on in. Welcome to the case. Chief Evans said he had a good man but I didn't know it would be you." Brandon held out a beefy hand with a firm grip.

"Hi, Brandon. It's been awhile."

"Meet the rest of the team." He introduced the others with a wave of the open palm. "Bill Tisher, Homeland Security; Greg Bowman, ATF; David Kreznek, FDLE and the Coast Guard; and George Khee, FBI. Gentlemen, Wilson is from the Fernandina Beach Police Department."

Wilson nodded and shook hands with each in turn. "It's good to do something a little different."

Tisher spoke up with a forced smile, showing small teeth reminding Wilson of a row of small corn kernels. "It's good to have a small-town cop with little to do join us." Wilson had to bite back a retort, but just smiled and gripped the man's hand a little harder than needed. He could tell from the twitch of an eyebrow that the small-framed man felt the extra pressure.

"I'll try to stay out of your way," said Wilson, looking him in the eye.

"Okay, let's get to why we're here." Brandon took some papers from a briefcase and spread them on the bed. "There's going to be a shipment of cocaine coming up here in a while, but it's not too big, a little less than eight hundred twenty kilos, bricked and packaged. Our team's purpose is to apprehend one man who's the security and is coordinating for someone with a street name of the 'Leopard.' We know this security guy is from Miami."

"Where's this Leopard from?" Kreznek asked.

Brandon took a drag on a cigarette and shrugged his shoulders. "We're not sure. We suspect somewhere in Florida. Phone taps have narrowed it down and we're closing in on this guy."

He tossed several photos on the bed. "Take one of these and memorize his face. His name is Alfred Benoit, he's the security guy and coordinator." The photo showed a tall, medium-framed man with a silicone blonde on his arm. She was smiling at the silver-haired thug.

"Hell of a name for a dealer," said Kreznek. "Is *chickie* going to be with him?"

"Not that we know, and he's more than a dealer. Hell of a lot more. He's been implicated in several murders but nothing sticks. Always armed and with a permit to carry."

Wilson looked at the picture and remembered seeing the face on the pages of the *Miami Herald*. Like every cop, he always wished that just once he'd make the "big one," the one that put a big-time hoodlum away. He turned the photo over and looked at the blank back, while he thought back to the day he stood face to face with Benoit.

Benoit had been detained concerning the murder of a minor drug dealer in Miami and Wilson had been in on the questioning. Benoit had maintained his relaxed demeanor and eagerness to answer all questions. His alibi was locked tight. Wilson's interest in the criminal mind had caused him to study the man and his actions. He and Benoit stared at each other during the interrogation. Benoit's only expressions had been occasional smiles interspersed among his rapid answers. Wilson had known the man was lying about his involvement, and Benoit knew that he knew. But Benoit had the upper hand...a good lawyer and tight alibi.

When Benoit had been released from interrogation, he went to Wilson, again looking him directly in the eye. "Someday, one of us will look in the coffin of the other." *Is that a threat or a prophecy?* "You're a good cop. Stay that way." Then he left.

"Wilson, you with us?" Brandon looked around to make sure everyone was listening. He continued, "The Leopard is the leader of the East Coast setup. Under this man there are several drug families controlling a territory that's broken into zones, each family controlling a zone. They stay pretty much out of each other's way. Sometimes there's local bickering, but when the family hears about it they take care of it, or worse, the Leopard takes care of it. They don't want any publicity."

George Khee spoke up, "Who's this Leopard?"

Brandon lifted his cigarette, letting the ash fall on the bed covers, and leaned back. "I wish we knew, but it's someone on the lower East Coast. We've intercepted some information and think he's between Savannah and Daytona." He inhaled then sent a blue cloud toward the smoke detector.

"Is the Leopard supposed to meet with Benoit?" Wilson asked.

"Not sure; we don't know why he's coming here. We have a contact within the people who're moving the goods, and he'll tell us the exact time of the shipment plus its handoff. He's also supposed to know if the Miami man is on board.

The transfer's supposed to go down on the Amelia River, and that's where Wilson comes in; he's familiar with the spots that would be good for the transfer." Brandon looked at him. "Right?"

"I've got some good spots picked out, but I'd like to know when it's supposed to go down, because at low tide, some places can't be navigated in with a large boat. Their timing will eliminate some of the spots we need to watch."

"I don't see why they want to come to some little jerk-water place like this one to transfer stuff. Why not meet out in the ocean? Just like two friendly boats getting together." Tisher looked at the Fernandina Beach detective.

Wilson felt his pulse pound. *I'll deal with you later, pinhead.* "Probably because we have good restaurants here," he said with a smile that brought a few chuckles from some of the others.

"Okay, let's get to facts and plans." Brandon laid out a large nautical chart of the area from Fort George Island to Cumberland Island. The map went west for five miles and east to just past the beach shoreline. "Go over the area. Wilson, where would you make the drop?"

He looked for a minute, then pointed toward the south end of the island. "I'd have some boats waiting down here, just above the bridge to Big Talbot Island. When the mother boat comes around Marker 11, here, I'd have them trail it, pull alongside and unload. There aren't many houses down there. If the transfer is done on the west side of the mother boat, no one should see it happening."

Brandon was silent as he studied this scenario. Wilson added, "If you have too much activity up here around the marina, you'll get noticed. There's a lot of water traffic. How are you going to stop the mother boat?"

"Khee is an FBI sniper and he'll disable the boat if we have to. We want the transfer operation to go as they planned and let them think it went off okay." Brandon pointed a thick finger to the lower end of the map. "If they transfer here, we'll let the mother boat get up here past Fernandina Beach and when they think it's a done deal, we'll board. I don't want any gunplay around the town. We'll have surveillance all along the way from local officials, but we think the Miami man is going to get off here and meet the Leopard. At least, that's what our informant says."

Bowman spoke for the first time. He was from Alcohol, Tobacco, and Firearms and assigned to Homeland Security. "Who is the informant and how will we recognize him? I mean if we get into some close contact, we don't want to eliminate him."

"Good point." Brandon sat back and finished his cigarette. "I only have his contact name — Ramirez.. He's a contract player. Both sides of the coin. Most of the time he's on the edge of both parties; we have to trust him and they usually trust him."

"Burning the candle at both ends, huh?" said Khee.

Wilson knew the type of person they were dealing with. He'd run into them in Miami. They were a necessity in law enforcement. Usually they were petty criminals who ratted on other petty criminals in order to cut a deal for themselves. Naturally, their life expectancy wasn't great. Sooner or later, the lower element got its revenge.

"What's in it for him this time?" Khee asked.

"Don't know. Probably revenge for some long-past infraction. He'll only reveal himself after he's in custody. Remember, if a guy says his name is Ramirez, move him to a different location."

Tisher faced Wilson. "Does your little town have a jail that can hold these bad boys?"

Wilson wanted to walk over and knock the smirk off the man's face. "We usually cuff them to a lamp post until a judge arrives."

"I mean, what if they're real mean?"

"Oh those, well, we take them over to Billy Bob's pig farm and shackle them in the waller. You want I should take you over there to visit your cousins?"

The smirk left Tisher's face. Brandon growled, "Okay, enough love talk. We'll go with Wilson's take on this. There's six of us and we'll split up into three boats. I've contacted the Nassau County Sheriff, and he's going to get us some help along the roads. Down here," he pointed to the south end of Amelia Island, "and over here. Jacksonville will have some officers stationed on the Big Talbot Island side. They'll pick up anyone who leaves the small boats, if there are any.

"If we have a mother boat and another large boat, we'll have to raid them together. I've got the Coast Guard in on this too. That's Kreznek's job."

Brandon looked at his watch. "I'm supposed to get a call from this Ramirez sometime this afternoon with details, possibly the drop area and time, I hope. I'll be in touch with you later. Any questions?"

There were none and Wilson moved to the door. He held it open as the group broke up. He said to Brandon, "See if you can get some description on this Ramirez. There's a new face in town that looks suspiciously like someone we used to bust in Miami. He may be Ramirez." Brandon nodded as Tisher walked by. Wilson looked down on the top of five-foot-three Tisher's head. *Must be a vertically challenged thing.* He hesitated, then turned back into the room.

"Jack, there's something about this I don't quite understand."

Brandon was shuffling papers into the briefcase and didn't look up. "What's that?"

"You have a drug kingpin coming up here, and you have only six people spread out arresting him and his goons. Don't you think they'll have a lot of firepower and they won't be afraid to use it when we close in?"

Now Brandon looked up. "You don't think I've thought this through? I've done this once or twice before and have the scars to prove it. Do you? No, I didn't think so. So, what's your problem?"

"Well, first, you're going into a dangerous situation with too few men. Second, we should have the Coast Guard helicopters along with a SWAT team to board this boat when the time comes. No, I haven't done this before, but common sense says you don't go in like John Wayne. You'll get your ass shot off and lose some good people."

Brandon lit another cigarette and blew the smoke toward him. "You afraid of getting shot? I'll call the Chief of Police and get someone else, if that's what you want."

"Let's don't make this personal, okay? I didn't like you when we were in Miami and I don't like you now. I think you're in over your head. I know every day when I walk out the door that I might not walk back in, so don't give me that crap about being afraid to take a round. I'm not going to give you a sermon." He walked back to the door. "You wouldn't listen anyway."

Brandon put his cigarette in the plastic cup and listened as the glowing tip made a hiss in his remaining gin and tonic.

———————— • ■ • ————————

"Hi, hon, how about a burger at T-Ray's?" Wilson gave Dianne a quick call.

"Okay. See you there in twenty minutes. Paperwork."

They walked across the Exxon station's parking lot and into T-Ray's, where they stood in line for a few minutes. Familiar faces greeted them and made small talk. Lunchtime at T-Ray's was a cross-section of Fernandina's population. Smartly dressed men and women rubbed shoulders with the laborers who were resurfacing 7th Street.

Dianne grabbed two unoccupied chairs while they were available, and Wilson ordered the small hamburger and a pork barbeque sandwich. From behind the counter, T-Ray kidded Wilson, "You're not going to get the Big T-Ray today?"

"I hurt myself the last time I did that. I would but I can't hold it today."

"When you're ready, we'll have it for you." T-Ray went back to preparing the orders.

Wilson sat down after filling the drink cups. "I'm always amazed at this place."

"Why?"

"It's not big and not fancy but he packs 'em in."

"Good food and a lot of it." She munched on her barbecue.

"Seems to work."

He was silent for a minute or two.

"What's wrong?"

Wilson leaned forward a little. "I see dead people…and they may be some of this task force."

"Why do you say that? I thought Brandon was good at this."

He lowered his voice even more. "He is, but he's trying to do too much with too few people. I have to talk to someone about this. I don't like the set-up. Someone is going to get hurt."

"Did you mention this to Brandon?"

"Sort of." He finished his burger and changed the subject. "By the way, I saw your old car at the Ritz the other day. The guy that bought it has dinged the right front fender."

Dianne frowned. "That was my baby."

When they left T-Ray's, Wilson gave her a quick kiss and she went back on patrol as he headed to his office.

Lisa and Michelle hopped out of the car and scooted into their grandmother's house before Wilson was able to gather the few groceries they had picked up on the way over. Dianne opened the door and he followed. "Food for the king," he declared. "Whatever it is, it smells good."

His mother turned away from the sink, "That's the pie I baked this afternoon." She gave direction as to where the various articles were to go. "And who's going to help with the chicken?" She eyed the girls.

"I will, Grandma!" Lisa was at the counter in a flash.

"Good. Wash your hands well and let's get started."

Lisa stood by her grandmother and watched as she placed the flour bowl next to the cutting board. "You put the chicken in there and get him good and frosted, like a snowman, as I hand the pieces to you."

"Okay." Lisa's eyes sparkled. When her grandmother rested her hand on the counter, Lisa gently touched the back of it with her finger. Priscilla smiled at her granddaughter as she continued cutting the chicken. Across the room, Dianne and Wilson had their soft drinks at the kitchen table while they watched the birds at the feeder just outside the window. Michelle began to set the table, and her father smiled at her initiative.

Perhaps six or seven times Lisa would put her finger on the back of her grandmother's and rub it gently.

"I guess my curiosity has the best of me, Lisa. Why are you rubbing the back of my hand like that?"

"Well, Grandma, it looks like you have chicken skin."

"Lisa!" Her father gave a strangled yelp.

Priscilla asked with a smile, "What makes you say that, honey?"

"You see, the chicken's skin is all rumpled up, just like the back of your hand."

Priscilla chuckled and Wilson was without words.

Stifling a laugh, Dianne said, "Lisa, let's go outside and see if we can find that pretty orange cat that lives next door."

"Nonsense," said Priscilla. "It's true now that I look at it. Don't worry about it. A child's innocence is fine with me, even if it embarrasses you two."

Wilson leaned back, looked at the ceiling and shook his head. Michelle came to the door from the dining room and declared, "Lisa, you're so—" She saw her father looking at her with a look only a parent can give a child that is about to get into trouble with her mouth. Closing her lips, she went back to finish the table.

Wilson looked at his wife. "See what you got yourself into?"

"I wouldn't have it any other way." She kissed him on the forehead.

Lisa turned to them. "Mommy, you and Daddy shouldn't kiss in public. It sets a bad example for us kids."

Grandma smiled and looked at Lisa, who was rinsing her hands of the mixture of flour and seasonings. "Wisdom beyond one's years." She looked over her glasses at Wilson and then said to the girls. "After dinner, we'll go downtown to get some ice cream." She leaned over to Lisa. "If that's all right with you?"

This question was met with hand-clapping response from both girls that sent flour dusting on the countertop and settling to the floor. Wilson put his head in his hands and calmly told Lisa to get a paper towel and clean it up.

The evening ride to Centre Street was quiet. Downtown, Grandma Wilson noted how the place had changed over the past twenty years she'd been living there. "New faces all the time. Of course, it's becoming an area for vacationers, too. Still, the faces at St. Michael's are changing. Younger people coming in."

"A lot of people work in Jacksonville or at King's Bay

Naval Base and live here," Wilson pointed out as they walked out of the Fantastic Fudge and headed toward the old train station turned visitors center. In the cool of the evening, they sat on the benches and watched people stroll by.

Wilson finished his Triple Chocolate Mint cone and studied the iron fountain in front of them by the sidewalk. "I know there's a story about that fountain." He pointed to it and cocked his head towards his mother.

"As a matter of fact there is, smarty." She gazed at the fountain, recalling the information she had gathered as a docent at the Amelia Island Museum of History. Wilson knew he was in for a five-minute history lesson.

"That's the Duryee Fountain. A bit of odd history about it, too. It was given to the city by a Mrs. W.B.C. Duryee. She seemed to like animals better than children, so the story goes, and her fountain was originally placed at the curb to water the horses from that big bowl at the top. The lower bowl was to give cats and dogs a drink. It certainly wasn't a fountain for people to drink out of. When autos came along, the fountain was moved to Fort Clinch for some fifty years." She motioned toward the top. "What's that thing called, that on the top?"

"Finial?" Dianne offered.

"Yes, the finial was lost somewhere at the Fort and when it was brought here in 1977 by the Amelia Island-Fernandina Restoration Foundation, they had it restored with grant from Bird and Son. George Davis, a local historian, used an old photograph as a model and found a finial in an Alabama ironworks yard that is very close to the original one."

Dianne walked over to the fountain, with the girls following her, and they stood admiring it. Michelle turned to her grandmother. "Whatever happened to Mrs. Duryee?"

"After Mr. Duryee died, she stayed in her house over on Broome Street most of the time. She was rarely seen outside."

She added quietly, "Mr. Duryee liked living here more so than the Mrs. I can't imagine why anyone would not like living here." She turned to look at the shrimp boats tied up at the wharf and the American flag flying at the Veterans' Memorial at the foot of Centre Street. Then she nudged Wilson and smiled. "I'm ready to go home now. History lesson's over."

Chapter 6

A few evenings later, Wilson lay in bed reading *Great Expectations* for the fourth time. Dianne's voice filtered down the hall as she read a story about a beautiful princess and her problems getting married to the prince of her choice. The girls were quiet, but every so often Wilson heard Lisa interject a comment. He had tried many times to get his older daughter to open up a little more and was dreading the coming years as she'd reach thirteen, thinking she was twenty-one. *And Pip thinks he has problems.* He heard a "Goodnight, Mommy," from Lisa, nothing from Michelle.

Dianne slid into bed and laid her head on her husband's chest. "What are you reading?"

"Charles Dickens. He was really able to get into his characters' heads. Girls asleep?"

"Nearly. I agree, Dickens was really something. It's almost like our work. We have to get into the criminal's mind to see what's next for us."

"Um-hmm."

She lay back on the pillow and picked up a magazine. "Is Tisher still being difficult?"

"Yeah." He dropped the book, knowing it was time for conversation and he wouldn't get any reading done until

Dianne had wound down. She put the magazine down and leaned on her elbow toward him.

"I was thinking. You're supposed to intercept the stuff soon, right?" Wilson knew that her wheels were turning. She continued without waiting for an answer, "Why couldn't Brandon check the airports and see who's out of town or leaving at the time of the drop?"

"Why?"

"Don't you see? That will give them an alibi to show they don't have anything to do with the drugs."

"It's logistically impossible. Not enough manpower. And besides, you can't go on *that* premise and hope to get information. You know the people on this island travel all the time. Sorry, it's a thought but it won't work out." He picked up his book again, hoping to resume his reading.

"How much is this transaction supposed to be worth?"

"About a million."

"That's a lot of green for drugs."

Wilson's mind clicked into gear. "What?" He put his book down again.

"I said that's a lot of green for drugs."

"Damn."

"What?"

"Do you remember at LaFontaine's funeral a few years ago, I mentioned that I saw Chief Cabe talking to a man in a green suit who looked familiar and that I couldn't place where I'd seen him?"

"No."

"Well, I did, and now I remember—he was a minor drug dealer in Miami I'd busted several times; he'd also gotten himself involved in a murder case, but had wiggled his way out of it. He always seemed to slither out any charges we ever brought against him. I think I saw him the other day here in Fernandina Beach. I wonder why he was talking to Cabe last year?"

"Ask Cabe." Dianne returned to her magazine, indicating the conversation was over.

———————— • ■ • ————————

Wilson left Amelia Island, crossing the Shave Bridge to the mainland. The sun rising this Monday morning was at his back. Its rays made the mist over the marsh glow with an opalescent sheen. He knew the mist would burn off quickly, followed by the warm spring breezes by noon. He noted all the new construction along A1A from Fernandina to Yulee and beyond. The four-laning of A1A from I-95 towards Callahan seemed to be taking forever, as the construction crews stopped traffic to let their machinery crawl up and down the highway.

Before long, he was through Callahan and cruising down US 301 to I-10. The short drive to MacClenny was uninteresting, and he stopped at the turn off to State Road 121 to break his boredom with a fast-food snack and a bathroom visit.

At the Florida State Prison near Raiford, he pulled into a visitors' parking space and walked to the entrance gate. He'd never liked driving by prisons when he'd traveled. They always gave him a feeling of hopeless emptiness he never could explain. Like it or not; he'd had to make this trip to try to get information about the man in green.

Wilson patiently endured the routine pat-downs and metal detectors, even though he was a police officer; he knew there were no exceptions. After signing in, he was escorted down several corridors, through more secure gates and into an interview room to wait for them to bring the prisoner to him. Echoes of the heavy metal doors shutting sounded horribly final, even though Wilson knew he would be able to leave later. The recently repainted pastel walls couldn't remove the drabness of the place. *How in the world can anyone who's been here once do something to warrant a return?*

He sat in one of the chairs beside the metal table, and listened as the footsteps coming down the hall got louder. The door opened and the corrections officer ushered the former police chief, John Cabe, into the cramped little room.

Cabe stopped short and gave a snort. "*Humph.* Looky who's here."

Wilson stood and nodded. "Chief."

"Not any more, sonny. Thanks to you." He looked back to the corrections officer and Wilson wondered if Cabe was calculating whether to deck him. "What do you want? Surely this ain't a social visit."

"Could be. It depends on you, I guess." Wilson nodded to the officer, who left and closed the door behind him. Both men sat down, taking opposite sides of the table.

"Whatcha want, boy? I ain't got time for you and what's this 'Chief' crap?"

"Whether you like it or not, I still think of you as Chief, even though you're here and Evans is Chief back there. You just screwed up bad and made some real dumb-ass decisions. I came in when you were wound tighter than a pig's tail, and it just fell apart for you."

"Enough recollectin' about *the good ol' days.*" Cabe gave a wicked smile. "I got two life terms to think about those days, sonny. And bein' an ex-police officer in here has its advantages. You know, like running into scum that I sent here. They wuz real happy to see me. Kinda like ol' home week." Cabe sat back and folded his arms. Wilson noticed that his old boss had lost weight but was still muscular and able to hold his own. After a moment, Cabe said, "Out with it, boy, why you here?"

"We've got a little problem back in Fernandina, and just

maybe you can help us with it." Wilson looked him in the eye.

"Oh, really? Too bad. I don't live there anymore, so it's not my problem."

Wilson leaned back and didn't say anything for a minute. "Chief, you were in law enforcement for...what twenty, thirty years? I don't believe all that's been thrown out the window. You still have a sense of right and wrong and you can help get some things right in a town you used to call home."

"Bobby Troop wrote me a letter not long after he retired and said you and Dianne got married."

"Yes, we did. Three years ago now." Wilson was surprised at the switch and wondered where this track was going.

"She's a wonderful woman. Be nice to her and treat her well. She was sorta like a daughter at times."

"She has mentioned that." He noted Cabe raised his eyebrows at that. "I think she's a wonderful woman, too."

Cabe looked at his fingernails. "Whatcha got in mind?"

"There was a man at LaFontaine's funeral who came up and spoke to you briefly. He had on a green suit. Who was he and what did he say?"

Cabe stared off at the barred window and was silent for a long while. He shifted in his chair a little. "Seems like you really have yourself a problem there, Wilson." He looked back to his interrogator. "I don't recall anyone of that description."

The room was quiet except for the sound coming from the air vent. *Playing for what he can get out of it. Don't blame him.* Wilson didn't speak, letting the tension build.

Cabe looked at him. "You know, son, you're playing with a pro. You better lay the cards down and let's see what you have. I've reconciled myself that I'm here 'til I die and from all my *friends* here, it may not be of old age." He leaned forward, folding his hands on the table.

Wilson did the same so their faces were inches apart

and whispered, "As a former peace officer you know I can't speak for anyone else but me. I was just hoping you would help us."

"Well, you know how memory slips in a place like this." Whispering back and with a wave of his hand, John Cabe looked around him.

Wilson scooted his chair back. "Have a nice life."

The correction officer heard the chair move and opened the door. Wilson stood.

"You make an offer and let's see what happens." Now Cabe's words had a clipped edginess that wasn't there before.

Wilson looked at him and then at the correction officer. He paused and sat back down. The correction officer closed the door again. "Like I said, I can't talk for someone else, but in conversations I've had with the Feds, I get the feeling that if you help us nab someone we're after, life could be a little easier for you.

"Like?"

"You know how it works. Our department can put a good word in for relocation to a minimum security facility or perhaps a re-sentencing hearing could take place." He watched the ex-chief mull over the tendered offer.

"Parole?" Cabe asked.

Wilson shook his head. "From life in here to a private room with a TV ain't bad. I need to know who the man in the green suit was and what he wanted."

"Where does he tie in? That was almost four years ago."

Wilson leaned forward again. "I recognized him from Miami. He was a petty drug dealer that we busted time after time. I noticed him at the funeral but couldn't place him until a few days ago when I saw him again in Fernandina."

"Do you know if he's talked to Evans?"

"Not that I know of. Why?" Wilson sat back in his chair.

Cabe looked past the wire mesh covering the small

window place high on the wall. "He might be fishing again. When would the process for your offers start?" He leaned back, looking like he was in charge of the negotiations now. The tapping of his fingers on the metal table slightly irritated Wilson. "My words could be hearsay. You know, something just to get a break for me?" Cabe was smart, Wilson knew.

"Not if entered as evidence against this guy and what you say is helpful in breaking this narcotics ring. You will have to make a statement to the Feds and after we clear the case up, you can proceed with your petition. How about it?" He looked at his watch. "Don't want you to miss lunch."

The room was silent for at least a minute as the two men studied each other. Wilson finally saw resignation in the other's face.

"You're right about his dealing; but he'd graduated to the big time; someone he called the Leopard wanted to finance my election bid. It was only the second time we met, the day of the funeral. I was seriously considering the financing bid after we first met, but I had told him that I had to think it over. Somehow they knew that LaFontaine had pulled his backing and money from me."

"They do have a network of spies," Wilson interjected. "What were you to do for the backing?"

"Furnish the duty roster. That was it. Just the roster." Cabe looked at his hands again. "They needed to know who was where and when. I don't think any of our people were on the take. Maybe one or two of our people were working on someone on the street who'd been in a bind. Who knows?"

"What happened at the funeral?"

"That silly bastard came to talk about the financing again. I was so pissed I sent him on his way and said I'd jail him the next time I saw him."

"What did he do?"

"Just smiled and said, 'The Leopard won't like that.'

When I told him to tell the Leopard to go and screw himself, the guy left." Cabe sat back. "That's all."

"I don't suppose he had a name."

Cabe looked at him. "Yeah, Jack Sprat."

Wilson put the notebook in his pocket. He got up and the officer opened the door.

"Wilson," Cabe called. Wilson stopped, not turning around. "Thanks."

He didn't reply but walked out of the prison, happy to get into fresh air and out of confinement.

———— •—•—• ————

The drive back to Fernandina Beach gave him time to fit more of the puzzle pieces together. The Leopard's name had come up often in his conversations with the others on the case. He was trying to figure out how the sighting in town of the man in green fit with what John Cabe had told him.

Once back in his office, he checked his voice mail before calling the State Attorney's office with the information about Cabe. One message was curt. "Wilson, Brandon. When you have time, give me a call." That was it. *Pompous ass.* The tone of his voice made it sound more like an order than a request.

He also had a message from Chief Evans asking him to come to his office. He decided Brandon could wait until he returned from seeing his chief.

"Come in, Wilson." Evans motioned him to a chair. "I've looked over some of the reports. How's Sarah doing?"

"Fine. She'll make a good detective." Sarah Grant had done some legwork for him on the LaFontaine case, and had been eager to move into Investigations.

"Good. Can you spare her for about a week? Jacksonville wants to use her as a decoy with some problems down on Phillips Highway."

"I think we can work it out." Wilson made a note in his pad. "Is that it?"

The chief hemmed and hawed until he got to the real reason for his summons: he wanted to know how the interview had gone with Cabe. Wilson filled him in on the details and said he was getting ready to call the State Attorney about it. Evans looked out his window and watched the squirrels chasing each other around the scrub oak trees. "You know, we haven't talked about that case much, and that's probably best. I've seen the reasons you did what you did."

"But?"

"Oh…there's no *but*. I don't think I ever told you, but I was impressed with your work then—although I was upset that it turned out that way. I thought you were crazy and just wanted to get attention, being from Miami and all."

"And?"

"And I have the greatest confidence in you; this case has the potential to be explosive, politically and physically. I want to warn you that there are some mighty big players involved. I won't keep any information from you. Rumors are that the Leopard is in north Florida."

"I've heard some rumors from Brandon and others."

"I want you to pass any information you get or any of your intuitions to Brandon, and not go out on a limb yourself. These guys have done it and it's their show, not yours or ours."

"Yes, sir."

"I still don't understand why you had to go see Cabe."

Wilson gave his boss a short version of his "man in the green suit" theory and hoped for some answers in return.

Evans leaned back and laughed. "Nobody in a green suit has tried to buy me off."

Wilson grinned and asked if there was anything more; he had to call Brandon.

"No, just be careful. Don't play the maverick cowboy."

"Yes, sir." He left and made the phone call from his office. Brandon wanted to have a final meeting about how this operation was going to go down.

Chapter 7

Wilson, we've just got to go into that garage and unpack those boxes!" Dianne put her hands on her blue-jeaned hips. "They've been out there almost two years, and they were in your mother's garage before that."

Her husband looked up from the Saturday morning paper. "I'll finish the coffee and we'll get to it. When are the girls due at the swim party?"

"In a few minutes. Jennie will be here soon to take them over." She turned to the hallway and shouted, "You girls better be ready. Carla's mom is in the driveway." There was a scamper of bare feet running down the hallway and into the kitchen.

"Bye, Daddy, bye, Dianne," Michelle said as she dashed toward the kitchen door.

Lisa kissed her father on the cheek and turned to give Dianne a kiss, too.

"Michelle, come here a sec." Dianne reached out and hugged both girls and gave them each a kiss on the cheek. "You mind your manners and tell Mrs. Grimsley that you had a good time when you leave. Okay?"

They nodded and were out the door in a flash, clutching towels.

Wilson opened the door to the double-car garage. It had

space for only one car since the other half was crowded with stacks of boxes. The windows couldn't let light in because of the boxes piled in front of them.

"Oh, Mom called and wants us to come over for dinner Sunday evening. I said that would be fine. It is, isn't it?"Dianne was opening a large box.

"Sure, we just have to make sure the girls are finished with any homework before we go." He sorted through the boxes, causing dust to fly.

"Michelle said she had some math problems she wants your help on." Dianne grunted while struggling with a well-taped box.

"I don't know what to do with her."

"What do you mean?"

"The way she responds to you."

"We've been over this before, honey. She will come around in her own time. She's not rude to me and we get along fine."

"I know, but it's just that…"

"Look. She's eleven. Her body is changing and piled upon all the angst of that, she remembers a mother who loved her and whom she loved back. Lisa was too young to have those feelings as strongly. It's okay, honey, really it is."

"Life would be less stressful if she didn't act like she had PMS all the time."

Dianne playfully slapped him on the shoulder. "You just wait until she's sixteen — it only gets worse. For some reason, when she's into her twenties, her brain will start working again."

He looked at the ceiling and shook his head. "Thank God you're around. I knew there was a reason I fell in love with you. I couldn't have handled this myself."

"Right now, let's handle these boxes. We'll start at the front and work our way to the back wall. St. Michael's is having a rummage sale in three weeks and we can take things over there."

With a *humph*, Wilson started opening box after box. Two hours later, that half of the garage was still filled with boxes, but now one section of them had tape over the lids. The smaller pile not marked *St. M* sat in the back of the garage. Dianne opened one last box and pulled out a heavy white shirt.

"What's this?" she asked holding it up for Wilson to see.

"Oh, that. It's my *ghee* top."

"What's that?" She pulled out what looked like very loose fitting sweat pants. Several long belts tumbled out behind the pants, each a different color.

"Those are the pants." He laughed. " I thought you could figure that out."

"No, smart butt. What's a *ghee*?"

"I took karate when I was younger."

"I didn't know that. What are these belts?"

He stopped taping a box and went over to her. "Each color is to distinguish rank in the *dojo*, or karate classroom, and you start out with a white belt and work your way to black."

She held up the black belt and said, "You're a black belt in karate?"

"Yeah, go figure." He sheepishly smiled.

"You'll have to teach me and the girls." She held up the shirt again.

"No way. I know the *sensi*—the teacher—over at the YMCA and he's good. You can take classes there if you all want."

"You're full of surprises, Wilson. What else haven't you told me?" She gave an impish smile.

They heard first the sound of a car door closing and then the patter of bare feet on concrete. Michelle and Lisa popped in, with damp towels wrapped around them. Dianne soon sent them skittering towards their room and hot showers. Jennie Brock came up. "They had a great time."

After thanking her and offering to play taxi driver the next time, Wilson went inside to answer the phone. Dianne couldn't hear any of the conversation, but he came out in a few minutes and announced, "I have a meeting." She knew the meeting was with Brandon.

"You two. Always cloak and dagger." Jennie laughed and turned to go.

"See ya, Jen. Thanks again." He waved to her before he turned to his wife. "It's Brandon and he's sitting on a burr. He thinks I told someone higher up the chain about our conversation to get more help on this."

"Did you?"

"Hell no; I don't operate that way. If I went over his head, he'd be the first person I'd tell that I was doing it." He reached into the box with the karate belts to retrieve the last one. Suddenly he jumped back, almost knocking Dianne down. "*Agh!*"

"What is it?"

"Spider! There! In the box!"

She glanced at the box and then at her husband, who was backing up and looking around for a weapon. He snatched up a shovel and stalked toward the box.

"What are you doing? That spider is so small I can hardly see it," she said while looking into the spider's soon-to-be tomb.

"I'm terrified of spiders. I know. I know it's crazy. Move and I'll get it." He crouched and circled the box.

"With that shovel you'll destroy the box and give the spider a heart attack. I'll get it with my sneaker." She removed her shoe and leaned over the box. *Wham.* Sneaker and spider connected. Dianne held up the spider by a leg with her fingernails.

"Drop it. It might be a black widow or a brown recluse, and both are very poisonous." He was still holding the shovel in the attack position. "You may have just stunned it and it could still bite you. Put it down." That was an order, not a request. "Now, Dianne."

She looked at him and dropped it. "Wilson, it's dead."

He ignored her and clobbered the spider on the concrete floor. Dianne looked up to see the girls in the doorway just as he brought the shovel down hard on the concrete a second time. This blow was so hard that its handle broke, stunning him back to reality as the shovel handle hit him in the shins. He jumped a little and looked at his small family standing on the landing.

"Well, Dianne, I guess you found out about Daddy and spiders." Michelle's calm voice was an admission that she'd seen this before and wasn't surprised by it. Lisa giggled and followed her sister into the kitchen, while Dianne and Wilson stood for a minute, facing each other. Dianne's startled expression was a cue for him to explain.

Quietly he picked up the shovel pieces and muttered, "I don't like spiders." He threw the remains of the shovel in the trashcan. "I'll be back after I meet Brandon. I have to run by the office too." He could feel the hair on the back of his neck standing up a little. He calmed himself down as he got in the car. *I'll have to apologize to Dianne when I get back.*

———————— • ■ • ————————

Wilson drove past the Sea Crest sign at the entrance of the new development where he and his family had settled. The turn on Sadler Road led him past the Mexican Food Market, then west past K-Mart and Publix. Being third in line, he waited for the light to turn at 14th and Sadler, and watched as two cars ran the light. *It'll catch up with them someday.* The light changed and he turned north on 14th, toward the city's new police station.

A young man in a noisy little import car rushed to pass him, loud mufflers announcing his youth. Wilson squelched an evil smile as the young buck slowed down to the speed limit when he recognized the unmarked car. He was so impatient that he occasionally goosed the gas, inching ahead of Wilson a little at a time. Wilson slowed down to stop, but as the light at the Wal-Mart corner changed, the boy was enough ahead that he felt it safe to run the red light. Wilson watched as a patrol car came out of The Travel Agency parking lot, but he knew the officer couldn't see the light-runner.

He lifted his mike off its hook. "375, 177." He recognized the new female officer in the patrol car.

"177, 375."

"The red sedan heading north on 14th ran the red light."

She double-clicked her microphone and turned onto 14th with blue lights flashing. When Wilson passed, the patrol car was in a parking lot, and the blond kid standing beside his car. Wilson finally turned on Lime Street past the theater, and then to the new-to-the-police building on the left. The building had a rather chequered past. *Then again,* Wilson thought, *what building in this town doesn't?* It had started our as an annex to the hospital, and had been filled with medical offices. Then it sat dormant for several years before the city bought it and moved its growing police department into it.

He punched in the door-lock code and entered. He was surprised to see Sarah Grant in the office on Saturday. Her back was to him and she didn't turn around.

"Hey, Sarah, whatcha doing here?"

"Just finishing the report and I'm out of here." She still didn't turn around.

Wilson walked over to her desk and she turned her head

slightly away from him. "I'll just be a minute more."

"Hey, look at me." She reluctantly turned to face him, and his jaw dropped. "Sarah, what the hell happened?" A blue bruise on her cheek and swelling under her eye marred her flawless complexion.

"Oh, nothing really." She shifted to shield her injured side from his scrutiny.

"A shiner like that isn't just nothing. Did this happen down in Jacksonville?"

"Yeah…comes with the territory. A john got out of his car and reached for me. I took a step back and knocked his hand away." She leaned back in the chair as Wilson sat on the edge of her desk. "He got really pissed really fast and really slugged me."

"Where was the backup and what happened to him?"

"Backup saw it and came running to rescue him."

"Him?"

"Well, then I got really pissed. As he made his second swing at me, I grabbed his wrist and broke it while I twisted him to the ground and jerked his shoulder out of joint. I think I may have broken his collarbone too. Sorry." She held her hands up, but the gleam in her eye gave her away.

"Damn! Good going. Is he in jail? When did this happen and why weren't we notified?"

"I wanted it kept quiet for a while, you know, until I heal a little. It happened last Tuesday night. He went to jail early Wednesday morning after spending the night waiting his turn at the ER. I didn't have to get medical attention; it was a glancing blow, anyway. We racked up five charges against him; the judge will assign us a court date Monday morning."

Wilson looked at the ceiling and shook his head. "You're sure that's all. You're okay now?"

Sarah laughed. "Yeah, just a bruised ego. I should have

seen it coming. But I will use the excuse that the light was low in that area."

He got up and patted her on the shoulder. "Take off Monday and Tuesday if you need it."

"And not get my purple heart? I'll be here." She grinned again. "Anyway, I need to show Wilbur what happens when you do real police work."

Wilson chuckled at the elusive detective Wilbur's well-known tradition of avoiding the office, and then he sat at his computer to retrieve some Fernandina drug stats. If he was going to see Brandon in a few minutes, he needed ammunition to back himself up. He knew what was coming; someone up in the chain of command had called Brandon.

———— • ● • ————

"You know you're not supposed to smoke in here?" asked Wilson as Brandon let him in.

"Yeah, the maid mentioned something about it. Sit down." Brandon had commandeered the desk. He leaned back in the flimsy chair. "You just couldn't keep your trap shut, could you?"

"If you're talking about what I think you're talking about, I didn't do it."

"Listen, I'm in charge of this operation, and I don't like anybody going over my head." Brandon's eyes snapped with anger.

"I didn't."

"Well, somebody did, and you're the only one who questioned what the plan."

Wilson leaned back in the easy chair he'd chosen, and took a moment to brush an imaginary speck off of the spotless brown slacks he'd put on that morning. "It looks to me like one of us thinks you're going at this a little too thin."

"My boss called me this morning," Brandon said, "and

now we have to plan on two Coast Guard helos, and a pot full of guys from the alphabet soups sitting around like fishing buddies just waiting for this drop."

How in the hell did you get put in charge of an operation this big? "I'm sorry about that, but I didn't rat on you." Wilson stood up. "This is Saturday and it's also a rare day off; I'm going to help my bride clean the garage. If you'll excuse me, I don't have time for your temper tantrum." *That ought to piss you off good.*

"Don't be such a smart ass, Wilson. I can still replace you on this team in a heartbeat." His voice quivered with indignation. Wilson watched as a vein popped up on the side of his head.

Pompous twit. "I'll keep that in mind." He quietly closed the door as he left the room. He dialed Dianne on his Nextel as he walked to his car. She and the girls would meet him at KP's Deli for lunch. *That should get the bad taste out of my mouth.*

Chapter 8

D ianne couldn't help checking herself out every tine she passed a mirror. She felt really good in her uniform and kept it razor sharp. She was delight to be a part of the Fernandina team– plus she got to work with her husband from time to time. She'd pulled her copper curls into a no-nonsense knot, held in place by a silver clip that Lisa had given her.

Dianne didn't particularly like the afternoon shift, because she would rather be at home when the girls got out of school; when their father would be home, she wanted to be there too. The good news was that she could make sure the girls had a good breakfast before she drove them to school. She and Wilson had arranged for Michelle and Lisa to be enrolled in an after-school program until he got off around five. Grandma had wanted to keep the girls, but she was rapidly getting to a point where she was unable to keep up with the two of them.

Dianne rode alone on routine patrol this afternoon, up and down familiar streets, through familiar neighborhoods. She knew many of the residents, and bemoaned the fact that more people came to live on the island every day. She had resented how the tone of island life was changing from the low-key atmosphere of the small fishing village it had been for decades. Dianne, who had been born at the old hospital on 14th Street and had lived here all of her life, was fast becoming a rarity as a native of Fernandina.

She reflected on the changes to her town. Most were for the good but "with any change in population base you will have changes in values." She remembered this from the sociology class she took at the University of North Florida. It was one of the required courses for her degree in Law Enforcement.

On a whim she had also taken an elective course in Meso-American art one semester and found herself fascinated. She wasn't sure why she found it so appealing unless it came with the genes—her mother was an artist. She certainly didn't expect her knowledge of the ancient art would ever help her in police work.

The shift was moving along slowly. Dianne stopped some teen-agers in a car going too fast in a residential area and gave them a warning. Her next call was equally boring; two cars had kissed in the Wal-Mart parking lot–Wilson called it "swapping paint."

She felt sorry for the elderly lady who hadn't seen that the other car had backed out just before she did. "Just be careful, please." She tried to be patient and sympathetic with the frightened woman. "It's dark out here and you could have hit a child instead of a Ford. Look around very carefully before you move. Okay?"

As she drove through Wendy's to get a cola to drink while she filled out the accident report, Wilson called her. "Hey, are you going to be able to come home for dinner?"

She looked at her watch, "I'll be there in fifteen minutes."

Dianne liked the way the kitchen was laid out in the new house. The bar separated the kitchen from the dining room, and a small alcove off to one side was fine for quick snacks; but when the four of them were together for a family meal, they ate in the dining room.

Wilson's spaghetti was on the menu for that night, which the girls liked. Lisa chattered about a field trip her class was taking to the Jacksonville zoo. "I want to take pictures of everything, Daddy."

"I think we can get you a disposable camera at Publix. Then you can take all the pictures you want." He made a mental note to pick one up the next day.

"What are you doing in school now, Michelle?" Dianne asked.

"Not much." The girl shrugged.

"She's in a play," Lisa announced.

"That sounds like fun. What's it about?"

"It's called *Rapunzel*," Michelle mumbled.

"What part do you have?" Dianne tamped down her exasperation and pushed the conversation.

"The witch in the tower."

"It's you!" Lisa exclaimed.

"Lisa, that's not nice." Wilson and Dianne responded, almost in unison. Both girls made faces at each other.

"Okay, you two." Dianne stood and gathered the dirty dishes. "I have to get back to work. Be nice for your daddy. He works hard just so you two monkeys can make faces at the dinner table."

The night was quiet until, just before 10:30, she got a call. "373, HQ."

She answered, "HQ, 373."

"Signal 63 at the Flounder's Gig." The dispatcher sounded almost apologetic, "Dianne, it sounds like Shorty Livingstone."

At the click of the microphone another patrolman came on, "373, 319, I'll be there in a few minutes, Dianne."

"10-4." Dianne dreaded this call. She remembered Wilson's encounter with Livingstone a few years ago; it had been painful for everyone. Now it was her turn, but she couldn't complain.   She'd been on the force for nearly two years, and had never been on duty when they'd had to bring him in.

She drove to the Flounder's Gig. It had been Sharky's Place when Wilson and Livingstone had met. After talking to the backup, she walked through the scarred front door and found a familiar sight. Everyone watched to see what such a diminutive female police officer was going to do with the feisty guy in the corner. The heavy smell of beer mixed with cigarette smoke. Despite Florida's public smoking ban, no one here had complained, so the crowd gladly overlooked the ordinance.

"What happened?" Dianne asked the little man in the corner.

"Aw man, why'd they send you?" Shorty's back was against the wall and he held a pool cue in one hand. His reputation of getting into bar fights was known all over the island.   Unfortunately, his favorite place was here with the local pool hustlers.

"Luck of the draw." She shrugged and parted the crowd. Her five-foot-five height still put her a little above Shorty's four-foot-ten. She asked again, this time with a little edge on it, "What happened?"

The sun-faded front door slammed and the crowd looked to see the husky, bald, six-foot-three-inch backup officer standing there with his arms folded.

The barmaid spoke up. "Shorty was taking a shot and he moved some balls out of the way."

"Hey, I'm short. My arm accidentally hit 'em and this prick, pardon me, Dianne, this prick said I did it on purpose."

Dianne's eyes cut to the barmaid, who volunteered, "Shorty looked around before he moved the balls. I was watching the game, and I think he did it on purpose. It looked like a fight would be next, and we asked him to leave—but he wouldn't get out."

"Excuse me," Dianne said as she moved past a huge man blocking Shorty. She positioned herself against the back wall with no one behind her. She leaned over and spoke quietly in Shorty's ear. His beer-breath made her take shallow breaths. "Listen to me, and listen good. I don't want to get mean and nasty with you, so just come outside with me nice and easy and I won't call that big ugly backup to come get you. These guys can bust you up good, *and* I think they want to." Shorty's breathing got heavier. Dianne knew how to use a soft tone to defuse a situation. "If we go outside and things cool off here, I'll talk to them and see if you can come back in tonight." She whispered, "Okay?"

"Damn it, Dianne. It was an accident."

"It's been happening too often, Shorty. Let's go." And they almost made it. As she put her hand on his shoulder to lead him to the door, the scowl on his face dared someone to make a remark. She neglected to collect the pool cue from him—a rookie's mistake she would quickly regret.

When they walked past a large scruffy guy who leered at Dianne and said, "Nice ass," things went downhill fast. There was a breathless half-second of silence before Shorty lost it; a snap of his wrist popped the cue into the oaf's crotch.

The guy bent over with one hand holding himself while the other reached for Shorty; Shorty ran to the door. Dianne put a hand up to stop the furious man as the towering backup officer stopped Shorty from making a break through the door.

"He's going to jail for that. Let me handle it," Dianne told the injured guy, who nodded and could only wheeze a reply that she didn't understand. "And watch your mouth next time." He nodded and sank to one knee under her stern stare.

Outside she faced her charge. "Shorty, I thought we had an understanding."

"But—"

"I don't care what they say, you stay out of it." She raised her voice.

He tried again, "But—"

"No buts." She opened the back door. "In."

Hanging his head, Shorty sat down but looked up to see a third patrol car pull up. Officer Watley got out. "Shorty, Shorty, Shorty, what are we going to do with you?"

"Screw you — pardon me, Dianne — screw you. Don't touch me. I'll file a police brutality charge against you. I remember the last time; I wasn't that drunk." Then he declared triumphantly, "I'm riding with Dianne." He added while slamming the door, "No need for cuffs tonight."

"That settles that." Watley laughed. Dianne grinned and shook her head, then slid into the driver's seat. Watley and the backup officer waved and got in their own cars.

A man came out of the Flounder's Gig to watch them drive away. The tail of his loose-fitting green shirt flapped in the night's warm sea breeze that brought the tang of salty air. He squinted in concentration. The relentless pounding of the waves just across the street made a good backdrop for his thoughts.

Chapter 9

E mma Love Hardee School's day was over with children spilling into buses, cars, trucks, and various SUVs. Michelle and her class had spent their afternoon rehearsing their play. After an hour, the teacher-director had heard enough missed lines and extra chatter. "That's it for the day — go home and, please, try to remember your parts for our next rehearsal!"

There was a flurry as the fourth-graders slung their heavy book bags carelessly over their shoulders, banging into whoever was standing too close. Michelle and her new best friend, Molly, walked slowly to the after-school-program room.

"This is a dumb play," said Michelle.

"Why do you say that? I think it's cool."

Michelle met that statement with her patent *puh-leez* look.

"Who's picking you up today?" They sat on a bench outside the door and watched Lisa and her friends giggling over some obscure and private event.

"Daddy and Dianne."

"It's neat to have your parents both work for the police. I bet they have all kinds of stories to tell."

"She not my mother. My mother died when I was little."

"I know, but she's married your daddy."

"So?" A puff of wind blew Michelle's blond hair into a tangle. "She's okay, I guess. She's not as bossy as I thought she would be. Still, I don't have a real mother now."

"You're lucky; two parents living at home. Mine don't get along too well and I think they're talking about divorce."

Michelle saw Molly drop her head and tried to be upbeat for her friend. "It might not be too bad. Belinda's parents got divorced over the summer and she gets lots of things from her mother when she stays with her."

"Big deal." A tear ran down Molly's cheek.

The helium-voiced screams of Lisa and her friends on the other side of the play yard interrupted the conversation. Michelle watched as they organized a round of drop-the-handkerchief.

"All I want is to be eighteen, so I can do what I want," she told Molly.

Ten minutes later Michelle saw Wilson enter the parking lot. Whoever picked up the girls was there at five o'clock sharp.

"Where's Mommy?" Lisa tossed her backpack into the rear seat. Michelle shot her sister an irritated look before climbing in beside her.

"She's at home. What do you want for dinner? This is family eat-out night and you get to pick." Dianne had started the popular tradition of going out to eat once a week, and the girls got to pick the restaurant every other week. The friendly squabbles always seemed to erase the last tensions of their day.

Michelle looked at her sister and said, "Tacos?" Lisa began to chant, "Tacos, tacos."

Wilson agreed, and after picking up Dianne at the house, they were on their way. Cheers came from the back seat as the car pulled up at Taco Bell and the girls scrambled out of the car. Inside, they looked over the menu, and Lisa, bursting with energy, fidgeted with a nearby napkin dispenser until Dianne told her to stop and find a place for all on them to sit. Wilson sat next to his older daughter and they all looked out the window at 8th Street and its traffic.

"The pulpwood trucks never stop coming, do they?" Wilson motioned to the caravan of three passing by.

"Those are the late guys;" his wife said. "It takes five loads a day before they begin to make any money so they run as late as they can. That's one of the reasons they speed down A1A."

"You know…" Wilson paused as he thought about the streets. "Wouldn't it be nice if the mills built a road just for those trucks?"

"Where?"

"Right off the bridge and straight to the mills. We've all seen the ruts on 8th Street."

"Well, it would be nice for the rest of us," said Dianne, "but it might not be too practical, having to go through the marshland."

Michelle watched as three girls sat at a table outside. After sliding their trays onto the concrete table, one of them took a pack of cigarettes out of her jeans and passed it around. Wilson watched Michelle as she stared at the teens.

"How old do you think they are?" he asked her.

"The girl in the red shirt is Sharon Miller's sister; she's in high school."

Lisa blurted, "They shouldn't be smoking. It's bad for you."

Michelle was silent and Dianne said, "Doing adult things doesn't make you an adult, you know."

"I know."

"I was your age once, believe it or not." Michelle's expression was blank, but Dianne slogged on, trying to make a connection. "I think I have an idea of how you feel. You want things to change a little faster than they are. Be patient, and the changes will come. Don't be in such a rush, okay?" She gave Michelle a warm smile to help soften the remarks.

"Yeah."

Later, when Wilson and Dianne were in bed reading, she asked him, "Do you think I was too stern with Michelle tonight?"

"No, we talked about this, you and I. They are your daughters now and I appreciate your concern for their welfare. You've shown them love and taken them as your own. And your patience with Michelle is extraordinary." He leaned over and planted a kiss on her forehead.

Dianne patted him in return. "She's had it rough, I know. She's lost the most important influence a young girl needs, even though she wouldn't want it sometimes. And big changes are coming—she's about to enter the wonderful world of being today's modern woman."

Wilson was stunned. "Already?"

"Yes. At least, it won't be long, and she's already heard from other kids a little of what puberty involves. She went to your mother, who told her to come to me, which she eventually did."

"And how did that conversation go…wait, I don't want to know."

Dianne laughed. "Very well, actually. It was about as close to a mother-daughter conversation as we've had so far. Don't look so worried, she already knew all about it. Young girls talk, you know, but sometimes they don't get all the facts straight."

"Good." Wilson sighed. "Can we change the conversation?"

Chapter 10

The sultry air blankets Miami's inner-city streets with a thick, moist heat.

"2413, HQ."

"HQ, 2413" Young Patrolman Wilson responds to a dispatcher call. The black and white car rolls slowly down the streets of Miami's drug district.

"Suspicious activity in the next block, possibly drug related." *How do they know where I am?*

"10-4." *I hate working this area. Sergeant Duarte knows it, and sends me here anyway. There they are, a whole damn gang. I'll call for a backup before I go in.* "HQ, 2413. Send in some backup."

"2413, no back-up available. Just you, buddy."

What the hell? That doesn't sound right. What's wrong with the radio? Come on, work. He tries several times to get the dispatcher on the radio but no answer comes. The lighted dial goes black. He looks up to see a dozen gang members coming toward him armed with chains, clubs and pipes.

This isn't real. I'm getting out of here. He puts the patrol car in gear and mashes the accelerator to the floor. *Damn it! Come on, move!* The car moves slower than he can walk. The gang leader stands in front and stops the car by putting his hand on the hood.

Sweat breaks out on the young officer's forehead and he draws his pistol. He can hear the jeers and accented voices yelling at him.

"Get away from my car!"

Now they're beating the car with their chains and clubs. One contorted face presses against the passenger window, and Wilson fires his Glock straight at it. The bullet goes through the glass without breaking it, and the face laughs and vanishes into a mist. *This crap isn't happening.* He opens the door, pushing gang members back, and points his pistol at them. *Get back, you bastards. I'll kill every one of you!*

The leader and his gang back off. Now there's silence. No night sounds, no street sounds, no traffic, nothing. Wilson discovers that he and the leader are standing on the sidewalk, separated by only a few feet.

"Come here and put your hands on the car. Now!" He hears his voice echo off the buildings.

The boy stands with his arms crossed, still holding a metal pipe. "Come and get me." He zips into the dim alley. Wilson does something he knows is suicidal and sprints after him into the darkness.

This is really getting nuts. Where did he go? Up there, in that doorway. He's not fully hidden. I've got you now, scum.

He inches his way down the back-lit alley, surrounded by the stench of rotting garbage. Thirty feet away, he can see a dark figure standing in a recessed doorway. He creeps on the balls of his feet, inching closer to the door. His pulse is pounding in his temples, and his weapon slips in his sweaty palm. *You're an ex-Ranger. Think! Calm waters, remember.* He blinks, and sees the figure step out of the doorway.

Standing there in a single shaft of light is the most beautiful blonde James Bond-girl he'd ever seen, and she's wearing a costume from the musical *Cats*. She's got the biggest pistol he's ever seen, complete with silencers. They both raise their weapons and fire.

He watches the bullet exit the silencer and even notices the puff of smoke following it. He watches the bullet travel in slow motion toward his chest. His bullet goes through the woman, yet she still stands. He tries to move out of the way of the spiraling chunk of lead, but it cuts through his uniform shirt. The impact hurls him along the dirty wet alley. As he falls, he closes his eyes, knowing he is dying. He finally hits the ground. He opens his eyes and hears the sweet sound of waves against the shore. He's lying on a sandy beach.

———— •■• ————

"*Arrgh.*" Wilson jerked awake and sat up in bed.

Before he was fully awake Dianne was holding him. "What is it, sweetheart?"

"Oh, God," He shuddered and wiped his face with trembling hands. "Just a bad dream, that's all."

"You're sweating. Are you okay?" She put her hand on his forehead to feel for a temperature.

He took deep breaths and fell back onto the pillow. "I'm all right. Just a bad dream about getting shot. You know how dreams are...they don't make sense."

"Have you had this dream before?"

"Not this one, but similar ones. It's nothing."

She laid her head on his chest. "If this assignment is causing these nightmares, get out of it now. Please, honey."

"Getting shot is a possibility we both face each time we put on the uniform. We know it from the first day we enter the academy. I don't know why this seems to be an issue now."

"Maybe you've suppressed it so much, it's coming out this way."

"I'm okay. What got me so upset was the shooter was this incredible blonde Bond-girl," he said, grinning now at the silliness, "dressed like a cat."

Dianne fell back on her pillow. "Take two aspirin and call me in the morning." She rolled over and was gently snoring before he could turn out the light.

Chapter 11

The weather was still playing games with Fernandina Beach, even though it was April. A chilly northeast wind swept across the island, scouring everything with blowing sand. Waves at high tide lunged over the granite rocks along the sea wall at Main Beach, and sent spray to wash the cars in the parking lot. Still more rain was in the forecast, but Wilson hoped it would hold off for the next few hours.

He stopped his car in his mother's driveway. She had been feeling weak for the past few weeks, so he made it a point to check on her every day. Today he'd brought the girls with him and they were going to dinner.

"It's a shame that Dianne can't go with us," Grandma Wilson said.

"She said she would try. Sometimes a routine traffic stop turns into more than you'd expect. She'll call when her supper break comes."

He helped his mother into the car and asked, "Where to?" After a flurry of cardboard hamburger suggestions from the back seat, Grandma Wilson suggested Shoney's. "Fine," he answered. "You girls can get a hamburger there, if you want, but remember they're huge."

"You know, girls, you can split one," Grandma added.

Wilson drove south down 17th Street and turned left onto

Atlantic Avenue. He wanted to drive over to Main Beach to see the surf. On the way, he glanced to his right to the expanse of new wetlands where acres of trees had recently been bulldozed. "The city got the shaft on that deal."

"What, dear?" his mother asked.

"Oh, nothing." They made the lap around the Main Beach parking lot, then went south on Fletcher toward the roundabout—known to some as a traffic circle—in front of Slider's. He chuckled, recalling that the management's comments in *The Fernandina Beach News-Leader* at one point referred to the roundabout as a traffic hazard. By now, most locals could swing around the circle with ease, but some tourists still appeared puzzled when approaching it.

"I've noticed a lot more vacation rentals lately; does it seem that way to you, Mom?"

"Well, yes, I guess. You know, at church there are a lot of new faces at each mass and you might see them once or twice and then they disappear." She went on, "It's like a lot of small towns that have been discovered. I was talking to Anne Harvey last Sunday, and she and her husband moved here from Montana, of all places."

"I haven't met Mrs. Harvey." Wilson slowed at a gap in the row of houses for a quick ocean view and saw the clouds had been turned coral by the setting sun. The girls didn't look that way; their earphones pounded something into their heads that he knew he wouldn't like.

"Well, if you'd come to church more often you'd know the new people." His mother continued, "Anyway, she said they found a pretty little town about fifteen years ago and settled in. Then it seemed like everyone retiring from Washington and Oregon found the same little town, and it was so overcrowded it was awful. So they've found Fernandina Beach, and they hope it won't turn out to be like that other place out west."

Wilson nodded and tried to pay polite attention to her musings about new residents. More people meant beefed up support systems, and he knew they'd have to hire more police officers as well as fire and rescue staff.

"Grandma, how'd you like my play?" Michelle asked from the back seat.

"Honey, that was the best *Rapunzel* I've ever seen. And you were very scary. What did you think of it, Prissy?" Grandma was the only person that Michelle let get away with calling her by her old nickname.

"Oh, okay. It was better than I thought it was going to be. Billy Roberts got sick when it was over."

Lisa chimed in, "I bet he threw up all over the place."

"Okay, enough barf talk." Wilson gave a stern look back in the rearview mirror. He parked the car at Shoney's and called Dianne's patrol car.

Fifteen seconds later he finally heard, "177, 373."

"Are you going to make it to Shoney's?"

"No, I'll call you later." Her voice seemed a little stressed, but he wasn't concerned; she could handle tough situations and would call for a backup if needed. He signed off and helped his mother into the restaurant, while the girls led the way.

———— • — • ————

"373, HQ."

"HQ, 373."

"Signal 13 prowler, possible signal 21." He gave the 4078 South Fletcher address.

"Roger, 373." Dianne was traveling on Citrona Street toward Fernandina Beach High School when she received the call. "I'll be there in two minutes. Call back and tell the homeowners I'll be checking the grounds with my flashlight on."

"373, Roger. We'll send a backup."

She made a U-turn in the school parking lot and sped toward South Fletcher Avenue. She leaned over and turned on the siren and blue lights. If a burglary was in progress, perhaps the sound of the approaching police vehicle would scare them off. She looked at the green numbers on the car's clock and remembered she was supposed to call home at dinnertime. She gave a mental shrug; it had been a hectic night with a lot of petty things happening.

In four minutes and forty-five seconds, she stopped several houses up from the address on South Fletcher to approach the house on foot.

With her right hand on the butt of the Glock pistol, she switched on the flashlight. She moved cautiously around the side of the huge two-story house, shining the beam around shrubbery and across the yard. After making a circuit all the way around, she walked up and knocked on the front door.

A man opened the door quickly. "Come in, please. I'm Sean O'Brien. Did you see anyone?"

"No, sir. Could you tell me where you saw the person?"

It was his wife who'd actually seen someone at the patio window, he explained, but the man had run when he'd seen her. He hadn't been trying to break in, but had stood there watching them. Dianne followed O'Brien through the arched doorway into the front room. He was about as tall as her six-foot husband, and his silver hair was perfectly combed straight back. His top lip sported a small, neat, silver mustache. His thin frame suggested a lot of tennis or running.

She tried to concentrate on the business at hand, but she felt as if she had walked into a museum. Two of the walls held floor-to-ceiling display cases filled with what she suspected were genuine Pre-Columbian artifacts. Looking back, she discovered paintings hanging over the doorway, one of a child in bright-colored Andean clothes, and the other a colorful plaza scene on market day.

The fourth wall surprised her; it was covered with floor-length earth tone curtains. Only at a slight movement did she see a woman sitting in a chair directly in front of the curtains. Dianne gave a small start and nodded to the lady of the house. Mrs. O'Brien was decked out in a black pantsuit accented by several pounds of gold jewelry. An ornate diamond and gold pin graced her shoulder. Dianne really wanted to go take a close look at that sparkling piece but she knew that would be tacky.

Mrs. O'Brien produced a semi-smile and a small nod. Dianne couldn't tell whether she was condescending or distraught. It wasn't important; there was work to be done.

She pressed the button on her lapel microphone and told the dispatcher to cancel the backup, as the scene was clean and, "…suspect Code Echo," indicating the suspect had left the scene. She heard the siren getting closer, and its shriek stopped abruptly.

She excused herself and went to her car to get the report book. The backup officer had just walked up at that time and they agreed Dianne could handle the incident. He said he'd cruise the neighborhood and ask questions if he saw anyone.

When she re-entered the home, O'Brien showed her to a high-back antique chair. Asking the routine questions, she noted the routine responses. "We'll step up patrol all along Fletcher and look for anything out of the ordinary," she told the couple. "Since there's no evidence he tried to break in, we can only guess that he just wanted to see what was around. Be sure to have your alarm on all the time, even if you're in the house."

O'Brien led Dianne to the front door, but his wife remained seated. As they passed one of the display cabinets, Dianne said, "Those are nice pieces. Are they Pre-Columbian?"

"Oh...yes. Thank you. My wife and I collect them." He hurried to open the door for her and stood on the porch until she was in her car. Another patrol car pulled up in behind her and sat there for a moment or two before moving off to check the neighborhood.

———— • ■ • ————

Wilson walked into Chief Evans' office just before 2 o'clock the next afternoon. He had been summoned but he had no idea why. The chief waved him to a chair. "I've got a problem and you and Dianne can help me."

"Whatever we can do."

"The assistant chief and I have to attend a conference in Atlanta this weekend. But Jacqueline and I were invited to an important dinner party here on Saturday night. It's one of those pain in the ass things that I have to show up at every so often." Evans shifted in his seat. "There will be a lot of influential people there. Can you and Dianne go, express the department's good will and my regrets?"

"Sure, we'd be glad to. What slant is the party?"

"This is the art crowd. They're trying to get an annual art festival going and want to pick our brains. Don't volunteer anything; just let them ask questions and tell them what they want to know. Dress is coat and tie casual."

"Got it. Time and place?"

Evans dialed his secretary. "Susan, when and where is that shindig Saturday night?"

She duly recited the information, and Wilson wrote it down. He wasn't overly enthusiastic about going, but dinner parties on the island usually had excellent food catered by one of the better chefs. "I'll give you a recap on Monday." He left the office, whistling all the way back to his office. He opened the door only to hear his telephone ringing.

"Investigations, Wilson."

"Is this line secure?" He recognized Brandon's voice.

"No."

"Meet me at a place called O'Kane's. Do you know where that is?"

"I think I can find it." *I've lived here for four years, jerk, and what's with wanting a secure line?*

"Good. Ten minutes."

"Right." He quickly hung up. He hoped Brandon felt the exasperation being aimed his way. However, since he was in charge, Wilson had to follow his lead.

He found a parking spot in front of the restaurant. Brandon was at one of the high round tables in the bar area with Tisher and Khee. Wilson gave his order to the waitress as he joined them.

"What's up?"

"We have to wait a week; boat's got problems." Brandon sipped a beer.

Wilson felt Tisher's stare and looked over at him. Tisher smiled. It wasn't a friendly how-are-you smile, but bordered on a smirk. *You don't know how much I'd like to put that smile in your pocket.* Wilson turned back to Brandon. "I've got a boat lined up so we can take a tour of the river whenever you want. How about tomorrow morning?"

Khee nodded, as did the other two. In a mocking Southern accent, Tisher asked, "Is y'all going to have some fishin' gear for us?"

Khee looked like he was waiting for Wilson to punch this guy's lights out, but he just leaned back in his chair. Brandon looked out of the window and said, "We'll meet you at 9. Where? Down at the marina?"

"Yeah, that sounds fine." Then he turned to Tisher. "Maybe we-uns could use y'all's wee-wee for bait."

This got a laugh from everyone except Tisher, who tried to mask his irritation, but his smile was too little and too late.

"Good one," he said, raising his beer in toast.

Wilson asked Khee, "Where are you from?"

"Pearl City, Hawaii." Khee broke into a broad grin. "You ever been there?"

"Yeah, my father was Air Force, and we were at Hickam for a tour. Loved it." He paused and reflected on the wonderful time he'd had as a kid in Hawaii. Deciding to mend some fences, he said, "How about you, Tisher?"

"Kansas City, Kansas."

"Jayhawks and Chiefs." Wilson raised his glass of iced tea. "May they always win, except when they play the Jags."

That evening when he told his daughters he was going on a boat ride early the next day, they wanted to miss school and go with him. He promised they would go out together soon, but this trip had to be a secret for now; he was counting on them to be good policeman's daughters and not tell anyone about the boat ride. Declaring that this was cool, they vowed to keep quiet about their "security briefing."

Chapter 12

Chief Evans' boat sped to Amelia Island's south end, toward the new George Crady Bridge. Wilson, at the helm with Brandon beside him, took the team past Marker 11, where the Intracoastal Waterway curls around marsh grasses and makes a lazy loop to the south behind Big Talbot Island. Marsh birds waded in the shallows and soared across the water of Nassau Sound.

He pointed as he turned around and headed back toward Fernandina. "Their boat will have to come up through here and go past that marker, Number 11. If they come at night, the best place to make a swap will be behind Big Talbot Island. If they come in the day time, there will be several places to swap."

Wilson guided the swift eighteen-footer around Marker 11 and headed north. Even though it was April, the early morning air held a little chill and the men zipped up their light jackets against the wind. Wilson pointed out a few places where they could put deputies "fishing" on lookout. He pointed out the obvious. "If done at night, it would be a new set of problems."

They needed to know as soon as possible when the trade was going to take place. But even more important—was the person they were looking for even going to be on the delivery boat?

Wilson slowed the boat as it approached the Shave Bridge. A few employees of the Down Under seafood restaurant were moving about the place, getting ready for the night's dinner. He reduced the boat's speed to a crawl. They saw a large cruiser coming out of the Amelia Island Marina's channel on the right, and Wilson slowed even more.

Just as they went through the open section of the railroad bridge, they heard it begin to rumble. The machinery began to rotate the center section around to meet the rest of the bridge, with a loud noise that startled all of them. They watched as the bridge fully closed, allowing a bellowing train carrying logs to the mills to cross the span.

"Where's the bridge tender?" Khee asked over the low-pitched rumbling of the heavy-laden cars crossing the span.

"There isn't one," Wilson yelled back. "It's activated by the trains that approach. One of our officers lives on a boat at that marina over there, and he says that sometimes a train will come barreling through the night, sounding like banshees are on their way."

Behind them, the cruiser from the marina had stopped near the closed bridge waiting patiently for the center span to swing back open again. Wilson pushed the throttle forward on their boat. "Over here is Jackson's Creek on the right, but I don't think our guys will stop there. Too narrow."

Slowing the boat again, he gave way to a tug and barge combination heading south on the Amelia River. The channel turned a little eastward and they passed the Rayonier mill, then turned north again to pass several large boats just leaving the city's marina. Early morning river traffic was picking up. Fishermen were returning from predawn expeditions and travelers along the Intracoastal Waterway were getting under way.

On the west side of the channel opposite the marina, several sailboats remained at anchor, and some occupants were moving about the decks. Wilson pointed out Bells River to the west, and after passing the Port, he pointed toward Egan's Creek. "Up there are two marinas and it's even possible that just one side or the other of those could be a place to make the drop. People around there would be mostly concentrated on their own boats, getting ready to go out or maybe having repairs done."

He urged his boat past two shrimp boats that were heading out to sea; the crews faced weeks of shipboard life as they gathered the ocean's crop of crustaceans. The outriggers were stowed high along side, and a young shrimper waved as Wilson and crew passed to port side.

"Was that a woman on board that first boat?" asked Bowman, the ATF representative.

Wilson strained to answer over the powerful thump of the shrimp boat's engine. "Yeah, some boats are crewed by husband and wife teams...or a guy and a girlfriend. The crew size often depends on how long they'll be out."

Up ahead, the *Miss Jane* was making her starboard turn to the ocean, and Wilson recalled his encounters with her captain during his investigation of the LaFontaine murder. As they slowly passed the *Miss Jane,* he saw William Carless working on equipment toward the boat's bow. Carless returned a brief nod to Wilson's cursory wave. *Hmm.* Assisting Carless was Shorty Livingstone.

Wilson finally eased back on the throttle and pointed the bow toward Cumberland Island. The depth gauge indicated they were still in deep water even as they pulled in close to shore. He made sure they were well out of the channel and kept the boat opposite a large brick structure on the point by idling against the incoming tide.

His Nextel vibrated on his hip.

He answered and listened for fifteen seconds. "Okay, Mom. I'm kinda busy now. I'll get back with you in an hour or so." The men turned and looked at him. He turned away from them and finished with, "Okay, an hour."

When he turned back around, Tisher was chuckling. *You know, twit, I really want to throw you overboard.* Wilson stared him down as the other man threw his toothpick over the side.

He continued with his tour of the area, "That's Fort Clinch, over there on the tip of the island. It's pre-Civil War and interesting if you have time to visit. The island over there," Wilson waved his hand to the north, "is Cumberland. In years past it was the haunt of Carnegie and his friends. He built a beautiful house—Dungeness—but it was burned, perhaps deliberately, about forty years ago. The Park Service manages most of the island, largely undeveloped."

"We're not here for history or tours, Wilson." Brandon gave him a wry look, raising his eyebrows.

"You never know when it might come in handy." Wilson laughed back at him. "The Kings Bay Naval Submarine Base is over there, too. Our guys wouldn't make a drop here because of all the surveillance equipment around." The men nodded and made notes in their little books they kept in their breast pockets between entries. "Submarines come into the Cumberland Sound heading to or from the base. Since their schedules are classified, there's no way of telling when they may appear. Obviously, the Miami boat can't afford any confrontation with the Navy tugs and security personnel who escort the subs."

After he turned their boat around, they traveled back to the dock with little conversation. Khee jumped to the dock and held the line while Wilson brought the trailer down to the ramp. Brandon said to meet in his room later that afternoon, after he'd checked for a message from the inside man.

———————•—■—•———————

Wilson took the boat back to the chief's house, but not

before he'd forked over twenty bucks for a neighborhood kid to clean it. Next, he took his girls on the promised trip to Wendy's. Dianne waited until they were seated to tell Wilson her news.

"I had a prowler call the other night—and guess what?"

He pondered a bit, and then looked over at Lisa. "It was a big lion that growled and snarled and scarfed all of the dogs in the neighborhood."

Lisa rolled her eyes. "Daddy, you're *sooo* silly."

"No, but you know that party we're supposed to go for the Chief — well, this is the same address." Her eyes sparkled, "A*nd* they have the greatest collection of Pre-Columbian artifacts that I could imagine."

Wilson, who knew of his wife's interest in such artifacts, had tried several times to get her a piece or two, but never found them or had the money to snag them. "Really?" He wondered if they might be persuaded to turn one loose for her birthday.

"It's like a museum in there." She gave an animated description when Lisa asked what was an artifact.

Wilson had always been uncomfortable socializing with Fernandina's upper crust; but he was getting better at it. He and Dianne were often asked to attend functions on behalf of the chief or assistant chief. Although their cars and toys were more expensive than his, he was discovering that these wealthy islanders were genuine and good people. It helped, he thought, that Dianne and he were a fairly interesting couple themselves, so they rarely lacked company at any of the fancy shindigs. He knew she was especially looking forward to seeing the inside of the O'Briens' house and its impressive collection again.

———— •■• ————

Dianne stood in front of the mirror for several minutes and then sighed. She retrieved a different pendant and earrings from her jewelry box and again gazed into the mirror, debating which would go better with the basic black dress.

"Honey, which looked better?" She turned to Wilson, who was putting on his shoes.

He looked up and smiled. "Sweetheart, you'd look good in either."

"Oh, you're no help." She went back and put on the first set of small diamonds. "I don't want to overdo it." She changed from the black dress to a slim fitting emerald green one.

Wilson was happy with her less-is-more philosophy of jewelry and dressing up. Diamond earrings and her grandmother's diamond pendant on a gold chain were enough to accent Dianne's loveliness. He told her the dress was going to turn men's heads and she said it bordered on "trashy tight" but she liked it, anyway.

He hugged her and whispered, "You look so gorgeous in it, I'll have to dust you for fingerprints when we get home."

"Thanks, honey, but don't get too close; you'll ruin my hairdo." She laughed and walked away.

Before leaving, they told the girls to behave for Grandma Wilson. They drove down Fletcher Avenue to the address. Sean O'Brien answered the doorbell himself and ignored Wilson to stare intently at Dianne. Then he held his arm for her and escorted her to the main room filled with people, while Wilson followed, feeling like a puppy tagging along.

Heads turned when the handsome couple entered. O'Brien had put his hand on top of Dianne's, making sure she couldn't get away anytime soon. She looked back at Wilson and raised her eyebrows, making Wilson grin at her predicament.

The wealthy and politically influential residents of the island filled the room. Wilson had finally gotten savvy enough to recognize even the quiet ones who worked better behind the lines than out in front. Their attendance tonight lent a certain cachet to the proposed festival. He watched as his host presented Dianne to several people. *She's got to be enjoying all of this attention. There are some real power players here tonight.*

O'Brien seemed to be enjoying his circuitous route around the room with Dianne, and they eventually met his wife coming out of the kitchen. "Kitty, meet Dianne. I'm sorry I've forgotten your last name."

"Wilson," she said, holding her hand out. "It's a pleasure, Mrs. O'Brien."

The woman took the proffered hand and studied her guest for a second. "Sean calls me Kitty, but everyone else calls me Connie." She paused and cocked her head. "I have this feeling that we've met."

"Yes, ma'am, we have," Dianne explained as Wilson joined them. "This is my husband; we're both on the city police force. I answered a call to your house a few days ago about a prowler."

Sean's eyes opened wide as he looked at her. "*You're* the lady policeman?"

She smiled at him. "Yes, sir." She turned to Connie. "Have you had any more problems?"

"No, nothing at all. It must have been an isolated incident."

"I hope so." Dianne paused before adding, "I must admit I was hoping that I'd get a chance to come back and look at your wonderful collection."

"You like Pre-Columbian?" Sean asked. His smile came close to being a leer. He wore his silver hair slicked down. His dark tan told Wilson he spent a lot of time outdoors. The only glaring anomaly was the man's narrow face, with a larger than normal nose that had a reddish tinge; the man liked his booze.

"Yes, I studied it for a semester at UNF," Dianne told him. "Fascinating. I love it."

"Sean, let go of the poor girl's hand and get Wilson a drink." Connie led Dianne over to a towering display cabinet at the side of the room.

"So, Wilson, what'll you have? Whatever it is, we've got it. Just tell the barkeep." Wilson nodded to the man behind the bar and asked for a bourbon and water.

"Wilson, I don't believe I've seen you around here."

Sean's strong hand was directing him over to a group of men standing near the hors d'oeuvres.

"I head up the detectives in the Police Department. And that means you've been a good citizen, since I haven't seen you either." He and his host both smiled weakly at the small joke. O'Brien introduced Wilson to the men, and then left him to fend for himself.

They were discussing when and where it would be best to hold the proposed art festival. One tall, slim man next to him had the annoying tendency to sniff every couple of seconds. *Allergies or a bad habit?* Directly across from him stood a round little man with what Wilson first thought was a bad haircut before he realized the man's toupee was listing badly to port. *Man, you gotta bury that dead animal on your head.* The fourth member of the quartet stood aloof from the rest. He had the habit when someone made a point in conversation of gazing up at the ceiling and murmuring, "*Hmm*, interesting." The first time he did it, Wilson looked up too, thinking maybe a drop of water had hit the man on the head.

He tried to be interested in their chatter, but kept an eye out for Dianne. He'd glimpsed her and Connie at the display cases, carrying on an animated discussion about the contents. "Well, Wilson, what do you think, since you would know about traffic flow and things like that?" A voice brought him back to the little enclave of men.

"Oh…I think parking space would be a big problem to begin with. You need to find a venue that would offer ample space or perhaps you could think of shuttles to move people to and fro." He hoped his bluff made sense, since he hadn't paid attention to the conversation.

The men looked him and then each other. The sniffer said, "You know, it takes an outsider sometimes to see the real solution to the problem. I like this Williams fellow."

"Wilson." he corrected. "My name is Wilson."

"Oh, don't make anything of it; he forgets to go home a lot too," Toupee said.

They all laughed at their inside joke, while Wilson smiled politely. He saw Dianne and Connie, clear at the other side of the room, and watched as Sean joined them and stood much too close to Dianne. Connie turned her head aside and said something and he moved on. *Dianne's a big girl and can take care of herself.*

"By the way, Wilson, who's that with Connie? She came in just before you did, and I don't remember seeing her around here, either," the ceiling-gazer said, drawing the words out slowly as if he were interested in making a play for her.

"That's Dianne, my wife, the lady of my life. Isn't she gorgeous?" Wilson rubbed it in a little.

The Sniffer sniffed. The round man cleared his throat and the other man looked at the ceiling. "*Hmm*. Yes."

Wilson smiled to himself and asked, "What line of work is Mr. O'Brien in?"

The Sniffer offered, "He was a VP in charge of something in a large food company, can't remember the name of it. Based in Chicago as I recall him saying." *Sniff.*

"Interesting. How long have they been on the island?"

"I think he's an old-timer around here, about twenty years." *Hmm.*

Wilson found the three a rather curious mixture. He discovered that the fellow with the sniffing habit was a retired accountant from an oil company; the gent with the toupee was a retired Marine colonel; and the third had been in textiles before retiring. He was about to leave the group when a hand touched him on the arm.

"Detective Wilson. How good to see you." It was the still lovely Mrs. Wadsworth-Langford, a resident of the Plantation who had needed police help a few years back.

"Oh, Mrs. Wadsworth-Langford, it's nice to see you again. How's Patton's Pride doing these days?"

"Call me Deborah, and it's great that you remember her name."

"That's one case I don't think I'll forget." He excused himself from the trio of men.

"She's fine and retired." Deborah took his arm and they moved to the hors d'oeuvres.   "She's one dog who's more valuable having puppies than in the ring now that she's a little older. But we don't have her anymore, now that Mother died. Nigel Spense has her: you remember Nigel, don't you?"

Wilson frowned as he tried to put a face with the name. Deborah helped, "You remember, the handler who was so upset when Patty managed to get loose and we had to get security and the police to help find her?"

"Oh, yes, now I do."

They chatted a few minutes more before Deborah excused herself to join her husband across the room. Wilson saw Dianne and moved in her direction.

She and Connie stood by one of the display cases, still deep in conversation. Sean joined them and suggested they launch the reason for the cocktail party. Connie agreed and squeezed Dianne's hand while promising they would get together again soon.

O'Brien moved to the fireplace and after getting

everyone's attention, he thanked all of them for coming, and moved smoothly into his announcement. "With all the artists and art lovers on our island, many of us — including both my wife and I — feel it's time for the island to have an art festival. We already have a book festival and a chamber music festival. This island is becoming known as a place where artists can find the peace and serenity that they need."

Wilson's gaze wandered around the room as people reacted to the pitch. He watched one or two slowly shake their heads, while others, as one bespectacled lady did, nodded *yes* to every point Sean made.

He saw Connie standing behind Sean and thought she looked a little bored with the proceedings. Her hair was swept up attractively, but the black color was tinged with gray, which surprised him. Surely she could afford a tint. Her slightly narrow face and strong chin combined to give her an elegant look. The only jarring note was the bright red lipstick on her too-thin lips. *She must have been a looker in her younger days.* Occasionally while her husband talked, she made a little face as if she had tasted something sour.

After Sean repeated himself several times, Connie jumped in to speak of the blossoming interest she had seen around town. "What we need for the first few years is a place to hold the festival. *And* patrons for the arts on Amelia Island." This drew a few laughs and good-natured remarks, like one man's, "That's why we're here."

Dianne held Wilson's arm while she listened intently. He eased himself from her and sauntered back toward the kitchen. He snagged a chair and positioned it near the door. *Will this ever end?* He mouthed a thank you when one of the staff handed him a cold drink.

Thirty minutes later, Connie spoke up, "Now that we have all kicked all these ideas out, let's get together in two weeks to see where we are. Tell Bertie Schuman what you would be willing to donate as a patron. She'll let everyone know when and where we'll meet. Now, continue to enjoy yourselves, and those busy bees in the kitchen should be ready for us in just a second." Wilson was taking the last sip of his drink as the entire room turned his way.

Later, when he stepped into the foyer to take a break from the crowd, he heard someone talking in the office. The door was ajar, and Wilson slowed down to eavesdrop. "Escucha, no me importa de tus problemas alla. Yo soy ú problema aquí. Traime las preubas y mas vale que seán pruebas de buena calidad…esta bien…tengo clientes listos y esperando, sin peros."

Wilson quietly walked back into the main room to meet Dianne, who was talking to Connie again. "Mrs. O'Brien, thank you again for having us. I'm sorry Chief Evans couldn't be here but, I'm delighted we were able to come."

"Oh, please call me Connie. You two definitely have to come back. Your wife, as you know, is fascinating. There're only a few people that I can talk to about my collection, and she's one of them. Please say you will come to dinner next week."

He looked at his wife, whose eyebrows were raised; he knew that signal. "We'd be delighted," he dutifully responded.

Dianne carried on a one-sided conversation all the way home, telling him about the O'Briens' fabulous collection. He interjected an occasional *um-hmm* to sound interested in such a dull topic. *Old clay pots and primitive work a first grader could do. And they'd probably look better,* he grumbled silently.

Chapter 13

It's a go. We have to be in position in two hours." A sleepy Wilson listened and then hung up the phone.

"Who was that?" Dianne mumbled.

"Jerk Face. He said it's a go. I've got to get going myself." He climbed out of his nice warm bed to dress. He looked at the clock, and the red number glowed 5:45 in the morning dawn. "Sorry to wake you, honey." He leaned over, brushed her hair back, and kissed her cheek.

"It's okay. Be careful." She half opened her eyes. Her evening shift had been long, rough, and tiring. She was too groggy to be coherent. *Been there, done that,* Wilson thought.

Two hours later he and the other men were in their boats with their baitless fishing lines in the water. The morning mist conjured up ghostly images on the Amelia River and sent a late spring chill through them. In Nassau Sound, separating Duval and Nassau counties, two men perched in a fast sixteen-foot boat on the ocean side of the new bridge. On the Amelia River side, two more were riding in a twenty-footer. Deputies from both Nassau and Duval counties were in place, despite grumbling over the short notice about the operation. Three men from FDLE had their boat anchored near Marker 11 and two men in a fourth boat a little further north toward Fernandina. All had their fishing lines in the water, and Wilson wondered if any of them actually knew how to fish. He could see honest-to-goodness fishermen in boats dotted along the river, so the law enforcement officers blended in. Each man knew where the other was; Brandon had given emphatic instructions about that.

Khee, who was near the Amelia Island Marina's entrance, looked at the rifle case at his feet and hoped he wouldn't have to use it. The railroad trestle began to groan and complain as it swung to a closed position. Khee could hear the train engine's horn in the distance.

Wilson and Brandon made their way to the mouth of Bells River in a twenty-foot boat that had been built for speed. Tisher sat in the bow of the boat with his feet propped up, playing with his .357 magnum. The chief had offered his boat, but Wilson had told him if any lead flew, he didn't want the boss's boat hit; there were always plenty of confiscated boats that the agencies could bring in to do the work.

The Coast Guard had two helicopters doing touch-and-go's at the Mayport Naval Air Station. They were monitoring the frequency set up for the operation, waiting to swoop down and snare the bad guys. At the entrance of Egan's Creek, hidden back against the sawgrass, was a SWAT team in a Zodiac boat. The six men sat and talked in low voices. Two other men kept them company, sitting on jet skis.

"Well, Bubba, now do you think we have enough men and fire power?" Sarcasm oozed from Brandon.

Wilson looked at him for a minute. "When this is over, let me know who to write to so I can give you a recommendation for Departmental Butthead of the Year."

"You never made it to the big time; now I see why."

Tisher jabbed, "You know, Jack, small towns for small people."

Wilson elected not to throw the man overboard this time. "What caliber is that pop gun, Tisher?"

Tisher quit messing about with his weapon and held it up to admire it. "Point three five seven."

Wilson couldn't help himself. "I've always heard that little men had a libidinous need for bigger guns."

Tisher glared at him. "I don't know exactly what you mean by all that fancy talk, but any time you're ready, sonny, any time."

Wilson laughed and looked at Brandon as the radio broke in, "Charger One, Charger Seven."

"Go ahead." Brandon liked the title of "Charger One."

"The subject is in view and rounding Marker 11."

"Roger. All Charger units: Be alert." Brandon moved to the bow to see if he could spot the *Well Behind.*

"It'll be about twenty minutes before it gets here from Marker 11," said Wilson.

The *Well Behind* rounded the marker and turned north. One of the Coast Guard helos flew along the surfline; the other stayed inland, but kept a visual watch on the boat. The men in Nassau Sound started reeling in their lines and slowly moved north up the Amelia River. Knowing that the transfer had to be done out of sight of other boaters, they stayed a fair distance away.

A twenty-foot boat anchored near Marker 11 started to move north not far from the *Well Behind.* Men, vigilant behind their sunglasses, stood on *Well Behind*'s deck, watching for any other boat activity. The men aboard the smaller boat, from several drug-running families, were there to make sure that each received his fair share. A crewman aboard the *Well Behind* hand-signaled the twenty-footer, which pulled alongside and easily kept pace with the larger boat. It took only five minutes to transfer the large blue containers filled with high-grade cocaine bricks. The bricks were destined to be cut several times by each dealer before ending up in the bodies of addicts in north Florida and south Georgia.

When the transfer was finished, the smaller boat veered off to the left and executed a turn to head down the river. *Well Behind*'s captain goosed the throttle forward and the large boat began to leave a wake that disturbed the birds looking for tidbits along the muddy shore.

Now the twenty-foot boat sped toward the boat ramp next to the bridge, where the dealers' cars and trucks were waiting. Eight members of law enforcement cleverly disguised as weekend fishermen were also waiting for them.

The dealers pulled up to the ramp, and one ran to get the truck and trailer. Once the boat was out of the water, the agents swarmed around it and had the men face down on the ground with a minimum of trouble. It was all over in less than thirty seconds. The agents read them their rights, in both English and Spanish, cuffed them and put them into waiting vans and headed to Jacksonville. The *Well Behind* was out of sight, oblivious of the takedown at the ramp. The Coast Guard helos, heading in a loose formation up the river toward Fernandina Beach, passed over the big boat. A man in green slacks and a white t-shirt, standing at the *Well Behind's* bow, nonchalantly turned to make his way to the aft, where the crew was assembled. Once he had their attention, he gave detailed directions. No one spoke, but they all nodded.

Wilson and Brandon craned their necks to watch the two helos fly over; they followed the river first, then made a gentle right turn to follow the Cumberland Sound out to the Atlantic. They were marking time until the moment came for the ground troops to board the *Well Behind* once it was past Fernandina's waterfront. The helos continued out to sea, paralleling the jetties and stopped at the jetty entrance to watch an approaching nuclear submarine.

Wilson noticed that Brandon was getting nervous, and that made him edgy in turn. Brandon could pull the trigger at any time and screw things up. His impatience, just one of his many faults, was going to get him in trouble someday. Wilson prayed that today wasn't the day. He watched Brandon gazing down river through his binoculars, waiting to see the *Well Behind* round the last bend in the Amelia River and into view. The radio chatter told them the drug transfer had already taken place.

Wilson carefully reviewed the scenario one more time. His attention to detail made him the good detective he was. *The Devil is in the details,* his mentor used to say. This case was nothing more than a drug bust with an arrest, but it was going to be the arrest of one of the biggest players in the East Coast drug scene. Worked right, that player could lead them to the Leopard.

Chapter 14

Y ou know I don't like this change in our plans. The Leopard didn't tell me about this." Alfred stood on the bridge next to the *Well Behind*'s captain.

"You know how the Leopard operates; likes to keep a finger on operations… felt that we needed a change." The captain double-checked the channel markers, making sure that nothing he did would bring attention to the vessel. He was proud of his boat and hoped that the next phase of this operation wouldn't make a mess too big for him to handle.

"And who's this Smith we picked up in St. Augustine? I don't like it. He doesn't look like any Smith I've ever seen, and I really don't like carrying the product while I'm on board." Alfred put his hands on his hips and turned to see who had come up the ladder. "And what do you want?"
Smith only smiled. "One of the crew wants to see you on the aft deck." He turned and went back down the ladder to wait for Alfred.

Alfred took the lead as they made their way aft. He stopped when he saw a large sheet of blue plastic spread out on the deck and four other sheets raised as a canopy to shield them from prying eyes. Four deckhands were standing there, each at a corner of the blue tarpaulin.

Alfred gritted his teeth. "What the hell is this for?"

With one graceful move, Smith thrust his stiletto up to the hilt into the man's back, just to the left of his spine and into his heart. The closest crewman put his gloved hand over Alfred's mouth. The other three crewmen lifted up the corners of the tarp as Smith held the crumpling man. Smith removed the blade and tossed it into the river before coolly assessing his victim; he saw only amazement in the dying man's eyes.

Smith leaned over so Alfred could hear him. "Sorry, ol' boy; business you know. The Leopard's claws are long and sharp." His smile was cold. Then he stood and said to the men, "Wrap up this present, boys." He walked back up to the bridge as the men held Alfred down during his last few seconds of life.

Smith looked ahead to the Shave Bridge. "Captain, it's such a beautiful day, let's get past this smelly village and put to sea."

The *Well Behind*'s captain laughed. "Yes, sir. To sea it is." He urged the throttles forward.

Wilson recognized Khee's voice on the radio, telling them that the boat had passed under the bridge. The plan was for Khee's boat to pass the *Well Behind* and lay by at a spot across from the mill just north of the bridge. They would anchor there until the larger boat passed them, then leapfrog again to a spot just north of the old pogy plant. Wilson had had to explain the name of this landmark and that pogy was a name for menhaden, a fish used for its oil. After the pressing process was over, the pogies were ground up for fertilizer. The Fernandina pogy plant had been out of operation for more than a decade, but its buildings were easily recognizable from the water.

Several boats sped past the *Well Behind*, and a couple of them carried guys who were really out for a morning fishing trip. Two of them, however, held law enforcement officers.

"Charger One, they are past the mill and on the way to

you." Khee's voice once again.

"Roger. All units, be sure to wait until I give the command to move."

Several clicks acknowledged his order. Brandon shook his head. "Sloppy radio discipline."

Tisher moved to the bow of the boat, then to the stern. He looked at Wilson, "You ready for some big-time law enforcement action. I mean this little town probably has...what, three drunks a year?"

Wilson measured his words. "You know Tisher, some people's names kinda fit them, just like yours does. But someone got the letters in the wrong order."

Tisher took a step toward him, but Brandon's hand on his chest stopped him. Brandon said, "Listen, pissant, did you ever hear the phrase 'get your foot shoved up your ass?'"

Tisher's eyes narrowed as the boss continued, "Wilson is a third degree black belt and when I worked with him in Miami, I saw him destroy someone twice his size. So stow your bullshit or I'll throw you overboard here and now. Understand?"

Tisher's face turned red. "Yessir," he said through tight lips.

Wilson didn't move a muscle as Brandon stepped back. "And you knock it off, too, ya hear?"

Giving him a mock sloppy salute, Wilson said, "Looks like company passing us."

All of them turned to see the *Well Behind* cruise past them. Wilson looked down the river and saw three boats loaded with the rest of their team slowly catching up. They would all meet once the *Well Behind* reached a point opposite Egan's Creek. Wilson could feel his pulse rate rise. He tried to breathe normally. Six minutes passed.

"Now!" Brandon yelled in the microphone.

Wilson shoved the throttle full forward and the V-8

powered boat leaped in the water. He could see the men on jet skis shoot from Egan's Creek to station themselves on either side of the *Well Behind*. The Zodiac was there in an instant. Crewmen from the *Well Behind* stormed out of the cabin with guns drawn.

"Guns!" Brandon yelled again into the mike.

The gunmen on the *Well Behind* opened fire on the Zodiac with automatic weapons. The men in the Zodiac returned the fire, as did the two on the jet skis. Even above the roar of the engine Wilson could hear the pops of gunfire and Brandon's cursing at the turn of events. They charged into the fray in less than thirty seconds. Wilson kept low and saw Tisher run to the bow to fire off a few rounds.

The *Well Behind* was now running at full speed, heading for Cumberland Sound. Two of the crew had been hit and were lying on deck; a third had fallen into the Amelia River. The Coast Guard Agusta 109 helos overhead were firing the M60 machine gun across the bow. Spray shot twenty-five feet in the air, and Wilson heard the *zzzzip* sound as fifty rounds came out in two seconds. The gunners only tapped the triggers, then let off. If needed, they could cut the cruiser in half in twelve seconds or less.

Brandon called for one of the team to retrieve the wounded drug-runner overboard, hoping he was still alive. By now the *Well Behind* had turned to her starboard to round the bend; Fort Clinch was in sight. Khee was in the bow squeezing off rounds of his 50-caliber rifle as fast as he could, into her transom. Black smoke belched up from a stern hatch, then from one of the exhausts, but the *Well Behind* traveled on.

The Zodiac had deposited four of her men on the drug boat, and they rushed to the locked bridge's door. In an instant, they shot through the locks, entered and slammed the captain to the deck. While one man cuffed him, another pulled throttles back to idle.

Wilson carefully maneuvered his boat alongside as Tisher stood and waved his weapon about and whooped, "We've done it!" As Tisher jumped aboard the boat, a crewman popped up from below deck, pointing an Uzi at him. Wilson was too far away and too busy to do anything but watch as fire spat from the Uzi. The 9mm rounds went through Tisher, the impact hurling him overboard. Tisher had blocked Brandon's line of sight, but now Brandon fired his Glock repeatedly, and the crewman went down. Brandon leaped on board and went up to the man lying on the deck. He fired two rounds point blank into the back of the man's head.

"Damn it, Jack, stop. Stop!" Wilson yelled at the shaking Brandon. He looked back at Tisher's body being carried by the tide toward Fernandina Beach. He called for another boat to retrieve the body. Brandon had finally holstered his weapon and came to the stern as Wilson tied off his boat and climbed aboard. As they watched, two lawmen hauled Tisher's limp body aboard their boat.

Brandon's only comment was, "Arrogant little asshole should have known better." He turned around to see who had been rounded up. Wilson made sure the men had Tisher aboard before he followed Brandon.

The crewmembers who had been hit were given rough first aid, cuffed, Meranda-ized. Brandon and Wilson took a nose count to make sure everyone was accounted for. The jet skis were tied to the Zodiac and other boats were tied up to the *Well Behind*, while some were returning to the docks. Wilson looked down at his shirt and saw the blood that Tisher had sprayed as he'd fallen past him. *Poor bastard went out in a flash.*

The plastic-wrapped body of Alfred Benoit lay on the deck, eyes staring at nothing. His mouth was open as if gasping for air. *I'm looking in your coffin, Benoit,* Wilson thought. A

SWAT team member said he had seen one of the crew trying to push the body overboard.

They walked back to the crew who had been lined up. Brandon aimed his first question at the captain, whose tanned face reflected many years in the tropics. "What's your name?"

He didn't answer the question, so Brandon tried Spanish.

"Captain William Jones-Brown," the man answered in English, with a swagger in his voice.

Brandon moved on. "And you?" They either mumbled names or remained silent, but no one mentioned Ramirez, the code name of the informer. Brandon moved back to the captain and crowded him until they were almost touching. "Would you have any idea how that body ended up on your cruiser and why someone was trying to put him in for a swim?"

The captain raised his eyebrows. "Body? What body?" His gray mustache twitched as he spoke.

"*Um-hm.*" Brandon moved closer. "There's this dead man on your deck. If there's a fatality of a Federal officer during a narcotics arrest, it's a Federal crime of murder. You also have attempted murder of Federal, State and local officers to add. And then there're several Federal drug charges against you. Most of them will probably result in life sentences." He grinned evilly. "We'll try for the death penalty on a few."

"I won't say anything until I have a lawyer." The captain didn't flinch. "I believe your men said that when they read me my rights. *Hmm*?" He smiled sweetly at Brandon.

Brandon grabbed the man by the lapels and shoved him against the bulkhead. "Listen, Fishbreath, I'll throw you overboard right now, still cuffed, and it'll look like you tripped. Don't get your ass on your shoulders with me." The captain's hat flew off and into the water.

Watching the hat disappear beneath the tannin-darkened water, the man only said, "That was an expensive hat."

Brandon slammed him against the bulkhead again. The

sharp crack of breaking glass brought Wilson over. "Jack, this isn't Miami anymore. Knock it off." He reached past Brandon to take the captain by the arm and led him back to the other men. Brandon watched them with an impassive face.

There's got to be one more. "Did you guys check the entire boat for anyone else?"

The SWAT leader nodded, just as they heard a jet ski start up. A man in a T-shirt and green slacks drove it rapidly into the channel.

"There's the other one!" Wilson jumped onto the Zodiac on his way to take the other jet ski. Its engine fired up immediately, then fell silent. *Damn government equipment.* The time gave the fleeing man even more of a head start. He tried it again and the engine caught. He opened the throttle full and was off in pursuit, momentarily thrown back by the quick acceleration. Three of the SWAT team boarded the boat Wilson and Brandon had used, and came roaring right behind Wilson, headed down the river toward Fernandina Beach's waterfront.

He kept an eye on the speeding jet ski, watching the man for any sign of a gun. Wilson recognized him—the man he had seen around town, and also at LaFontaine's funeral. He was chasing the man in green. This character had eluded him too many times in the past; he was going to nail the guy this time, even if it was for nothing more than an accessory to the murder on the cruiser.

They zipped past the abandoned pogy plant. The spray kicked up by the other ski stung Wilson's face. He was gaining on the man, despite having to maneuver to avoid his wake. He looked back to see the SWAT team guys catching up. He wouldn't mind their assistance, but he wanted to make this collar for himself.

They raced past the shrimp boats lined up at the wharf. As they approached the city's marina, Wilson saw a tugboat pushing a long barge just out from the docks, heading north. He saw his objective move over to the river side of Dock 1. *So you're going to make a run for it on foot, eh?* Brandon had already called ahead and Fernandina Beach Police Department officers were waiting with weapons drawn.

The SWAT team finally passed Wilson and was now ten yards behind the fleeing man, but suddenly, he veered to the left and down the chute between Docks 1 and 2. The SWAT team had to turn sharply to the right and pass the barge, hoping to be in front of their prey when they emerged on the stern of the tug. But their boat couldn't make the sharp turn like the jet ski.

Wilson zoomed into the closed-off chute, hoping he had the other man in a deadend situation. The fugitive slowed, but then he saw an opening between the dock house and Dock 2. Gunning his jet ski, he went through the slot between Docks 2 and 3, then shot back toward the river. Wilson was right on his tail through the small space and spun the throttle handle, jolting himself against the seat.

When the SWAT team didn't see the man they were chasing emerge from behind the tug's stern, they made a wide turn to the right, hoping to catch him coming out of the marina. But the speeding jet ski turned left, barely avoiding getting run over by a large pleasure craft towing a dinghy. Wilson, right behind him, winced as the captain of the pleasure craft gave a long angry blast of his air horn. Shouts and hand gestures reinforced the horn's message.

The SWAT boat came into view in front of the slow moving barge that nearly blocked the way. Taking advantage of a narrow space just ahead of the barge, the man on the jet ski zoomed through. He and the SWAT team passed inches from each other, going in opposite directions. Wilson followed his path, barely missing the barge, and turned to head down river just yards behind the other skier.

The SWAT boat's driver cut the wheel hard, as he was headed toward the marina's Number 1 dock. It was a valiant effort, but the speed and size of the craft wouldn't allow it to turn as much as needed. The boat struck the dinghy of the yacht, sending its own bow in the air. The SWAT boat went airborne over the dinghy, landing on an open-cockpit twenty-four-foot ocean-going fishing boat. The collision catapulted the SWAT team off and rolled them onto Dock 1. The two jet skis were on their own, barreling down the Amelia River toward the Shave Bridge.

Wilson didn't know how much gas he had left, but hoped it was enough to catch the man. The open railroad bridge was straight ahead.

He was only an eighth of a mile behind the other skier as they neared it. He saw a sailboat in the left passage; that meant the man would go to the right. Once past the sailboat, the jet ski made a sharp turn to the left, as if to head back north. Wilson followed him closely, but his view was blocked for a moment as he passed the sailboat.

A riderless jet ski shot past the sailboat, headed for open water. Wilson looked from side to side, hoping to spot the man in the water. He saw the sailboat's crew pointing at the bridge and looked up to the trestle where a triumphant figure stood. Wilson found a spot to pull his own ski over so he could climb up and join him.

He called, "Okay, it's over. Let's go."

The man held his arms open. "Where? Your ski is on its way to Miami, how're ya gonna take me anywhere?"

Damn. "We'll wait until the train comes along. I've wanted to talk to you for a long time. Turn around and put your hands behind you." He reached for his handcuffs.

"I don't think so." Grinning, the man ran to the end of the trestle. Wilson followed him at a leisurely pace. They were stuck until a train or boat came by. *Where you gonna run to, jerk?*

"Let's make it easy on both of us, okay?" Wilson dangled the cuffs.

The other man chuckled. "No…no. You see, I don't like jails. I can let you chase me around this tinkertoy, if you need the exercise, but I say we call it a draw and wait for a train."

"Since you were on that boat, maybe you can tell me who killed Benoit. And, just to satisfy my curiosity, who the hell is the Leopard?" Wilson still advanced on the dealer.

"Benoit who? And what's a leopard got to do with this?" The man reached the end of the trestle and looked up at the ironwork.

"Come on, now, let's play nice." Wilson looked around and weighed his options. *I could charge him and try to get him cuffed before the next train comes.* He looked up the Amelia River and saw boats coming around the bend. *Maybe I can convince him that one of those boats is our guys coming down here.* "See those boats? That's the rest of the task force. You, my man, are history. And don't even think about trying the river; the currents will drown you for sure."

The man looked down at the swirling water. "Hate to say, you may be right. Can't swim, so that's that." He began to climb an iron girder. "Maybe one of you big strong policeman can shoot me off the top of this thing. Like in the movies, make it a dramatic ending."

"Nah. That'll just make you a cult hero and us the bad guys. Come on down." Down river, an outboard motorboat with two fishermen in it was making slow progress against the tidal flow. It was putting along toward the trestle. Wilson reached behind him to retrieve his Nextel from his left hip. It wasn't there.

The other man laughed and climbed the last few feet on the trestle ironwork. Then he began to cross the top of the span. "Did you lose your walkie-talkie? Too bad; it would have come in real handy about now." He laughed again as if he were enjoying this game.

Wilson took careful steps on the crossties to follow him to the other end of the trestle. A train whistle sounded in the distance. The automated trestle would start moving soon. "You know, you really need to come down from there before something knocks you off your perch."

The man sat down on a crossbeam. "Oh, I'm okay right where I am."

If he goes in the drink, I'm not going in after him. But if he comes down, I'll have to move in on him in a hurry. He discovered his empty holster. *Damn, lost my gun, too.*

Now, they heard relays clicking, followed by a motor's whine. The trestle gave a sudden jerk as it began to rotate into position, with loud squeals of metal gears meshing together. Wilson moved to the end, hoping the fugitive realized he had few options.

The man twitched at the sound of the motor and grabbed an iron truss just in time to keep from losing his precarious position. His eyes widened in alarm when the train engine rounded the corner and he began to climb down.

Wilson moved to intercept him; if he knocked him out, he had time to drag him to the end of trestle and drop to the ground with him. Maybe. He waited until they were eye level before he aimed a quick karate punch to the solar plexus, but his opponent twisted to the side. The punch only grazed his chest, allowing him to come back with a roundhouse punch. Wilson ducked and tried to counter with a backhand to the neck. The man blocked it with a raised forearm and continued the motion to catch Wilson below the eye. *Damn, that hurt.* He drew in a calming breath. *Now you've made me mad, sucker.* He was vaguely aware of the little fishing boat and the long, warning blasts from the train.

The man in green tried to kick him, but Wilson raised

his knee and twisted to block the kick. As the trestle jostled again, the man lost his balance and fell backwards. Wilson leaped and grabbed the man's wrist. As the man dangled below the trestle, Wilson struggled to pull him back up before the two lengths of track met.

He shouted down, "Who's the Leopard?"

"How should I know? Pull me up! I can't swim!"

"Come on, tell me." The gap narrowed as the track swung closer to closing. "Tell me or you'll get crunched."

The man looked at the fixed train track on shore, which they were rapidly approaching. "Don't know." Then he smiled broadly. "By the way, my name's Ramirez."

Bastard! You're the plant. Wilson heard the putt-putt of the fishing boat's outboard motor as it passed under them. He started to pull hard on the man's wrist, just as a large gray spider crawled from underneath the crosstie not two inches from his face. "*Ugh!*" He reared back and let go of the man he had held suspended above the water.

Ramirez landed with a muffled thud in the fishing boat to the surprise of its occupants. The drop had been only six feet, so he quickly jumped to his feet, ready for his next move. Wilson gave a fleeting thought to jumping too, but forgot it as the tracks locked in place. The clanging of the trestle stopped, only to be replaced by the steady blare of the train's horn. Now Wilson looked for a place to go before the train squashed him like a bug.

He shouted to Ramirez, "Who's the Leopard?"

The man yelled back, "Vaya con Dios, Senor." With a grandiose sweep of his arm, he gave a low bow. He turned to the fishermen and ordered them to go to the city marina, explaining that he was a federal agent and needed to get to the docks. The men hesitated a moment to look at Wilson and his predicament before they sped off at the "agent's" urging.

As the train reached the far end of the trestle, he could feel the vibrations throughout his body. He grabbed a vertical piece of iron and swung himself out over the water. He caught a glimpse of the wide-eyed engineer yelling at him, as he searched around for a better grip. Pushing off sideways to get a little swinging motion, he looped his hand through a hole in the beam. Adrenaline pumped through him and he suddenly realized he needed to breathe. He gasped in a lung full of air and looked around for a better handhold.

Wilson coughed at the dust the train kicked up. Its cars carried pine logs bound for the mills and coal for the mill's generating plant. He pulled himself up a little and saw that he could now put his feet on the long crossbeam hitting him in the waist. He felt exhaustion creeping upon him as he swung a foot up on the cold iron and finally managed to pull himself up to stand. *That was fun—now all I have to do is wait for the train to pass, and then head for the nearest phone.* He smelled the logs' strong pine scent as he counted how many cars were left.

He rested a moment and watched the gentle sway as they passed. The last car was in sight, the engine had already made the turn to parallel 8th Street. A small piece of coal fell just as he turned back to check the end of the train. It was only about the size of a chicken egg but it hurt like hell when it hit him on the cheek Ramirez had failed to smack. He felt the trickle of blood and touched the spot to see how bad it was. *Just great. Press on it.* He was going to look like he'd gone ten rounds with a Golden Gloves champ.

When the last car passed, Wilson walked on the crossties toward the Down Under Restaurant. Someone from there had seen the fracas and had already called the Nassau County Sheriff's Department. Three patrol cars were kicking up dust as they stopped in the restaurant's parking lot. *Oh, great.* He recognized a couple of the officers walking across the gravel lot.

They had grins on their faces. "Out for a morning stroll, Wilson?"

"Yeah, something like that." He tried to grin back but it hurt too much. He was covered with dirt and saw a Nassau County Fire and Rescue vehicle stop next to a patrol car. The EMTs cleaned his cuts and applied something that stung like the devil. He barely heard their suggestion that he get a tetanus shot as he swiveled his head to look for the fishing boat with his answers in it.

He used a deputy's radio to see if someone could intercept the boat. Since they weren't on Brandon's operational channel, the relay took a few minutes. Brandon sent word back that no boat had come up the river.

At the City Marina, the fishing boat had dropped off its passenger. The man went inside and asked for a small briefcase marked for Simms. The attendant, barely glancing at his bogus identification, gladly followed the instructions to give the case to a man named Simms. Ramirez, alias Simms, strode up the gangway and to dry land. He sauntered past Brett's Waterway Café and up Centre Street, whistling and gazing at the shops like any other visitor to Fernandina Beach. The lure of the twenty-five-thousand-dollar payoff had him hoping he could escape Wilson without revealing his made-up identity.

Brandon and his armed flotilla, nestled outboard of the moored shrimp boats north of the marina, were blissfully unaware that one of the town's newest arrivals was the man they'd spent the last four hours chasing. Lunchtime diners at Brett's munched and sipped as they watched the *Well Behind* being tethered to her temporary new berth at Dock 3.

Chapter 15

Wilson woke with a throbbing headache. The day after the operation with Brandon wasn't starting out well. He sat on the side of the bed, rubbing his eyes and wincing at the ache on his face. Both eyes were black and blue; one was thanks to Ramirez, and the other could be blamed on the lump of falling coal. He gingerly touched the two stitches it took to close the cut on his right cheek.

Dianne walked into the room. "The girls are ready for school."

"Okay, I'll be there in a second. Let me get some clothes on."

Dianne stifled a laugh. Wilson raised a questioning eyebrow. She sat beside him and put her arms around him. "I'm sorry, baby, you look like a raccoon, with those black eyes."

He laughed at the prospect of going to work like this. "Yep, I reckon I do." He pulled a pair of pants on and went into the kitchen. The girls were standing at the door, waiting for Dianne to take them to school.

"Daddy, you look terrible." Michelle stared at him.

"I know." He leaned over to give each girl a kiss.

"Does it still hurt?" Lisa asked, her small face scrunched

up with concern.

"A little. You both be careful at school and I'll be there to pick you up when you get out. Now, off with you—I love you!" He kissed Dianne and mumbled something about a shower, as he turned his back to the flurry of gathering up backpacks and racing out of the door.

Standing in front of his mirror, he gave a chuckle. *She's right. I do look like a raccoon. I'll be in for it at work. Not looking forward to that.*

At the station, he walked right to his office without stopping by the reception desk. Fortunately, he didn't run into anyone on the way. He had called in after the foray yesterday and said he'd be in late. Wilson checked his voice mail and Brandon had left his typically abrupt message. *What a sweetheart.* Brandon wanted to see him and get a final debriefing before he wrapped up the operation. *I hope this is the last I see of him.* The message continued, saying that he wanted Wilson to meet him, to but call him first. He made the call and told Brandon to come over to the station. That didn't sit well with him, but that was too bad.

Once in Wilson's cubicle, Brandon never mentioned the detective's black eyes. They spent the next hour going over details of the operation from every angle. Occasionally Brandon would ask a question to "make sure we're on the same page," as he put it, which Wilson interpreted as a subtle invitation to alter the events so Brandon look better than he deserved.

Wilson gave his own account of Tisher's death, but emphasized that his view was partially blocked by Brandon standing at the bow of the boat.

"Do you think Tisher acted as a responsible agent during the action that led to his death?" Brandon asked.

Wilson leaned back in his chair and looked at the ceiling. *What are you trying to do, clear yourself from any blame?* "I can't say that he acted irresponsibly, just prematurely." Brandon noted the answer in the black folder on his lap.

"Did the man called Ramirez tell you his name, or did you even bother to ask?" Brandon kept his head down, his pen ready to record Wilson's answer

You're pushing it, Brandon. "He told me his name just before I dropped him in the river." *I'm not going to tell you I'm afraid of spiders and let go of him on purpose.*

Brandon paused and looked up at Wilson. "You dropped him?"

"He slipped out of my hand."

"I'll say he's being hunted and I'll let it go at that." He scanned the office with a bored look. "Are there any events, in your opinion, that could have changed the outcome and avoid any bloodshed?"

Who's on trial here? "Who's to say? You know quite well that if we had just boarded on the other side of the cruiser, the whole thing might have come out differently. So you can say that doing things differently could have prevented agent Tisher's death." Y*ou're right; he shouldn't have jumped up like he'd just scored the winning touchdown.*

The telephone rang. "Wilson, Investigations."

"Honey, were you in that awful drug thing yesterday?" Again Grandmother Wilson didn't wait for an answer. "I just know you were. I wish you'd been a lawyer or something else. You're giving me gray hairs."

"Mom. I'm okay."

"I know that *now*. Please don't do that again. You have other detectives there, don't you? Of course, you do."

"Mom, can I call you later? It's really a bad time and we're wrapping up things here."

"Y'all come for dinner. No argument. 6 o'clock. Goodbye and take care of yourself."

"Bye, Mom." He rolled his eyes, hoping for sympathy

from Brandon, but none came forth. Wilson wanted this session to end. "So, that's about it. I can't think of anything to add."

Brandon reviewed his notes for a few minutes before he closed the small black notebook. "That about does it. Give my regards to your chief, and thank him for me."

"I can get him for you; he's three minutes away."

"No, that's okay, I have to catch a plane and head to Atlanta. Take care of yourself." He left without offering his hand. *Still the same ol' boy.*

Wilson turned to his computer and filled in the lines on the prepared report. He quickly finished it and filed it in the system, with a copy heading out to Chief Evans. He had to fill out an incident report about the loss of his cell phone and the Glock in the Amelia River. Under the circumstances, he wouldn't have to pay for the loss.

The Jacksonville television stations called and wanted to interview him and his "spin on the action," as one reporter put it. They were going to air what information they had on the 6 o'clock news. He declined, saying the investigation was still ongoing and the department would issue a press release.

———— •■• ————

"The Surf for lunch?" Dianne asked.

"Sure. When?" Wilson leaned back in his chair. He almost missed the squeaking and nearly being pitched out of his old chair.

"I'll call you, but it looks like 1 o'clock."

At 1:15 he looked at his watch just as he saw Dianne pull into the last parking spot in front of the popular beach restaurant. "Sorry, you know how it goes: the paperwork, then I had to run a license plate." She sat next to him.

"Ah, those were the days." He brushed her cheek with the back of his hand. "Plate check out?"

"Yep, some guy from Atlanta. The sticker looked out of date, but was okay. Listen, Connie O'Brien called and wants us to come over for dinner on Wednesday. How does that sound?"

"A little out of our league, aren't they?"

Her shoulders slumped a little. "She's nice and I'd love to hear more about her collection. Do you know she has several pieces from each period of Pre-Columbian work?"

He frowned, and she put her hand on his arm. "I'd really like to go."

"Sure. I'd kinda like to talk to What's-his-name again. This isn't coat and tie, is it?"

"Sean is What's-his-name, and no, you can be casual."

"Wilson, come in, and Dianne, so good to see you again." Sean placed her hand at once on his arm and put his hand over it as he led her into the living room. Wilson closed the door and followed. *I'll kill him, if he touches anything other than her hand.*

Their hostess approached. "Wilson, do come in and let me fix you something. What shall it be?" Connie appeared more relaxed than during their last visit. Her hair was shorter now and looked better, combed straight back with a little fullness on the left side. She wore an expensive but casual pantsuit accented by a diamond brooch on her shoulder. Sean, on the other hand, wore simple "guy clothes," clearly not trying to out-dress the wife.

Once the initial pleasantries were over, Connie said, "Dianne, later I want to show you a special piece I got a few days ago." She turned to Wilson. "Did Dianne tell you I collect and deal in the Pre-Columbian artifacts?"

"I believe she mentioned it a few days ago." He sipped his bourbon and water.

"It's a hobby that can sometimes be lucrative."

"Who are the buyers?" He tried to warm up to the collection and the conversation..

"It depends on the item itself. The market's just about split between museums and private collections. The more rare objects usually go into private collections, because the museums can't afford the price. Since the '80s, importing artifacts is frowned upon, but pieces continue to show up on markets, even though most countries these days want to keep their heritage in the country, not sold and scattered all over the world. The British robbed Egypt of untold wealth, and the Egyptian government is now trying to get it back. The Pan-American countries see what happened in Egypt and don't want it to happen to them."

She went on, "Still, there are times when a piece can be legally bought and leave one of these countries. Museums sell items to get other items. It's a circuitous route, but some artifacts end up in the hands of private collectors like us. Fortunately, I acquired my personal pieces before the embargos went into effect. I deal with museums mostly, but occasionally I sell to private collectors."

Wilson looked around a little closer and noticed that the cabinets were not the only containers of pricey items. During his last visit, he had also missed seeing the grand piano in its own alcove, as well as several oil paintings that graced the walls. The spaces in the house blended into each other and made the eye follow the design. *This ain't a tract house.*

"Dianne, let me freshen up your drink." Sean took the glass and Wilson noted that O'Brien's Italian leather shoes didn't make a sound on the hardwood floors. He heard his host talking around the corner of the bar to someone in the kitchen. Returning, he said, "Linda says dinner will be ready in about five minutes. Shall we be seated?" He watched Dianne rise and escorted her to the dining room table. Wilson gave his hand to Connie.

As they walked the length of the room, Connie took his arm and pulled him close so she could whisper, "Don't fret about Sean—he likes women, but he's forgotten what to do with 'em when he catches 'em." She giggled.

"She's a big girl. I'm not worried." He patted her hand.

Once they were seated, they were served the salad course. Wilson wondered if the domestic helper was a regular employee or had been hired for the night. The wine had already been poured into crystal glasses.

"Wilson, I heard on the news about your terrible experience with those awful drug runners," Connie gushed.

"Yes, I'd rather not go through that again, especially the part about losing someone on our side."

"You know how TV people sometimes gets facts bass-ackwards; did someone chase down one of the men all the way to the railroad bridge?" asked Sean.

Dianne smiled and pointed at her husband. Sean gave a little laugh. "Was that you?"

"'Fraid so. That's how I got to look like a raccoon." They all had a laugh at his expense.

"I always said you looked good in purple and green, honey." Dianne patted his arm.

"I noticed that you had a little color around the eyes but thought you might not want to go there." They laughed at this, and O'Brien continued, "I guess the investigation is over then?" He looked from Wilson to Dianne.

"That part of it is. Homeland Security, the umbrella agency, has finished most of its inquiry here. The people arrested on the boat are in federal custody, as are those who were apprehended down near Big Talbot Island." He watched his host to see if he had any reaction.

"Hmm. They've got to be singing like canaries." Sean finished his glass of wine and poured himself more before offering any to his guests.

"One person slipped through, and we're still looking for him. He might want to bargain, but it could be tough with some of the charges he's facing."

"Such as?" Sean pushed his salad plate away, and the domestic removed it immediately.

Wilson's intuition kicked in; he wondered why Sean was so curious. *Maybe he's just being interested in my work in general, or has he got a vested interest?* "We didn't find any drugs on their boat, but we have pictures of the transfer they made down river. They might try to wiggle on that."

"The TV said there was a body on board." Connie shook her head in disbelief. "I mean, here on Amelia Island?"

He hadn't had time to watch any television, so had missed that bit of news. "The TV said there was a body on board?"

"Why, yes. This man who seemed to be in charge of the whole thing was interviewed and said a body was on the deck, when the drugs were seized. He said the street value was about two million dollars. According to him, they were hot on the trail of a man who got away and they'd probably have him in custody in a few days." She motioned for the plates to be taken away.

Wilson sighed at Brandon's grandstanding. He'd babble confidential information all over the media so he could look important—and put the entire case in jeopardy. There was no telling what his ego had him say, beyond what came out in the broadcast interview. *I wonder what else he said. I'll have to call Channel Four tomorrow and get a copy of the entire interview. All for a twenty-second sound bite.*

He was desperate to change the subject. "I understand you were in the food business," he said to Sean. The domestic brought out a platter of roast lamb with delicious-looking side dishes.

"I was vice president for marketing for Amherst Food

Company for the last fifteen years with them, but I had thirty years with the company."

"What's their main product? I don't believe I've heard of them," Dianne asked.

Sean laughed and said, "I bet 99 percent of the country hasn't heard of them. They are suppliers to the big guys. All the name brands you see on the shelves at the stores? They don't grow all that stuff themselves. They look for brokers, like Amherst. We dealt mostly with what's called accessory items. Most everything we eat that's processed has salt in it. One of Amherst's contracts is between salt producers and companies that use a lot, such as soup companies. Another thing they do is contract a whole farm crop somewhere in the Mid-West and broker it to large grocery chains."

"Interesting. I never dreamed that there was a business like that." Dianne turned to her hostess. "Connie, this lamb is excellent."

Connie nodded toward the kitchen. "Linda has been with us for years, and it was tough to convince her to move down here with us. I wouldn't hear of her staying behind. She's a whiz with spices and such, but I have a tough time boiling water."

"Your beautiful artwork reflects your travels." Wilson knew just enough to appreciate the wall hangings as well as sculpture displayed on pedestals.

"Most of it is from Meso-America, you know, Central and South America as well as Mexico. Kitty and I traveled there extensively while I was with Amherst, and that's where we made a lot of friends and contacts for business. And we've been to England several times. Amherst was working on getting into the European market."

Connie remarked, "He calls me Kitty because I'm fascinated with the jaguar and its influence in the art of Pre-Columbian societies."

"I noticed the aquarium over there. Those fish are beautiful."

"Oh, those." Sean smiled. "They belong to me and Linda. They're saltwater fish, rather exotic, so we have to be pretty careful with the salinity."

Wilson continued to look around the formal dining area and its antique English oak furniture that the O'Briens had purchased on one of the "over there" visits. The architect had elevated the dining room two steps above the living room, which allowed those seated at the table to see the shoreline. Tonight, the large bay window showcased a full moon rising over the ocean.

"Let's adjourn to the living room for our coffee and liqueur," said Sean, pushing back his chair.

When they were seated around the coffee table, Wilson turned to his hostess. "Did you work for Amherst Food also?"

"No, we met at a friend's party thirty years ago and fell in love immediately," She directed a syrupy smile toward Sean, who was busy charming Dianne. "I must say that I am intrigued by your name." She looked at him over the rim of her wine glass.

"Oh?"

"Calling you just Wilson all the time doesn't seem quite right. You must have a first name."

"It's an old, old family name and, in the old days, names were unusual according to today's standards. I prefer to use Wilson; it just makes life easier. My school days were sometimes…well, bruising is an easy way of saying it."

"Well, I won't press it." She laughed and said to Dianne, "Let me show you what came in a few days ago." The two women took their after-dinner liqueurs with them to the display cabinets.

"You never said much about that body; do you know who it was or anything more than what the TV said?" Sean leaned back and sipped his glass of twenty-year-old port.

"We're trying to identify it at this point of the investigation. It's difficult to say much more until we can identify him. Drug deals always teeter on the edge of violence. No one trusts anyone and everyone has a quick trigger finger. It's out of my hands now anyway; they are up on federal charges, but we also filed charges to cover any loose ends."

"Do the Feds keep you informed about their progress?"

"No, it's their case. They might come around us asking some specific questions about the operation or want to know if we have any information about local people who might've been involved."

"I was curious about the law enforcement procedure in something this big. I mean, there was a bunch of people involved from what they said on TV. Coast Guard and several branches under the Homeland Security's direction, for example. How did you know about the thing, anyway?"

"Trade secret." Wilson gave a wry smile. "You know about trade secrets, don't you, Sean, in your line of business?"

Sean laughed. "Talk about fierce competition; those big companies would try bribery *and* anything else to get information to get the jump on their competition. Our company demanded loyalty, and paid us enough to get it."

The phone rang and Linda came to the kitchen door. "Señor Sean, a gentleman wishes to speak to you." Her accent and lovely brown skin spoke of her Latin heritage. O'Brien left to take the call in the same room where Wilson heard him talking in Spanish a few weeks before.

He couldn't make out Sean's end of the conversation, even though he tried. At first he thought it was just garbled by distance, but he suddenly realized that Sean was speaking Spanish again. He wandered to where Dianne and Connie were standing; which brought him closer to Sean. The cabinet's motorized sliding door was open and Dianne was holding a small figurine.

"Look at this, Wilson. It's over three thousand years old."

"For God's sake, don't drop it," he whispered.

"Aren't these fascinating?" Dianne handed the small piece back to Connie. "These are from the pre-Classic period, aren't they?"

"Yes, that's what I concentrate on. The early *preclásico inferior* period is my interest." Connie looked at Wilson and smiled. "*Preclásico inferior* is a snob's way of saying it's from the period from 1660 to 1000 BC. It's just a way of dating the different styles. I find it's easier on the nerves and pocketbook to narrow one's interest."

He now had a chance for a closer look at the pin on Connie's shoulder. The sparkling array of diamonds demanded attention, detailing the profile of a jaguar from nose to tail, with accents of gold. Her black and gold blouse provided a perfect backdrop for the stunning two-inch-long piece. She smiled when she noticed him looking at the pin.

"This is what got me started collecting, believe it or not. Sean got an absolutely huge bonus, plus a trip to Mexico years ago, and had this made for me while we were there."

Dianne scrutinized it. "I didn't want to be rude earlier, but I've been checking it out too. It's beyond belief." She turned to her husband and batted her eyes. "Honey, get me one." They all chuckled.

"Sorry, Dianne, it's one of a kind." Connie didn't sound sorry at all.

Wilson smiled at his hostess and returned to perusing the cases. He stopped in front of one and leaned down to look at two small bowls. He heard the door slide open as Connie removed one and handed it to him.

"Hold your hand open and let the bowl rest in your palm. That's the safest way to hold it. That piece and its companion," she said, pointing to a similar dish, "are reproductions—we dealers don't like the term fake. The bowls are called tripods and were sometimes used in ceremonial rites."

Wilson held it up to eye level. "I don't know about these things, but I'm not sure I want to know what ceremony this one was used for."

Connie removed the other dish and turned it over. "You see, you're right." She laughed. "That one you have has three legs that are phallic symbols and these supports..." she flipped her own bowl over for the others to see, "...these are breasts. The legs on many tripods are decorative or symbolic, depending on their use. I sold the originals for $250,000 each. They're one of a kind and cost me $200,000 each, so there wasn't much of a profit. You have to pay, let's call it an export tax, to every hand that you pass through on your way out of the country."

They gravitated to the coffee table to replenish their coffee and drinks, and Connie continued, "All of the Latin American cultures had many gods, and their effigies were displayed throughout their houses and temples." She pointed to one case. "That holds mostly reproductions that I've had made from the authentic pieces. These are my favorites and several here that are legitimate, as the tripods over here are genuine." She pointed to a row of four- to six-inch diameter dish-shaped artifacts. "I like the two tripods, male and female, as I call them, because they are unusual conversation pieces. The other case is all merchandise I sell."

Dianne looked closely at the other tripods. "Aren't those the jaguar effigies?"

"Yes, the jaguar god was involved heavily in the religious ceremonies. It was probably one of the most reproduced symbols in the Meso-American regions. Since Sean had this pin made, he has purchased a lot of jaguar pieces for me. He likes them more than I do; he's a big Jaguars football fan. But those pieces are in such relative abundance, they don't bring the high prices of other pieces." Connie pointed a chest-high shelf. "The death mask in this case, the one with the turquoise and gold, is being auctioned now among three museums and the price is now up to two hundred and fifty. I expect it will top out at three quarters, maybe a little more."

Of a million. Wilson silently finished the sentence for her and gave a low whistle. "Are these insurable?" *And she ain't talking small change.*

"Yes and no. I know; bad answer." She laughed. "You can't put a price on a unique item, the only one of its kind in the world."

He looked around. "But someone could break in and take just one piece and have a lot of money in his hands."

"We've taken precautions, believe me."

Sean came in from the office and pushed the door almost closed before motioning for Connie. "That's Raul on the phone for you. I told him not to call during the evening." Wilson watched as his host washed a small white pill down with his expensive after-dinner drink.

Connie seemed perturbed by the interruption. "What's he want?"

"Something about a shipment for me and a find for you." He came over to the Wilsons. "Sorry about this. We've tried to tell him not to call us at night." He coughed. "Doggone heart pills, they always want to get stuck." He moved to help himself to yet another gulp of port.

Wilson could hear only enough to know that Connie was speaking in English. He continued his lap around the room, stopping occasionally to examine a mask or a clay figure. Dianne came to his side. He motioned with a nod. "The sex of these figures is never in doubt, man or woman."

"No, and that's typical of all of the human pieces. Look at these."

"They look different. Are they from the same place?"

Connie rejoined them. "Sorry about this interruption. Are you talking about this group of head figures? They are unusual, and that's why I collect them." She pointed at several of the clay head. "These have the distinctive African features, while these are definitely Asian. No one can come up with a reason for these differences. For some years, anthropologists thought that Africans came to the Yucatan, while Asian peoples came to Peru and the mid-Americas, which includes Mexico. Who knows? But it's fun to speculate, maybe they're both right."

Dianne spoke up, "Honey, we have to run. Your mom must be run ragged by now with the girls."

"Yeah, look at the time. I had no idea so much history could be contained in a few ounces of clay." The Wilsons said their goodbyes and left, heading north on Fletcher Avenue to Atlantic.

During the drive home, Dianne was so pumped up about the O'Brien collection that she kept up a running commentary the entire trip. Wilson managed an *mm-hmm* now and then, but his mind was elsewhere. He needed to call his friend at the FBI in Jacksonville in the morning.

Chapter 16

The gray Wednesday morning dawned with a drizzle. Wilson insisted that the girls wear light jackets to school. They left the house grumbling. He checked his voice messages when he arrived at the station. Nothing noteworthy, but one he needed to follow up on later in the day. Another message informed him that Wilbur would be late because of a flat tire. Wilson made a mental note to have him check into some information about three recent burglaries that may have related.

The partitions creating cubicles allowed the detectives to talk to each other, while still providing a small illusion of a private work area. From where Wilson sat, he could see the status board above the coffee pot. He heard rapid clicks coming from a keyboard and knew it was Sarah. She was becoming an integral part of the investigative force and Wilson recognized she had the sixth sense that a good investigator needed. *Odd that I can tell who's on the computer by the clicks.*

Another new detective, Jon Stewart, came in and asked, "Did you see the pictures on the front page of the *News-Leader*?"

"Not yet. What's it about?"

"The drug bust with pictures of the team coming in at

the marina." He handed his boss the front section of the newspaper.

Wilson took it and read an almost unrecognizable story about how Jack Brandon about single-handedly brought the criminal activity on the island to a halt. Brandon was quoted as saying one fugitive was still on the loose, but should be in custody soon. He explained that he was in charge of the operation, and had directed that several law enforcement agencies be asked to participate. When asked if any Fernandina Beach or Nassau County officers had been involved, his reply had been, "Yes, in an advisory capacity about the topographic layout." *Crime would be rampant if it wasn't for Brandon.*

Wilson snorted. He folded the paper and gave it back to Stewart. "Thanks, I don't know how we didn't know about this." Stewart's smile helped relieve the sting.

"Hang in there, boss. Someday you'll get to be famous." They chuckled and Stewart disappeared down the mauve-partitioned path.

Wilson speed-dialed his FBI contact in Jacksonville. After two rings, Greg Dalton answered. "Greg, your buddy Wilson from the Fernandina Beach Police Department; how's the weather down south?" Wilson swiveled around in his chair, ready for a long conversation.

"Fine. Heard about the bust y'all made up there. Good job. I guess Brandon did it all. What did y'all do, hold his hat while he did all the work?" They had a laugh at the man's absurd hogging of the spotlight.

"Yeah, he did it all himself. I think we were here just to verify his per diem voucher."

"Whatcha up to these days, Wilson?" Dalton got a little more serious.

"Right now I'm chasing a ghost or something else just as elusive. What have you got on the Leopard?"

"Let me check." Wilson heard Dalton's efficient clicking

on the keyboard. "I think I have your fax number; what I can do is send you this file. Do you have a lead?"

"I'm not sure. During Operation Brandon, I heard about the Leopard a couple of times. The thought occurred to me he would be operating in this geographic area. I'm kinda keeping my ear to the ground."

"Man, if you caught him, Brandon would turn blue. You'd really have a feather in your cap." Wilson heard more clicks. "I'm shooting the file to you now. Anything else?"

"Not yet. Let me look over the file and go from there. I appreciate this; I owe you one."

He ended the call and turned on his printer. He was still smiling about Dalton's humor as he went to get a cup of coffee. On his way back to his desk he asked the other detectives for updates on the cases.

The phone rang before he could start looking over Dalton's incoming information. "Investigations, Wilson."

"Are you the chief detective?" came a small voice from the phone.

"Yes, how can I help you?"

"I told the operator that I wanted the chief detective and nobody else. It's very implicit that I am to talk to the chief detective."

Implicit? "Yes, ma'am. I am who you're looking for. How can I help you?"

"Well, you see, I've just killed a man."

"You have just killed a man?" Wilson kept his voice calm. "Where are you and where is the man you killed?"

"I'm at home, residing here in Fernandina Beach, and he's dead living in Oklahoma."

Wilson looked at the ceiling and rocked back in his chair. *Why do I get these?* "You say the man is in Oklahoma? Just when did you kill him?"

"Last night. You see, I put a spell on him, and then I had

Irma kill him."

We're getting nowhere. I see where this is going.
"Ma'am, can you come down to the police station so we can
talk about it?"

"You mean you're not going to send out a patrol car and
haul me in?"

"We'll have to call Oklahoma and make sure you really
killed him. And, oh, who is Irma?"

"Irma is the ghost who lives with me."

"Okay, ma'am; come on down to the police department
and we'll call Oklahoma while you're here. Another detective
will help us."

"Is he good… I mean, as good as you," she paused,
"detectively speaking?"

"Yes, ma'am, it's a lady detective and she is very good."
Wilson hoped the conversation was winding down. "When
can you come over here?"

"He's a lady? He's not one of those morphalized people
is he? Don't matter, I'll be over in a few minutes."

Wilson thanked her, got her address, phone number, and
after hanging up, called out, "Sarah Grant, I have a deal for
you. You better get your dictionary out, because you're going
to learn some new words."

———————•·•·———————

The fax machine spat out the information Dalton had
sent. Over his cup of reheated coffee, he found the files gave
details and names of the higher echelon of the Leopard's
organization, the late Alfred Benoit among them—but not a
hint as to where the Leopard's operations were located. There
were references to Daytona, but the FBI agents hadn't turned
up anything over down there. Several references to the
Brunswick, Georgia, area showed up, including a seized
shrimp boat with three tons or marijuana and kilos of cocaine.

The name, Leopard, had come up during that investigation, but only as one reference and nothing definitive. Buried in the inch-thick information was one line: "Telephone tap on 24 July 2000 indicated the presence of the Leopard in Fernandina Beach, Florida."

Wilson carefully read the whole file twice; that one statement was the only item that suggested the Leopard was in this area. He was going to have to check in with his local contacts on the edge of the drug scene. He looked up the list of individuals arrested in the last few days to make sure his contact snitch wasn't already in custody. He grabbed his coat, but the light rain shower stopped long enough for him to get to his car. It started again before he got out of the lot.

He turned onto 14th and headed north. Just past the fire/rescue station, he slowed to a stop as the light turned red at Atlantic Avenue. Waiting for the light to change, he thought back to the day when, being brand-new in town, he'd made the trip farther out on 14th Street to look for a character named Cajun Jack. Today was the first time he'd thought of Cajun Jack in years; he wondered if the treasure map had ever been located. *Probably not; it would really cause a furor in this town.* The last time he's seen that map had been on a foggy night four years ago. The parchment that many men had died for had been floating down the embankment on its way into the Amelia River. Last touched by Cajun Jack himself.

The light changed and he drove down Atlantic. Downtown, several people waved to him and it made him feel good to return the greetings as he made his way to Front Street. Turning right at the railroad tracks, he passed the few shrimp boats at the docks and stopped at a corrugated tin building. The bit of grass around the building was still damp from the early morning rain and little puddles reflected the blue sky.

The *Miss Jane* sat quietly, her mooring lines slack as the gentle rocking lifted and lowered them. His nose twitched as the smell of the shrimping industry came to him. He walked up to the boat where William Carless leaned against the gunwale, mending a net. "Hi, William. Mind if I ask a few questions? Do you remember me?"

Carless, who had figured prominently in the LaFontaine murder a few years ago, looked up and shrugged his shoulders. "Yeah, I remember you. To what do I owe this displeasure? Did you find some more of my wonderful relatives dead?"

"A few answers to a few questions." Wilson stepped aboard. "It seems there's been a recent influx of illegal drugs in the area." He waited for a response.

Carless kept weaving the repair and didn't look up. It was a cat-and-mouse game now, who was going to talk first. Wilson leaned back against the gunwale. Carless stopped work, took out a cigarette, lit it and blew the smoke in Wilson's direction. The wind carried the smoke back in his face. He looked at the detective for a minute, then returned to work.

"Yeah, that's a real problem," Carless said. "Don't want little babies getting mixed up with any Mary Jane." He looked up. "Do we?"

"No, I suppose not." Glancing away, Wilson added, "Do you know any of these guys that might be bringing stuff in from a mother ship?"

"Nope."

"Seems like an INS plane spotted some boats about your size up against a coastal freighter. Just looked suspicious, that's all. You know how those INS guys are." He tried the lie as a gambit, knowing that such activity wasn't outside the bounds of possibility.

"Any names on those boats?"

"Oh, they took some pictures and are waiting on the blowups." Wilson paused for a minute then smiled. "Hope your boat don't show up in those pictures." *He won't tell, have to try something else.*

Carless rolled his eyes up at him and back down, all the while shaking his head.

"Do you know where Shorty Livingstone might be? He always seems to know what's going around."

Carless re-hung the mended net. "That little turd hasn't been around for nearly two months."

"Strange, I just saw him on your boat a few days ago."

Carless frowned. "Are you spying on me again?" He squinted at Wilson through the cigarette smoke, "Oh yeah, he was, wasn't he. Well, let's see." He looked around. "He might be down at the *Emma Lou*, down there four or five boats away," he said, pointing toward the yacht basin.

You still look like a squirrel. "Thanks." Wilson gingerly climbed over the bow and onto the small wharf. He looked back at Carless before heading toward the other boat.

Shorty was sitting on the bow of the *Emma Lou*, feet dangling over the side. Wilson called out, "Mr. Livingstone."

Shorty's face lit up with a grin. "Hey, Mr. Policeman. How's it going? Ain't seen you in a long time."

"Oh, I've been around. You stayin' out of trouble?"

Shorty laughed, "Yeah, I guess so. I've had pretty steady work." He cocked his head, clearly curious why the chief detective would come looking for him.

"Come over here and let's talk." Wilson moved out of earshot of the *Emma Lou*'s crew, who were also interested in why he was there. When Shorty joined him, Wilson said in a quiet voice, "We're having a pretty bad drug problem and maybe we can help each other a little bit."

"Hey, drugs ain't my thing. You know ol' devil whiskey is where I go."

"I know, but you hear things that might help. Are those guys dealing or hauling?" He nodded toward the boat Shorty just left.

"You tryin' to get me killed? They see me talking to you

already. If something goes down, guess who they will come looking for?" Shorty realized he was talking too loudly and lowered his voice, "I wouldn't tell you if I knew. You guys have banged me up pretty hard lately; besides I don't think they are." He gestured toward the boat. "If anybody around here does haul, it's small time. *And* that's all I'm sayin'."

Wilson smiled. He had run into Shorty enough over the past few years enough to know he had to put up a front, at least while the crew was standing at the railing watching. "Fair enough, I just thought we might at least *try* to work together for this town." He wanted to appeal to Shorty's feelings.

"Listen," Shorty reiterated, "if something goes down they will always look at me as the rat. I don't have any other place to go, know what I mean?"

"I see your point. Just tell me what you know about someone called the Leopard." Wilson went in a new direction.

Shorty eyes narrowed. "I see. You really want me to get killed. You're outta your freakin' mind?"

"No." Wilson grinned at him. "What would we do if we didn't have you to keep us busy?"

"That guy you whacked the other day was somebody big from Miami. That's all I know and that's the word on the street." Shorty started to walk back to the boat, and then turned around and stepped back toward Wilson. "You're a nice guy and married to a beautiful woman, with kids too. Don't go too far. Mess with the little people and you're okay. You start runnin' up the ladder and you'll wind up like that dude did the other day. What you are asking, I don't know. You need to get the Feds in here, to protect your ass." Shorty paused and gave the detective a long look. "Know what I mean?" He stomped back to the boat.

Well, that tells me that the Leopard is probably in the immediate area, if Shorty hasn't heard of him. Now, I need to flush out a few more contacts.

Chapter 17

It was late afternoon when Wilson made it back to the office. He was beat but wanted to look over the day's reports and let the conversations with Carless and Shorty percolate in his mind. Sarah came in and stopped at the partition. He rolled his eyes when she picked the loose lint off the mauve partitions. *God, I hate these partitions.*

"You've stuck it to me this time, boss." She had one hand on her hip.

Wilson cocked a wary eyebrow at her. "What?"

"The lady who murdered someone in Oklahoma?" She raised her eyebrows, making it a question.

"Oh, yeah. How did that work out? Sit down," he said with the wave of his hand.

Detective Hughes' dark hair was pulled back and secured with a silver clasp. He liked Sarah's offbeat humor and suspected that when not on duty, she would usually be dressed in anything black, sparkling with silver jewelry. At the Police/ Sheriff's softball game she had arrived wearing black shorts and a black tank top with the legend in bold white letters: "Outta my way, Punk!"

Now professionally uniformed, she leaned back with her fingers intertwined. She'd been on patrol duty ten years before getting her chance to move up into investigations. Wilson knew she was sharp and her recent stint with the Jacksonville Sheriff's Office showed she was willing to take necessary risks. Sarah never questioned him as to why he made a decision but asked questions to gain knowledge into the investigative process. Now she wondered aloud, "Why on earth did you think this woman had something worth sending me over to interview?"

"Why?" He half smiled.

"She comes in here with a story that has me ready to make a call to the funny farm, but instead I make like I'm really interested in what she has to say…"

"And?"

"And she tells me she had Irma, the ghost, kill a guy in Oklahoma." Sarah threw her hands up.

Wilson made believe he was looking for a pencil. "What did you find out?"

"I called the sheriff out in Armpit, Oklahoma, or wherever it was. He said there was a homicide about 1:30 yesterday morning. A jealous wife caught her husband and his girlfriend going at it in a motel, killed him and wounded the girlfriend." Wilson started to speak.

"Wait." She held her hand up. "There's more. Small town, everybody knows everybody. The motel clerk saw the wife go into the room and he heard shots. The wife came out to her car and drove away. Hasn't been seen since. Here's the topper, though…" An impish twinkle showed in Sarah's eyes. "The wife's name is Irma."

"What's the relationship between the Oklahoma people and the woman here?" Wilson snapped his fingers in frustration. "Darn it, what's the woman's name here?"

"Mrs. Boxer. She's the victim's ex-wife. The motel clerk ID'd his last visitor as the man's last wife."

"What's the problem? Irma called here and told Mrs. Boxer that she killed the cheating scum."

"The sheriff out there was baffled; Irma's been dead for four years."

"Ah huh...and the clerk said the visitor was definitely Irma?"

"Yep, small town." Sarah nodded toward Wilson. "Irma was his cousin."

"You checked Boxer's alibi?"

"She was here in the hospital with pneumonia for the past week—only got out yesterday afternoon. The hospital staff will swear to it."

"Sounds like the Oklahoma sheriff has a problem with ghosts." Wilson rocked back and chuckled.

Sarah got up. "I'll send a report to the sheriff out there if you think it will do any good. Who knows, maybe the lady here knows more about spirits than she lets on."

He chuckled. "Maybe so, but the sheriff has our number if he needs us." He looked at his watch. "Rats, I'm late. I have to go pick up the girls. Lisa's class went to the zoo today, so I imagine I'll get an earful on the way home. I keep threatening them that I'm going to leave them there sometime." A smile came across his face.

"I'll have to call Child Protective Services to keep an eye on you." Sarah laughed as she went back to her cubicle, wondering at how the mention of his daughters could melt his composure.

———— •━• ————

Continuing his hunt for clues about the Leopard, Wilson made a list of questions and passed out copies to patrol officers. They were to use them when they busted even the most petty drug users. Four days later, he received a letter with no return address and a Lake City postmark. He turned it over and felt something slip around inside. He smelled the envelope before he slit it open and carefully looked inside.

Four photographs fell out on to his desk.

The color drained from his face. He picked them up by the edges, trying to preserve any fingerprints. The photos were of Lisa on the school trip to the zoo. They were obviously taken with a telephoto lens, and she and her schoolmates were completely unaware of the photographer.

He turned the photos over to see if there were any messages on their backs. Nothing.

The only other person in the office was Newman, and Wilson called for him. He carefully handed a photo to the other detective. "What do you think of this?"

Newman, like Wilson, had had enough of big city crime. Phoenix's loss was Fernandina's gain. The six-foot-four detective looked the pictures for a second, also holding them by the edges. "Telephoto of kids…at the Jax zoo having a good time."

"Don't you think the prints were done here on the island at Publix?" Newman's experience gave Wilson the confidence to think of him as his number two man. Wilbur, who had been with the Fernandina Police Department for twenty-three years, was talking retirement.

Newman turned the photo over and looked closer at the imprinted marks. "Looks to me like it was. See here, it's faint but Publix is what it says. That's where we take our film to be processed."

"That's what I thought, too. Thanks." Wilson phoned the evidence technician and arranged to take the photos over and be dusted for fingerprints. The only things visible were smudges at the edges. Nothing to get a reading on.

Ten minutes later, Wilson was waiting his turn at the Publix Photo Lab counter. He introduced himself and made sure no one else was near by. He looked at the nametag. "David, I need to know if these photos were processed here. Hold them by the edges, please."

David smiled his easy smile and adjusted his glasses as he turned the photo over. There'd been no need for the lieutenant to introduce himself; David couldn't remember names all the time, but he had a wonderful facility for faces. "Yes, sir, see here's our store number and name,"

"Do you know which one of you processed it? It's been about a week."

"I think I did. Kids at the zoo?"

"Yes. Do you remember who brought them in or picked them up?"

"Not who brought them in. It was after hours, so no one was in the lab. I vaguely remember a man picking them up. It's a little unusual to see a whole roll of telephoto shots; most photos are of family and vacation stuff taken with everyday cameras. We keep an eye out for anything suspicious, especially involving children."

"These didn't raise a flag?" Wilson tried to keep the irritation out of his voice.

"Not really. Those you have are only four of a roll of twenty-four. The other photos were of animals and other people. Over all, there was nothing unusual except the use of the long lens. If they were all of one child, done with a telephoto, then I'd think the guy was a predator; that would be enough to raise the flag, and we'd take action–you can count on it!"

"Tell me everything you can think of about this guy picking up the photos."

David gave him a general description and added, "The man said he was down from Georgia and went to the zoo with his sister and her kids. He didn't know much about Fernandina and asked a lot of questions about our different housing areas. You know, where different streets are."

"Do you remember any street names?"

"Will Hardee was one. I think another was Regatta, but

I'm not sure."

"How about Reatta?"

"Could've been. We have a lot of visitors passing through who ask a lot of questions; unless they say something unusual, I hit *delete* and dump the chatter."

"I wonder if your surveillance cameras would have a shot of him?"

"It's hard to say. His back would have been to the camera coming in, and walking out of here, he may have had his head down. I'll call the manager and let you talk to him." David paged Mr. Docket, who was eager to help and ushered Wilson to his office.

Fifteen minutes later, Wilson was back at the photo counter. "David, if that man were to come back, is there any way you could get a photo of him without him—or anyone else—knowing it?"

"Sure."

"I mean, a good photo so I could ID him?"

"Easy to do. I'll bring the equipment in tomorrow and set it up. I'll show Brenda and Vicki, the other photo technicians, how to do it and we'll have you covered."

"Here's my card; call me as soon as you get something." They shook hands and Wilson left to send the pictures to FDLE's lab to see if they could lift prints.

Michelle and Lisa kept Wilson and Dianne occupied that evening helping with homework assignments. Then the girls wanted to start a game of Monopoly. When 9 o'clock came, Dianne sent the girls off to take baths; they talked and giggled through the bubble bath. Then she tucked them in, saying, "Daddy will be in to kiss you goodnight in a few minutes. Then you chatterboxes have to go to sleep." After the girls were finally asleep and Wilson and Dianne sat in bed, he told her about the photos.

"Why would he take pictures of Lisa? Is it a warning?"

"The Chief and I talked it over, and I must be onto something here. Everybody knows I'm working on the Leopard thing, and I was in on the drug bust a few weeks ago. I've asked the photo people at Publix to see if they can get a picture of the guy if he returns." He went on to tell Dianne about the conversation with the photo lab clerk.

She was sitting up now, no longer sleepy. "If the guy's asking questions about neighborhoods and streets, he's looking for our home. I'll tell the school that we will physically come in and get the girls daily. What else can we do?" Her voice held a high, strained note, and Wilson struggled to reassure her.

"I'll talk to the Hansons across the street; if they agree to it, Chief Evans said we'll set up a stakeout over there for a while. Until this guy makes another move, we have to wait."

"I guess I'm supposed to be able to sleep now." She lay down and stared at the ceiling.

He ignored her fretting. He needed her police brain to kick in. "What doesn't make sense is that the envelope was postmarked in Lake City. I'm going to have a talk with our Mister Livingstone first thing tomorrow morning." He laid his head down on his pillow and turned off the bedside lamp. "Sweet dreams, sweetheart." He moved to kiss her goodnight.

But she wasn't ready to call it a night yet. "Speaking of sleep and dreams, have you had any more nightmares about being shot?" She stroked his face as she spoke softly.

"Not really." he admitted reluctantly.

"What does that mean?"

"I woke up before it really took off. It didn't spook me, either. It's okay, honey. I think it was just the tension of working with Brandon and Tisher."

Dianne kissed his cheek and whispered, "As long as you are okay with it. I won't ask any more, but if you wake me like you did before, we're getting us some help. I'm in this too, remember? No argument, buster."

————————•—•—•————————

"Shorty, get your butt over here." Wilson wasn't in the mood for niceties. He had stalked up to a tin building about twelve yards from the moored shrimp boat

Livingstone left the *Emma Lou*'s deck and sauntered to the side of the building. "What do you want now? Every time I turn around lately, you're there, in my face. I've been a good boy, lately anyway."

Wilson grabbed him and lifted him up against the wall until he was on his tiptoes. The thump of Shorty's five-foot-tall body hitting the metal reverberated, causing the other two crewmen to look over to see what was going on. One started to come over, until Wilson pointed to him and said, "I'd stay there if I were you." The man stopped but didn't retreat.

"Shorty, you need help?" the man yelled.

"No—we've had this dance before. I can take him if necessary."

The man reluctantly went back to cleaning the deck but kept a close eye on them.

"You got something on your mind?" Shorty grinned.

Wilson twisted his collar. "Who did you tell I was asking questions around?"

Shorty gasped as his face reddened. "No one, I swear. Hey, you oughtta know, we got this game goin'. You know, you cops and me. I don't give you no trouble but once in a while." Wilson tightened his fist, causing Shorty to gag. "Honest, maybe someone saw us talking, but I didn't say nothin' to nobody. A couple of guys asked me about the other day you was here, but all I said was you was checking on a wallet someone lifted at the bar."

Wilson's eyes flashed as he shook the guy one more time. "Somebody is threatening me through the mail. Scary mail.

So scary that I'll wax 'em in a heartbeat when I find 'em. You got anything on that?" Wilson leaned close to the man's face so Shorty could see the seething anger in his eyes. "If you want to save your ass, you better tell me what you know. I still owe you a couple of nights in the can for that thigh bite at Sharky's."

Shorty swallowed hard and his voice squeaked. "Honest, Wilson, I don't know what you're talking about. Honest. I don't never, ever threaten no cop. Uh-uh. No siree." He had tears in his eyes. "Lemme down, okay?"

Both of the crewmen were standing at the gunwale, apparently waiting for Shorty to call them. They held heavy clubs.

In the quiet around them, all that was heard was the squawk of seagulls overhead. He wasn't about to tangle with the two crewmen with Shorty thrown in for aggravation's sake. He looked Shorty straight in the eye. "You better be squeaky clean from now on, 'cause I think you know something."

"Man, I don't know nothin' about any threats but if I hear somethin', I'll find you. Okay?" Color was coming back to his face. Wilson dropped him to the ground, and walked away without looking back.

———— • ■ • ————

Chief Evans put a twenty-four-hour surveillance on the Wilson house. The watching policemen operated from the home just across the residential street. There was nothing that happened in the area that wasn't reported. The Hansons were excited about playing a part in a "stakeout." They kept their promise not to tell anyone, and when asked they said friends from out of town were visiting. One officer kept a still camera equipped with a telephoto lens pointed at the Wilson home, while another manned the video equipment. They were always in radio contact with dispatch as well as patrol cars. Dianne and Wilson didn't let the girls know what was going on across the street, but did remind them–again–to be careful of strangers. They reviewed what to do if a stranger approached them. The school principal was more than happy to keep an eye on the girls both during and after school. Wilson didn't tell his mother, who was frailer than ever, because he was afraid she would worry herself into the hospital.

"You don't bring the girls around as much anymore, honey. Why not?" Grandma Wilson had asked one afternoon. He took her shopping at Publix each Thursday.

"Mom, they're so full of energy." He paused. "I know their boisterous clatter makes you nervous and that's okay, they make me nervous, too. They are a handful."

Whenever he mentioned the subject of having a live-in helper, his mother would get upset and say, "I'll tell you when I need help. Until then, I'm okay by myself. I've had to do it since your father died and I'm not about to start having a stranger tend to me."

———————————•━•——————————

Wilson touched base periodically with the men on stakeout. There were no reports of anything unusual, but each officer was hyped about a threat made on a fellow officer. No one ever let on about the reason for the Hansons to have houseguests. Wilson had to work to keep his mind from having a flash burn. He was torn between being the concerned parent and the police detective trying to nab whoever took those pictures. He kept himself busy by helping other detectives on their cases and spent time repeatedly going over the FBI file on the Leopard. He read the Leopard's bio, but it was too sketchy to construct much of a profile. Under the heading of nationality, the form was marked *unknown,* and Wilson stopped to ponder that one. The Leopard's operating area was limited, so far, to the East Coast, which meant that he had connections around the country in the chain of drug lords. Wilson leaned back in the chair and interlocked his fingers behind his head. Looking at the patterns of the ceiling's acoustic tile, he wondered if there was a pattern or if they were created in a random manner. *Patterns… patterns…patterns. Let's see if I can come up with a pattern here from what we know and what's in the FBI file.*

He took out a legal pad and started making notes and drawing diagrams. He listed facts in one column and questions in another. He assigned numbers to each fact and tried to match them with the questions. After an hour of writing, he looked at his scribbles. *Hell, I'm not any farther along than I was before.*

His Nextel rang. "Wilson, Investigations

"How about lunch and do you have anything yet?" Dianne called twice a day to check, even though she knew he'd call her immediately if something came up.

"KP's Deli in twenty minutes and nothing to report, sweetheart."

"Sounds good; see ya." Whenever Dianne was on patrol now, several times a day she made it a point to drive by the girls' schools. Lisa was now at Atlantic Elementary and Michelle had moved up to Emma Love Hardee School, which held fourth and fifth grades.

After they placed the order she said, "I got a call from Connie O'Brien this morning. She wants us to come for lunch next Saturday." She and Wilson were sharing one of the deli's huge BLTs.

"But we're supposed to go to the beach and fly the kites with the girls."

"Until we catch this pervert who's taking pictures, I'd like to keep everyone inside, behind locked doors."

"We can't let him dictate what our lives are going to be." He paused, and smiled at his wife. "But I see your point." He finished his iced tea. "Call her back and tell her we have to spend time with the girls."

"She wants the girls to come too. She said there will be two other children there, so that should work out well, but she did sound kinda put out about a friend of Sean's who's visiting. Apparently she doesn't care for him—or her—I forgot to ask."

"Okay. Maybe we could go to the beach later. I was looking forward to a little beach time, and you know the girls are always ready."

Dianne patted his hand. "You can play with your toys after we go to the O'Briens."

"Thanks, Mommy."

———————— • • • ————————

At 12:30 the following Saturday, the Wilsons drove from Delainy Street onto Reatta and then to Will Hardee. The girls had gotten a thorough review about behavior before they left the house, because the O'Briens weren't used to having children around. Dianne also explained about Connie's collection, and this seemed to draw Michelle's interest.

Wilson followed a BMW sports car, not paying particular attention to it, until it pulled into the O'Briens' driveway ahead of him. Since they had only been there at night, he hadn't noticed a little driveway off the main drive leading to the house. The sports car went down that way and Wilson decided that the driver must be the domestic help, Linda. She disappeared behind a large retaining wall as Wilson pulled up in front of the home.

The O'Briens were delighted to see them, and introduced them to their other guests. Harvey Blackmoore was introduced as former Western regional vice president of the food company where Sean had also been an executive. Blackmoore's granddaughters were roughly the same ages as Michelle and Lisa. Connie took Sylvia Blackmoore, Dianne and the little girls on a tour of the house.

"When we first came to Amelia Island, we bought three lots on the ocean at what then was a scandalous price of twenty thousand dollars each. When Sean got several nice year-end bonuses, we had an architect come up from Jacksonville and design this house with the attached apartment." Touring the guestrooms, everyone oohed over the great walk-in closets. The den had a huge television surrounded by soft leather lounge chairs at one end and a billiard table and bar at the other end of the room. The master bedroom had floor to ceiling windows affording breathtaking views of the beach. Opposite them was a fireplace with Italian marble facing to the ceiling. She led them past the bathroom with its Mexican onyx tub and vanity, into an area where a live palm tree grew in the middle of a round room. She pointed up to the octagonal skylight. "This has a retractable cover so we can regulate the amount of sunlight coming in. I try to prevent the direct sun from hitting the carpet and fading it."

The tour concluded in the kitchen where Linda was preparing lunch. "We have a formal dining room, but we usually eat in here or on the patio. Sylvia, you remember Linda, who's been with us forever." The women smiled and nodded.

They went back into the living room and joined the men. "What are you guys talking about now?"

"I was just telling them about the real estate agent who came by the other day wanting us to sell." Sean got up to freshen up everyone's drinks. "She said it would be easy to get six million for this place."

Wilson and Dianne looked at each other and raised their eyebrows. Connie said, "We're not even interested in selling. This is such a nice place to live."

"So, Wilson, you're a police detective." Harvey looked at Dianne. "And your wife is on the force too?"

"We're in different departments. I'm in investigations

and she's on the street."

"Hey, don't make that sound like I'm working the streets," Dianne said with a laugh.

"I'm sure he didn't mean it that way." Harvey smiled at Wilson. "Sean was telling me you were involved in a large drug raid recently."

"I played a small part; we got the bad guys and the cocaine they were transporting." Wilson didn't like talking to strangers about ongoing investigations. "So, you and Sean were in the food business together?"

"That and other adventures. Do you have many unsolved crimes here?" Harvey laughed and winked at Sean.

"Mrs. O'Brien, lunch is ready." Linda had the dining room table set and ready.

They all rose and went to the table, giving Wilson an excuse for a brief reply. "Occasionally, but we eventually figure it out." He wanted to steer the conversation away from local crime. "What are some of your other adventures?"

"I own a small electronics company, mostly government contract work. We have a plant in Virginia, outside D.C. And I have a little office downtown here, too, because I have work at Cape Kennedy and King's Bay Submarine Base. Can't say much about it, of course."

"Of course."

"Any other unsolved mysteries going on now? Maybe my company could be of service to Fernandina's finest."

"What would that be?" Wilson held the seat for Dianne.

"Electronic surveillance and the like." Blackmoore, like O'Brien, sat and their wives seated themselves. Wilson replied casually, "We have some equipment and what we don't have, we get from other agencies as we need it."

"Always looking for an opportunity, you know?"

"Sure." Wilson was beginning not to like Blackmoore.

"How about mysteries? Do you get many in a small town

like this?"

"We have a couple of open cases that are giving us a run for our money, but we'll solve 'em, even if it takes a few years. The county sheriff recently arrested a man for a crime he committed in a town on the other side of the county and we have tied him to a murder committed in Fernandina four years ago."

"I was chatting with our yard boy the other day, and he said he heard that the body on that yacht you got a few weeks ago was a drug lord from Miami," Sean interjected.

"We're not sure about that yet." Wilson hesitated, then added, "But who knows?"

"Let's talk about something besides dead bodies," Connie spoke up, and the conversation turned to the girls, their schools, and how they were doing.

Dianne looked up and noticed a large crucifix hanging over the buffet table against the wall. She was sure the crucifix hadn't been there the night of the party.

———— •■• ————

On the ride home, Wilson was thinking about the conversations. Dianne saw his wheels turning. "Okay, what are you working on?"

"You know, this Blackmoore fellow's questions were like he'd either known beforehand about some of the things going on around here or…"

"Or?"

"Or he was prompted to ask them." Wilson turned down Simmons Road.

"By whom?"

"Only three people live in the house. Might be any one of them. Oh, I forgot," he said as he pulled into their driveway, "Forensics called, and found nothing on the photos I told you about."

Chapter 18

A week had gone by and the stakeouts had come up empty. Wilson's life was settling down to a comforting routine and he was beginning to adjust to his eldest daughter's morphing into a teen. Michelle and Dianne were working on their relationship, even if most of the work was by Dianne. Michelle was beginning to realize that she again had a family, and more bright moments were cropping up.

Wilson strung a badminton net across the back yard in an effort to keep the girls closer to home. It was working, because they played the game often. The children had been told only that someone who had a grudge against their father might want to intimidate or frighten them, to get even. They were reminded yet again to be alert and watchful. Wilson hated to do it, but the normal carefree bicycle rides throughout the neighborhood were now confined to Delainy Street, and not more than four houses away from their own.

Lisa was too young to question what was behind all the new rules, but Michelle was more astute: she recognized that their lives had changed and they weren't being told all that was happening. She didn't press the issue, but when she got vague answers, she would remark, "Well, something's going on." She made sure they knew that she realized they were taking different routes to school or to shopping centers.

One Friday afternoon, Dianne picked up the children from school for what had become a weekly tradition – going to Publix to shop and then to Wendy's for a Frosty. Dianne was amused at the way Lisa liked to play make-believe, even when opening the family junk mail, pretending that it was from some important person. She would make up thrilling stories–for instance, being invited to meet the Queen of England—when in reality it was an ad for tires. This Friday when they got home, Lisa took the mail out of the box and thumbed through bills and circulars.

"Mama, I've got mail from the President of the United States! Can I open it?"

Preoccupied with putting things in the refrigerator, Dianne called back, "Okay, but we can't go to Washington until Monday." She smiled and went along with the fantasy.

Lisa looked over the selection of circulars and ads, then picked up a plain envelope addressed to The Wilsons. She tried to be careful opening it, but the envelope ripped apart, spilling photographs all over the floor. Lisa stared down and frowned. Dianne came to the doorway and recognized what was happening. She was across the room in a flash and, trying not to upset Lisa, took the photos from her by the edges. Glancing at them, she said, "Honey, those were meant for me to see. Where's the envelope?"

"Here." Lisa held its mangled remnants.

"Okay, put it down and go wash your hands. And use lots of soap and warm water." Dianne tried to remain calm but her heart pounded. She took out her Nextel and called Wilson. "We've got another group of photos."

Her terse words hit him hard. He had hoped that the first set was a prank, but now he knew they weren't; things suddenly became more serious. "Okay, hang on to them and don't let the girls see or touch them."

"Too late, Lisa's already done both."

"What are the pictures of?"

"The girls in the backyard playing badminton and riding their bikes in the street."

"Damn. I'll be right there." Wilson killed his phone and raced over to Chief Evans' office.

He knocked once and walked in without waiting for an answer. "Dianne just got another envelope with photos of the girls at our house." He stopped just short of the desk and was surprised to realize he was puffing.

Evans picked up his phone and growled, "Get me the roster of the Wilson stakeout, now, and get all the men in here." There was a short pause. "I don't care if they're off duty. Get them in here now." He slammed the phone down and looked at Wilson. "What happened?"

Wilson sat down. He'd kept the Chief up to speed about the photos and now told him about the call from Dianne. Evans had been fiddling with a pencil and now tapped the desktop, "Where will we go from here?"

Wilson snapped his fingers. "I just remembered; I talked to that guy over at the Publix Photo Lab." He called Dianne and asked her to check the back of a photo for any marks. She called out numbers and letters. "Okay, have Mrs. Hanson come stay with the girls. I'll meet you at Publix in five minutes. Chief, have those officers stay here until I get back. I shouldn't be long." He went out the door and down the hall, nearly knocking into an officer entering the hall.

He got out of his car and dashed to the photo lab counter. "David, have you had any luck?"

"As a matter of fact, I was trying to call you a few minutes ago; I left a message on your voice mail." He turned and took several photos from a drawer. "Here's your man, and I made a second set of photos, just in case."

Dianne joined her husband and they both looked at the

picture David held out. "Did you get only one shot?"

"Yes, the way we had it set up, we couldn't get more than one at a time. I did, however, zoom in and make it a little clearer."

Dianne took one of the photos. "This is the guy I stopped a few weeks ago. You remember; it was the car with the Georgia plate that looked funny."

"Vaguely. David, how did you take this without him knowing it?"

"I have a long air-operated shutter release I use to take pictures of birds at feeders. I put the camera on this counter and hid it with paperwork." He pointed to a counter behind him. "I ran the rubber air line down the side of the cabinet and taped the bulb on the floor. When he came up to get his photos, Brenda was here, and she stepped on the bulb to take the photo. Simple, really."

Dianne asked, "Are you sure he didn't know he'd had his picture taken?"

"Yes, ma'am. If fact, Brenda's a good-looking woman and he stayed around and hit on her."

"Do you still have the information about him?"

"Yeah, it's here in this record of film taken in. Let's see…Robins is the name he gave us but no telephone number. Again, said he was vacationing here and looking around to maybe buy a place."

Wilson turned the photo over several times, thinking. "Did Brenda say that he might be back?"

"No, she's married and didn't give him any encouragement, but she was extra nice to him."

He reached to pay for the photos, but David waved his hand. "Remember, the manager said to help you any way we could, so there's no charge. We're always glad to help."

"Thanks. Uh, it's best that no one else knows about this." Wilson shook David's hand.

"About what?"

"Exactly. Thanks again." Once they were in the parking lot, Dianne brought up the girls safety again. Wilson stopped at her car and said, "I don't think he'll try anything. These photos are to scare me away from the hunt for the Leopard. I don't think the girls are really in any danger." He put his hands on her shoulders and shook her gently. "Now, I'm going back to the department. Evans has all the stakeout guys there except for the one on duty now. I've got to run." He gave her a quick kiss and left. Dianne watched him go, hoping he'd called it right.

He went straight to Evans' office. Seated around the conference table were the five men involved in the surveillance team. Wilson let them know that he was upset; since they'd started the stakeout, the stalker had been able not only photograph the girls on their bicycles but also had invaded their backyard. He threw the duplicate set of photos onto the table.

"What in the hell are you guys doing? How could this guy get this close to my house in broad daylight and you not see him?" He was livid and the men couldn't look at him. Each was afraid that the photos had been taken on his shift. "Here, look at these." He shoved them at the officers.

Chief Evans stepped in and his quiet voice calmed everyone, "Okay, Wilson, we all understand why you're upset. Believe me, we want this guy just as much as you."

He ran his hand through his hair. "In all honesty, Chief, I don't think you do." He paced while they watched in silence. He stopped and looked at the men he had come to trust; the bonds among them were strong, but the threats to his daughters had weakened them.

One of the men looked at the photos more closely. He began to turn them to make them lie right, since they had been taken at a slant. "These of the girls on the bicycles were taken in the afternoon, about 4 p.m., I'd guess, same for the backyard shots."

"How can you tell that?" Wilson began to calm down, now that somebody else was talking.

"Shadows. I worked in photo interpretation in the Air Force. Since your house faces south, you can see the length of the shadows and the color of the light. Colors of the sunlight on objects change according to where the sun is in the sky. People don't generally know that. But the day they were taken…that's a guess."

"There has to be a reason that he was at your house besides taking pictures," another officer added. When Wilson just looked at him, he continued, "One reason would be to visit you or Dianne, but you haven't had any visitors. Another would be a service call. Have you had any work done at the house in the last couple of weeks?"

Wilson shook his head and finally joined them at the table. "What could someone do that would let him freely roam through the neighborhood?"

"Oh hell," someone said and they all looked at him. "I saw a utility guy walking through the neighborhood reading electric meters. Where's your meter, Wilson?"

Wilson picked up the photos and scanned them for a second before whispering, "Right where these photos were taken. Son of a bitch." He looked up at the man. "Do you have any recollection of what he looked like or had on?"

"I couldn't see your meter and he moved in and out of my view several times. Generic. Gray work pants and shirt. Nondescript. Sandy hair, maybe five seven, five eight… medium build. He went to the other houses. In fact, he ignored the little dog that was following him and yapping at him most of the time. That's the only unusual thing."

"Dianne says she stopped him a week ago—his Georgia license plate looked a little odd but it checked out. She recognized him from *this* photo." He held up the surveillance photo David had taken at Publix. "Does this look like the meterman?" He shoved the photo across the table.

"Could very well be. I didn't put the binocs on him."

The chief looked at the team and then leaned back. "Okay, let's get the record of Dianne's stopping the suspect, then put out a local APB. I'll call Sheriff Goodsend, notify Jacksonville and FHP. This guy has guts and a brain. He may very well be armed, so we'll assume that. We'll keep the team watching your house, Wilson, and you guys, damn it, let's start questioning anyone going near the house. Phillips, you brief whoever's at Wilson's right now." He nodded to dismiss them.

Chapter 19

Chief Evans called Wilson to his office the day after the APB went out. Evans sat behind his large desk and offered him a cup of coffee.

"Charles, you didn't call me in here for a cup of coffee." Five years of working together closely had built a friendship that allowed some relaxation of protocol behind closed doors.

Evans laughed. "You're right. I know you're on edge regarding this photo thing. Let me toss some ideas out and see what you like. This guy is probably still in the area. Not too many people in Fernandina know of the Leopard. By now, those guys we captured in the raid have been in touch with their lawyers in Miami. I feel sure the Leopard has to know that someone in the department knows about him. And it's a given that all Feds are after him. All that leads me to a new strategy." Evans rocked his chair back and forth.

"How 'bout we go public with this? In a big way. I can talk to the *News-Leader* and *Nassau Neighbors;* their editors should go along with us."

"You mean do a front page story?" Wilson frowned a little.

"Not only that, but do a series on the drug scene. Expose it, blow it up. We'll put the heat on."

Wilson thoughtfully sat back in his chair. Neither man

spoke for a minute. "We couldn't put the information about the photos in; it would put too much pressure on the girls."

"No, I wasn't thinking of that. Just tell the community that you are leading the investigation into the identity of the Leopard. We'll also tell our side of the recent bust, not just Brandon's take on it. There isn't a town in America that doesn't have a drug problem. You remember that conference Bill and I went to a few weeks ago?" Wilson nodded.

"The police chief of...I can't think of the name of that podunk town in southwest Georgia. Anyway, his city's population is about three thousand, and he made a heroin and cocaine bust last year that was close to half a million dollars in street value. He was the new guy in town elected to clean up the drugs. He's doing all right, but it's at a price." Evans paused. "I don't have to tell you, it's everywhere."

"Chamber of Commerce won't like it," Wilson pointed out. "Little Fernandina with a major drug problem."

"It's also to clean up *their* town. They'll have to like it. By the way, how long has it been since you've taken a vacation?"

"What's that got to do with anything?"

"When this story breaks, you might want to be out of town. Take the girls to Disneyworld or to the mountains."

"No, that's running out. I'll face it head on. You know me better than that."

"Yeah, I do. But I wouldn't blame you if you did get away for awhile."

Later that day, Evans made a call to the publisher of the *News-Leader*. George Mallory said he was always happy to work with the department "in any way that would improve life in and around Fernandina," when he offered to send a reporter out the next day. Evans emphasized there were to be no photographs of Wilson with this story.

Wilson wanted to wait until he got home to tell his family

about the upcoming story. He called Dianne to give her a heads-up, promising to fill her in later. As expected, she was concerned about the plan but said she trusted his judgment.

After his conversation with the chief, he called an old acquaintance at the Jacksonville Sheriff's Office who was now the head of the Burglary Division. Wilson wanted someone who was familiar with breaking and entering to come and look at their house, to point out its weaknesses. He wouldn't waste any time before strengthening those points; his family was vulnerable.

That afternoon he sat the family down at the kitchen table and told his daughters about the photos. After they had time to absorb this, he told them about the plan to catch the man who'd taken the pictures. Dianne assured them that they weren't in any danger as long as they followed some pretty simple rules. After the talk, Wilson gathered Michelle and Lisa in his arms and told them he loved them very much; he explained that he was on this case so they could grow up in a better place.

Lisa went over to Dianne. "Mommy, are you going to help catch this man?"

Dianne took her hands and looked at her, "Baby, this man doesn't even want me to catch him."

"Why not?"

"Because I'd hurt him so much that Chief Evans wouldn't like it." She smiled at Wilson over Lisa's shoulder as she stood up.

He spoke up again, "Okay, let's get ready." He had promised them dinner out if they paid attention at the family meeting.

Lisa asked, "Where are we going for the nice dinner?"

"McDonalds!"

"Oh boy," was Lisa's enthusiastic squeal.

Michelle rolled her eyes and put her hand on her sister's

shoulder. "Lisa, Daddy's teasing you."

"It's a surprise. Both of you, get ready."

As they scampered out of the kitchen, Dianne called, "Michelle, your yellow dress... Lisa, put on the blue one."

He turned to her as the girls ran down the hallway, "See how tall Michelle's getting? She's almost as tall as you are." He shook his head and mumbled something about "...growing too fast" as he went to get ready.

The sunset over the Amelia River settled the quiet day's end on the island. At Brett's Waterway Café, the Wilsons watched the clouds in the west change from white to shades of pink, then corals splashing boldly across the horizon before a fire-red sun disappeared. The low light of the fine restaurant softened all shadows.

His mother had told him how this restaurant had started out in what was now Motorcity Cycles on 8th Street. Then, when the telephone company moved out of its nice brick building farther up the street, Brett had moved right in. Now Horizon's Restaurant occupied that spot, while Brett's Waterway Café overlooked the Intracoastal Waterway and the city marina.

Wilson ordered an appetizer and they whispered occasional etiquette hints to the girls. Sitting back, he looked at each of the women in his life. They were all especially beautiful tonight, and he loved the happy spontaneity of the girls, Michelle was looking more and more each day like her mother. He felt a sudden pang of sadness.

"Why are you looking like that, Daddy?" asked Michelle.

"How am I looking?"

She gave a little shake of her head. "Weird, with a grin on your face."

"Oh, I was just thinking how much you look like your mother." He turned to Dianne to see if he'd made a mistake in saying it out loud.

Dianne put her hand on his and said, "She does look like that picture of Grace that's on her dresser, doesn't she?"

"That's what I was thinking, too." He remembered when his daughter put it on her dresser in the new house. It showed all four of them, Michelle at six and Lisa, two, standing next to Mickey Mouse.

Michelle had explained as she put the eight-by-ten photo in just the right place. "I'll see it before I go to sleep and first thing when I wake up."

Dinner was served and interrupted their reminiscing. Lisa gleefully shared all the second-grade gossip at school. Her sister joined in with tales of the goings-on in her grade. The chatter went on until Lisa came out with, "I saw Michelle holding Harold Brady's hand yesterday."

Dianne and Wilson looked at each other. Lisa licked the back of her spoon in satisfaction and Michelle gave her a stare that should have melted it.

Wilson asked Michelle, "Has he asked you on a date yet?"

She rolled her eyes up and said with a hint of exasperation, "No."

"Well, you tell him your daddy said you could start dating when you're twenty-five years old."

She looked at her father and didn't say a word. He put his hand on her arm, "Okay, twenty-three then." She wrinkled her nose at him.

"Thanks. I know girls that say they're going steady."

Dianne piped up, "I went steady with a different boy every week. I loved telling the other girls that so they'd be jealous."

His three ladies began to talk about boys in school, and Wilson was astute enough to stay out of this territory. He used the time to formulate a plan to release information to the newspaper a little at a time. The Leopard was tough, and

Wilson wanted to see who would blink first. A passing couple broke his train of thought.

Wilson didn't notice the man, but the woman was tall and thin, with blonde hair streaming down to the middle of her back. As he watched them being seated nearby, he was sure he'd seen her before. She suddenly looked at Wilson and smiled. It was then he realized that Dianne was talking to him.

"…so Wilson, what do you think about the atomic bomb going off in Fernandina?"

"Yeah, that's bad… what?"

"Come on now, that young thing had all of your attention." She gently kicked his leg.

"No, I wasn't or she didn't. What are you talking about?"

"Daddy," Michelle whispered, "I *saw* you too."

"Well, if you busybodies must know… she just reminded me of a girl I saw when I was in college, years ago. I only saw her twice, but I'll never forget her face."

Dianne looked away. "Wow; she made quite an impression."

Wilson sighed. He knew he'd stepped in it. He had to come clean.

"Okay, here's the story: I was only a student number among thousands, and a shy kid in a place I had no business being. The campus newspaper, *The Alligator,* ran her picture as 'Co-ed of the Month' and she was all us guys could talk about. Her name was Sheena. One day we happened to pass each other during class change. I gawked and she smiled and said hello. I wasn't much good the rest of the week, let alone that day. It happened the next week too. That time I was cool, I said hello back at her." He paused. "I never saw her again," he finished and took a sip of wine.

Swinging her feet back and forth, Lisa said, "So, what happened to her?"

"She's fat and has six kids," Dianne quickly remarked, making a face at her husband.

"I don't know. But I knew how Don Quixote felt about Dulcinea." He chuckled.

"Daddy, you're getting weird again." Michelle finished her ice cream.

Later, as they were getting ready for bed, Dianne said, "Sheena, huh?"

Wilson rolled his eyes; he knew what was coming, so he might as well play along. "Yes, and you know, it's funny; I hadn't thought of her that much this week."

Dianne fired a pillow his way. "This week? So, I guess you fantasize about her a lot, huh?"

He walked over to her and put his arms around her slim waist. "I was teasing." He kissed her nose. "It's really been about a month."

She pushed him away slowly. "Maybe I can make you forget her."

"I was hoping you would."

Chapter 20

Dianne was traveling east on Atlantic in her patrol car when a call came over the radio. She turned into the Recreation Center's parking lot and listened as another patrolman called in that he had the APB suspect's car in view and was stopping him.

"360, 373. What's your 20?" Her heart rate increased.

"Blockbuster Video parking lot."

"HQ, 373. I'm en route." She turned on her blue light and made a beeline back on Atlantic Avenue and swung left on Citrona. She kept telling herself to be calm. Not sure where Wilson was, she called the dispatcher requesting that he meet her at the scene. Reaching Sadler Road, she accelerated toward what she hoped was the scumbag who'd taken the pictures.

When she turned into the lot, she saw Perkins had the driver out of the car and was talking to him. She felt her face flush with heat and told herself to remain calm and professional.

The man glanced at her when she approached. He was the man in the Publix surveillance photo. She stepped so that she and Perkins were on either side of him. She nodded to Perkins and he told the man, "Put your hands on the roof and spread your legs apart."

"You still haven't told me why you stopped me," muttered the driver.

Perkins frisked and handcuffed him, and then pushed him off balance so he was leaning against the car. He handed Dianne the man's driver's license. Looking at it, she said, "What are you doing in town, Mr. Mason? You're a long way from home."

"Trying to get a job."

"Like taking pictures of little kids and mailing them to people?" Her throat tightened up and she raised her voice.

Perkins put his hand on her shoulder, gently but firmly easing her back. "Dianne, let me put him in the car." She backed up and the man got into the patrol car's back seat.

Wilson drove up and she went to meet him. "He's the guy in the photo, the same one I stopped a few weeks ago." Her hands were shaking.

"Okay, listen—go sit in your car and I'll get someone to cover for you. You're too upset to be any good now. I'm going to go over and try not to kill this guy. Call HQ and have Driscoll's Auto Service come get his car."

She started to walk away. "I want my shot, too, ya know." She glared at the guy in the rear seat as she passed Perkins' car.

Wilson stopped at Mason's car and looked inside. The only thing visible on the passenger side was a camera, complete with a powerful telephoto lens. A suitcase lay on the back seat, and the entire area was littered with fast-food bags.

When he questioned Perkins about this man he'd stopped, it was pretty much the same as Dianne had told him. He'd said he was John Mason, here in town looking for work. Perkins hadn't had a chance to run a check on either the car or driver. Detective Sarah Grant drove into the lot and went to Dianne's car, where she leaned over to talk through the window. Wilson caught sight of Linda, O'Brien's domestic helper, driving by, rubbernecking.

Later, at the police station, Wilson had Mason put in the interview room after the patrol officer fingerprinted him. Wilson went to his office before heading to the interview room. He had told Dianne that he didn't want her in on the interrogation, because he was concerned her emotions would get in the way. She grudgingly agreed she'd probably lose it and went home, after extracting a promise that he'd tell her everything.

Wilson called for Sarah Grant to be present. "Mr. Mason, you've been read your rights and said you understand them."

Mason nodded. They inventoried all of his personal effects, penned his name across the top of the envelope they were put in.

Sarah sat at the table across from Mason and fixed her eyes on him, looking for something, anything that might be helpful. She opened a small notebook and clicked her ballpoint pen. Wilson silently looked out the window, with his back to Mason. The air conditioner blower kicked in and cool air poured into the room. Wilson began by tossing paperwork on the table, face down; then laid the photos of his girls on the table. He didn't say anything, but put them face up, all in a neat row. He watched Mason as he touched the edges to straighten them. The man's eyes traveled from one photo to the next.

Wilson leaned on the table and spoke just above a whisper. "Do you know these little girls, Mr. Mason?"

The man shifted in his chair, cleared his throat, but said nothing. He licked his lips and looked away from the pictures.

Wilson worked hard to keep his voice calm. "These are my little girls, Mr. Mason. And I'd like to know why you were photographing them." The suspect had a thin line of sweat on his forehead.

Sarah flipped a page of the notebook. "We have your prints on these photos, so we know you're the one that took them."

Mason gave a nervous laugh. "You haven't had time to process the prints. How could you know that? You're bluffing."

Wilson flipped over the set of fingerprints he'd taken from his office ten minutes earlier. "These are your prints and they match." Wilson snatched them back up. "The game's over, Mason. Who put you up to this? You aren't smart enough to try to extort money from me."

"Give me a name and address." Sarah waved the pen over the notebook.

"We believe you're a sexual predator, a child molester. We know you made those pictures. That's pretty good proof to a judge. Do you know who those little girls are, Mr. Mason?" He leaned over and yelled into his face, "My little girls. And you know what?"

Mason stared at him, and Wilson said, "You took those photos of my two innocent little girls without their knowledge or consent. Without my knowledge or consent."

Sarah saw Mason's composure slip a little. He looked in shock, not believing that he was here and in this trouble. He turned away from Wilson's face. She asked, "Who put you up to this, the Leopard?"

"I'm guessing that you'll get twenty to thirty years for this." Wilson stood upright suddenly, knocking over his chair. He slammed his fist on the table. "Who are you working for?"

Mason jumped, but remained silent, staring at the scarred surface of the table.

"We've been following you for the past two weeks and know your every move. You went to my house dressed like a meter reader, and you live out of your car. We know a lot about you, Mr. Mason. By the way, what are you doing with nearly a thousand dollars in your pocket and not staying in a motel? You said you haven't been arrested before and, believe me, we're checking on that right now, Mr. Smart Guy." He pointed his finger at the man. He slammed his chair upright and started pacing the room.

Mason shifted again in his seat and began trembling. Sarah looked at Wilson.

She clicked her pen, laid it down and turned to the man. Belying her cherubic face, the tone of her voice was hard. "We're not playing good-cop-bad-cop. I'd like to take you out back and cut your nuts off." She never blinked while staring at the man.

He took a long deep breath and looked at Wilson.

Wilson spoke slowly, "She would do it, too. Do you know what they do to people like you in prison? Let's say the judge is lenient on you and you get only twenty years. You might survive four or five years, but I wouldn't count on it."

Mason wouldn't look up from the table. Wilson and Sarah spent the next forty-five minutes trying to get him to open up. Chief Evans came by and stood at the window for a full five minutes. Evans had no expression on his face, but just stared at Mason, who tried not to look back. The chief had considered taking Wilson out of the room and putting another detective in for the interrogation, but dismissed the thought.

Wilson's experience gave him a wide array of approaches and now he moved to one that he hoped would hit close to Mason's home.

"Do you have kids, Mr. Mason?" The other man's eyes flickered a little. Wilson plopped into the chair and added, almost nonchalantly, "Yeah, I bet you do. Nice looking guy like you." Wilson shook his head, then violently slammed his fist down, "Talk to me, damn it!"

When Mason turned his head away. Wilson saw a tear

on his cheek. "You better cry, you sorry piece of crap. Go ahead and cry… cry for yourself because the person who put you up to this is going to let you swing in the breeze. He isn't going to raise one finger to help you."

"If they raise a finger," Sarah said to Mason, "it will be like this." She had her middle finger up.

Wilson threw his hands up. "If anybody helped you, he'd be an accomplice. Now here you are, trying to figure out how do I get myself out of this mess, and you know what?" He stood erect again. "You ain't going to get out of this." There was a knock at the door. "You hold that thought, sport, while I get the door."

When he opened it, a uniform stuck a sheet of paper in his hand. He read it as he made his way to his chair and then held up the sheet. "Know what this is? It's a police report from the Broward County Sheriff's Office, and it says you were picked up on April 3 on State Road 997 after someone had beaten the crap out of you. You refused medical attention and said you'd taken a wrong turn. They bought this story until, as misfortune happens, a K-9 unit pulled up and the dog smelled cocaine on you. You were clean, but you know what, Mr. Mason? I used to work Miami, drug runners would have a residual smell of cocaine on them that was easily detected." He paused. "Yeah, go figure. Just like you, they'd be clean, but we knew that eventually they'd end up in the morgue or swimming with the alligators in one of the canals."

He casually took a stick of gum from his pocket, unwrapped it slowly, and put it in his mouth. "Still don't want to talk about it…Mr. Mason?"

He stared at the clean-cut looking guy. *How old are you? Thirty or so?* "C'mon, tell me. Who put you up to this?"

Mason tilted his head to one side and finally spoke, "They'll kill my family if I talk. You should know that if you're really from Miami."

"I know and you know these people are heavy, but we

can hide you and your family," Wilson told him. "I have contacts at the FBI and we can all work this out."

"Are you stupid, man? They have informants everywhere. No way you can hide me good enough I won't be found."

"Maybe that's what they tell you to keep you in line, but it's not true. Think about this for a second: If the top guys go down, there's nobody to rescue them; they'll take the people below with 'em. We both know that some of *those* people are waiting to take their place." Wilson paused. "It's a game, Mr. Mason. A game that little people like you lose. They sail away to Aruba in their yachts with hot women and cold beer to keep them company and…and you become somebody's wife in prison."

He let the silence grow to give the man time to grasp what he'd just dropped on him. He pushed his chair back and stood, looked at Sarah and with a slight nod said, "He's not talking. Put him in a cell until we can take him to County. You'll see a judge in the morning, Mr. Mason." Wilson shuffled papers and made ready to leave.

Sarah looked at the suspect, glancing at the ring impression on his finger. "Mr. Mason, you've got a wife and kids and no one knows you're here but us. All the information we've got on you can be lost in the files. If you cooperate and we take down the Leopard, the Mason family could disappear," she snapped her fingers, "into thin air." She looked at Wilson, who waited to see what the man's reaction would be. She softened her voice. "You know, Denver is nice and so is any big city where people can get easily lost."

They waited for another five silent minutes. They could see Mason weighing the options. He looked at them and then around the room. "Screw it, you had your chance." Sarah stood and noisily got her handcuffs.

"Wait. What information do you need?"

Chapter 21

Wilson called back to the duty desk to have an officer come take Mason for a bathroom break and get him a cup of coffee. Things were a little more relaxed now. After setting up the tape recorder, Wilson settled at the table again and prepared to listen to the man's tale of woe that would undoubtedly end his unwelcome stay in Fernandina Beach's jail. Mason started by claiming that his contact was by telephone. He gave Wilson the phone number, which Wilson dialed while they were sitting there. It was an 800 number, and the voice on the other end said it wasn't in service at this time. *They must be through with Mason or know he's here.*

Mason said he didn't know anything about the Leopard, the name had never come up. He was a pilot, and all he did was fly stuff up from Colombia to Miami—and then got mugged for his payment. Later his contact had called him on his cell phone. They'd said all he had to do was take the pictures in Fernandina and then leave town. He was on his way out of town when he got stopped.

"We'll get you back over here tomorrow for a formal statement," said Wilson. "Right now, you're headed over to the county lock-up, where you'll at least get something to eat. In fact, we might go over there for your formal statement.

We'll see."

It was late in the afternoon by the time he wrapped up the interview. He called to see how Dianne was doing. She apologized for her emotional outburst at the scene and he told her not to worry; it was a normal reaction. He had his own trouble controlling himself around Mason.

The following day Wilson and Sarah met Mason at the county jail. They had the tape recorder again and a stenographer to transcribe Mason's every word. He repeated what he told them the day before, including the telephone number he'd been given. Wilson had already made contact with AT&T and they were going to get back to him, but things didn't look good. They told him the number had been disconnected the day before.

Mason claimed he had met his contact through a guy he met at a small outlying airfield in the Miami area. The man had known he was in a financial bind with three small children and a wife to support. One flight, this man had said, would make him financially free, and he would be able to move elsewhere to start over. The plan they hatched seemed foolproof, until he was left to meet those three guys on the road. He now thought that the muggers already knew he had a lot of money, and that he was tied to the guys who had collected the cocaine from his plane.

"Hell, I can't even provide you with names; even if I could, you know names change in this business—just like the weather."

Wilson's next move was to contact the FBI in Jacksonville to see if they wanted to interview the man. Either way, he'd send his FBI counterpart a copy of this transcript.

Mason was arraigned later in the morning, and the only charge the DA would file was stalking; he'd confessed to taking the photos of Wilson's daughters. They couldn't bring any drug charges against him, because there was no evidence.

Wilson would get in touch with some old friends at the Dade County Sheriff's Office and see if they wanted Mason. No bail was set.

"I'm sure they don't have any evidence down there either," he told Dianne later. "Once his battery case was cleared, they probably closed it. And Mason couldn't provide then with descriptions of his assailants. You wouldn't believe how dark it gets out there in the middle of the swampland. He was no good to them and couldn't even help them track any runners."

"So he gets out of here with nothing but a stalking charge." Her face darkened again.

"I know you're upset, but you're a police officer so you know how it works. He'll either spend some time at County or, since this is his first time, he'll walk and be told to hit the road."

Just before going home, he looked over a report that Wilbur had filed on a case he was deep into. Wilbur, on his way back to the station after investigating a theft at a warehouse near Front Street, had seen two men shoving Shorty Livingstone around in a vacant lot. Wilbur had jumped out of his car to see what was happening. Shorty and he went back a few years. Very few people in town knew that at one time they were in-laws; Wilbur had been married to Shorty's sister. Before Wilbur's ulcer became a permanent fixture, the two men used to hit the bars a couple times a week. They remained friends over the years, in spite of the divorce and Shorty's run-ins with the police. Now Shorty was in the middle of something and Wilbur, once again, had to bail him out.

Shorty told Wilbur it was a personal problem between him and the two guys who were bothering him, because he'd quit working on that shrimp boat. The two men made some mumbled posturing threats and left when Wilbur showed up. The officer left Shorty standing in the lot and returned to his car. "I could've taken them if you hadn't interrupted," Shorty muttered—the only thanks Wilbur got.

Wilson liked the idea of having a hard copy of reports, in spite of the wonders of the computer. Side notes could be made on the hard copy, but not in the computer. He had just filed Wilbur's report copy when the secretary at the main desk called and said there was someone to see him.

He went out and met a tall man in his late forties who held out his hand. "I'm Robert Potter, and I own several shrimp boats. I was wondering if we could talk."

Wilson took him back to his office, where Potter began by mentioning that the word was out that the police were investigating drug business filtered through some shrimp boats. He had come down to find out what was going on.

"I appreciate your directness, Mr. Potter. As with all agencies, we're stretched thin. We've helped the INS and Border Patrol from time to time in catching drug runners using our port. We know that a lot of boats that are docked here from time to time are home ported somewhere else. We don't want to scare our shrimpers, or those who come in for provisions, into thinking we're sitting with spyglasses waiting for them to make a wrong move. But we do keep an eye on the docks."

Potter nodded. "I appreciate that, and I know the men will."

"You'd be amazed. We've caught drug runners in huge pleasure yachts, airplanes and one guy was brave, foolish, and stupid enough to drive a tractor-trailer here with false bottom containers loaded with marijuana."

Potter frowned. "There's that much of a demand for weed here in Fernandina?"

"The last guy told us some of it was for here, but the most of it was going to be loaded onto small boats, like cabin cruisers, and sent up the coast to Georgia. So you see, it's not the shrimpers who are our targets; we haven't singled them out. In our line of work, we have to look at anyone who has the capability to be a drug runner. In fact, we've had tips from local boat owners about suspect boats coming into our port." Wilson gave a short laugh. "I don't think I could physically tackle being in the shrimp business."

"It is physically demanding when you're hauling in the nets. You've made me feel a lot better, Detective Wilson. I appreciate your honesty." The man shook Wilson's hand and left the office.

It had been a long, emotional day, and he couldn't wait to log himself out on the status board; a quiet evening at home sounded wonderful. He walked to his car a little faster when he remembered Dianne saying something about a small pork roast for dinner.

———— •—• ————

Dianne convinced her husband to take some time off on Saturday morning. She made a picnic lunch and he got the kites ready for the beach. She felt better about going places now that the stalker was in custody; the beach was where they all had fun. They watched the girls from the shade of a covered table.

Occasionally a strong gust would send dust from the demolition of the Beachside Commons building swirling into the air. Wilson watched as a small cloud wisped its way across Fletcher.

"What are they going to build there? I forget," he said, squinting against the sun. He felt in his pocket for sunglasses.

"I forget too. That corner has a lot of history." Dianne took a sip of her cola.

"Like what?"

"Do you remember Alice Walsh? Your mother introduced you to her after Mass a few Sundays ago?"

"Yes, I do now. Doesn't she work for the *News-Leader?*"

"The same. Her parents were the Moores, Morris and Claire; they built the first building over there in 1929." Dianne pointed to the rubble. "The only other building out here was a casino, built where we're sitting. The Moores had a home on Ash Street, but built a small place here by the shore, and soon Claire was selling the beach-goers cold drinks and snacks from her porch. Morris was a barber on Centre Street but later they lived here at Fernandina Beach. There were two towns then, you know—downtown was Fernandina and out here was Fernandina Beach."

Wilson watched the girls while listening. "How'd all that…" he nodded toward the pile of broken concrete, "get to be there?"

"Morris built a two-story place with a restaurant and grocery on the bottom floor and rooms to rent upstairs. The family lived in a cottage in back of the place. When it burned down in 1932, they moved back downtown, but came back and bought more land and built a bigger place."

Lisa came running up. "Daddy, Michelle's making her kite hit mine and she won't stop."

"I can't help it. It's the wind making it do that." Michelle tried to pass this off, but Wilson saw how things were going between the sisters.

He turned and gestured to the area behind them. "Michelle, go over there to fly your kite, and Lisa, you go in front of the light pole." Michelle walked away, shaking her head, and Lisa ran to her appointed spot. He turned his attention to Dianne again.

She gestured with a hand. "Over there they built a motel and gas station. The original place was added onto, so by 1941 there was a private dining room and dance floor. Things went well because he put in a one-chair barbershop and laundromat."

"Sounds ambitious. What happened to it all?"

"Time. Their son bought the place in the 1960s, and another fire hit a year or two later. The son rebuilt and eventually sold it. The Beachside Commons was built on the original foundation, and some of the walls were used."

"Interesting." Wilson reached for a sandwich.

Dianne turned and called the girls for lunch. They came running over, out of breath, and asked first for something to drink. They sat in silence, listening to the gulls crying to each other and watching the people strolling along the walkway.

Slowly nibbling her sandwich, Dianne gazed toward the old Moores' site. Wilson looked at her and then at the site. "I can see the wheels turning. What are you thinking about?"

"*Mmm*... well, a few years ago your mother had Alice and some women from St. Michaels over for a luncheon, and they were talking about family get-togethers. Alice told one of the most touching stories about the place. She said the Moores closed the restaurant on Christmas and had a big family dinner. The four Moore boys were in service during World War II, but were home at the time.

"About halfway through the meal, Claire saw four Army soldiers, who were stationed at Fort Clinch, peering in the window, thinking the restaurant was open. She got up and invited them in for Christmas dinner. Later Claire found one boy, about eighteen, sitting by himself at a table, and he was crying. When she asked what was wrong, he said it was his first time ever away from home at Christmas. Your mother said there wasn't a dry eye at the table when Alice finished the story."

Wilson was silent for a few moments. Michelle said, "That's sad."

Lisa took a drink of soda and asked, "What happened—to the boy, I mean?"

"I don't know, honey. I don't think anyone here in town knows. Let's finish and get ready to go home. Remember, we're supposed to go to Regency Mall this afternoon."

This prompted the girls to get their things quickly into the car. Wilson teased Dianne with the remark that he wasn't so sure that teaching the girls that shopping and spending money was fun was a good thing.

"Get used to it, buster. It only gets worse when they're both teenagers." She rolled her eyes at him.

————————•●•————————

The Wednesday edition of the *News-Leader's* top headline read: Does Fernandina Beach Have a Drug Problem?

Wilson read the article at the breakfast table. He'd given the interview a few days before, and was glad to see it covered everything he wanted to say. The reporter had asked him if the person who'd escaped during the bust had been captured. He'd lied and said the suspect had been caught in Georgia and was waiting extradition back to Florida. *Ramirez is probably busy selling information to someone else now. One day he'll get his butt caught in a real jam and no one will be there to help him.* The story went on to bring up the Leopard's name several times and emphasized the law enforcement team's idea that the Leopard was in the area. The story ended with the hint that several agencies were closing in on this key figure and had inside information that was pointing them in the right direction.

Wilson hoped this article would work, but he was still apprehensive about this whole newspaper idea. It meant making his family a potential target for someone as powerful at the Leopard, and he knew the big cat wouldn't hesitate to eliminate his opponents. He and Dianne had talked to the girls at length, and made it quite clear that this media coverage might cause their friends to ask questions. Dianne had suggested, "Just tell them you don't know anything about it, and that your parents don't discuss police business with you."

Chapter 22

Sean O'Brien sat reading the same *News- Leader.* He put it down and drained his cup of coffee before pouring himself another from the silver service. Clear golden sunlight spilled into the room, and a gentle breeze played with the palm fronds at the edge of the patio. He took a moment to appreciate his surroundings before he sat back, falling into deep thought. The past few years had been so hectic that he rarely seemed to have the luxury of trying to tie his thoughts all together.

Connie came up the steps to the dining area, but paused to watch her husband staring out the window. She moved to her own chair. "You're sure thinking hard. Worrying about your visit to the heart doctor today?"

Linda brought in Connie's breakfast and set it before her. Sean didn't answer his wife right away, but looked at her until Linda went back to the kitchen. He sipped his coffee.

"There's a very interesting story in the paper that tells me our friends the Wilsons are pretty astute observers."

Connie buttered her toast. "How so?"

"There's a front page story all about some East Coast drug lord they're calling the Leopard." He set his coffee cup down carefully. "Does that name ring a bell?"

"No, should it?" She looked up to see Linda standing in

the doorway. Connie frowned, and Linda moved out of view.

"Well, I was just putting a couple of things together in my mind."

Connie gave a little chuckle. "Don't overdo it, darling."

"It's all fitting now." After a few moments, he spoke, "I think, my dear wife, that you could tell everyone all they wanted to know about the Leopard."

Connie burst out laughing. "What a ridiculous idea. I'm loving this, how did you come to that conclusion?"

Sean wouldn't look at her as he calmly elaborated on the number of phone calls from people in Central and South America she'd been getting, and how many more there'd been recently. He'd noticed she'd seemed edgy lately, especially when the story broke about the murder and drug bust on the Amelia River. Then there was an increase of phone calls from her "art dealers," supposedly about delicately negotiated purchases.

Another thing that stood out in his mind, he told her, was the ease of going through the Customs when leaving Colombia. And now that he thought of it, they usually had the same customs agent every time they'd come back to the States. There were the occasional quick trips to museums about some of the clients' purchases, yet most deals took months.

"In short, my darling wife, I think this pottery thing you have going is a large and lucrative front and a damn clever one at that."

Connie sat back and stared at him in disbelief. "I think your medicine is making you delusional."

He waited while she went on to debunk his theory. He folded the paper, took out a pen and circled a spot in the paper and handed it to her, watching for a reaction. The paragraph read:

"Recently police arrested John Mason in connection with

child stalking and taking unauthorized photographs of children. Detective Lt. Wilson went on to explain that he felt there might be a connection between Mason and recent drug shipments in and out of the Miami area. Mason mentioned the name *Leopard* in his interview with the police lieutenant. The suspect is being held in the Nassau County Jail and will be turned over to federal law enforcement agents as soon as the paperwork is processed, according to Lt. Wilson."

Connie tossed the paper on the table, pushed her plate aside and drank her coffee. "So?"

Sean snorted. "Your worthless cousin is named John Mason, and he was recently involved in some sort of trouble in Miami, remember? He called you here to get some money so he could get back to Atlanta."

She gave a short laugh. "Oh, it's not him, I can assure you. John went straight back to Atlanta. Where else would he go? His wife and kids are there. He wouldn't do anything that stupid again." She looked tired as she leaned back and watched her husband. "What are you going to do now...call Wilson?"

"No, you'll hang yourself soon enough." He got up and left the room.

She sipped the coffee slowly. Linda came in and sat in the chair next to her, putting a hand on her arm. "What now?"

Connie lit a cigarette and blew the smoke toward the ceiling. "I guess it's time for a special seafood dinner." She began tapping the cigarette lighter on the table.

"What about cousin John?"

"He knows little to nothing." She dropped the cigarette in the unfinished cup of coffee and watched the waves rolling onto the beach with the incoming tide. "I'll make a phone call to Jacksonville. They'll see to it he's dealt with."

———•—•—

Wilson checked into the office by placing his peg in the

In hole. He sat down but got right back up to fill his coffee cup. He returned to his desk and the ringing telephone.

"Wilson, Investigations…oh, Wilbur, where are you now? Uh-huh…Okay, get that information over to the State Attorney's Office…yeah, that's fine, see you then." He hung up, took out his personal phone book and dialed.

"FBI, Dalton."

"Greg, Wilson, Fernandina Beach. How's it going?"

"Fine. One of our agents lives in Fernandina and brought in a *News-Leader*. You're stirring up a hornets' nest, you know."

Wilson rocked back in his chair. "Yeah, the guy we caught was taking picture of my girls and mailing them to us to scare me off the chase."

"Why didn't you call us?"

"We caught this guy by a lot of luck and quick thinking. He's a pawn and doesn't count for much in the big picture. He doesn't know much, or seem to, anyway. Scared mostly."

"I was about to call you. I have some information that might be of interest to you."

"Oh?"

"The dead guy on the boat, Alfred Benoit, was—as we suspected—a player with the Leopard. His occupation was listed on his passport as used furniture dealer. The yacht he was found on is registered in Panama to a company called Kitty's Koffee Kompany, all with K's. There are several owners scattered all through Latin America, and any of them could be a front man."

"Interesting. What else did you get?" Wilson was making notes by now.

"We had gotten a judge to issue a wire tap order about two months ago, finally, and Benoit made a couple of phone calls; we got a partial number of 904-26. There are five 26 prefixes, four in Jacksonville and one in Fernandina Beach, in the 904 area code."

"Why did you get just that bit and not the whole number?"

"After the six, we'd get static on the line, and the phone company doesn't know why, either here or Miami. The static lasted for anywhere from three to six minutes. Not long. Then the line was closed, like the call has ended. Make any sense?"

"Not yet. Let me get back to you."

"Okay. Remember if you get something good going on, let us know. This is an international thing, and a lot of agencies want in on it and—"

Wilson started to pull Dalton's chain. "And you want me to call the IRS boys, and INS as well, and FDLE and on and on."

"Good one. Keep us informed, okay?"

"Greg, you'll be the first I'll call. I still have your cell number. Take care."

"You too."

They hung up and Wilson grabbed the telephone book.

———————— •■• ————————

In the O'Briens' home, Linda announced that dinner was ready. The couple sat down while she brought in her special seafood gumbo. Connie snapped her cloth napkin and laid it across her lap.

"Sean, I have been stewing about this all day, and I just want to say that you have made this a truly miserable day for me. I think your accusations this morning were completely out of line."

He looked at her with no expression while she continued, "You know that I do very well with the artifact transactions. You have a comfortable retirement, and this windmill that you're chasing is nice, but I don't think you're going to topple it with your accusations. You have your little secrets and I have mine." She smiled over the wine glass.

"Mine don't involve ordering murder," he said through clenched teeth.

"Oh, Sean, grow up. I'm talking about your coffee venture. I'm not involved in any drug thing. I agree that from what the paper said and from what Wilson said, there is a remote domain of possibility that someone like me could be doing things like this so-called Leopard character. Let's face it, the improbability of it is much greater than the probability. Besides being nonsense, they need to sell newspapers. Let's not let this excellent gumbo go to waste by arguing over something that isn't."

Sean silently finished the gumbo and began on the pasta salad while Linda brought in the main dish. He brooded and drank several more glasses of wine as they finished the meal. Then he left the table without a word to his wife and sat in the large leather chair facing the wide flat-screen television on the wall. He set another full wine glass down on the end table.

Connie calmly sat at the table and slowly sipped the dry wine. Nearly a half hour later, he glanced over at her, still at the table. She looked like a cat ready to spring on its prey, carefully watching, waiting for the right moment.

Sean put his hand to his lips and massaged them a little. Connie looked at the kitchen door where Linda stood with a frown on her face. They both watched him flex his fingers and wring his hands a little.

"What's wrong?" Connie called from the table.

"I don't know. I feel tingles and my lips are numb." He rubbed his legs and arms.

"Oh, sit back and relax. It's your nerves. You're just upset." She sipped her wine.

"*Ugh!*" He grabbed his stomach. Linda started to go to him but the look from Connie immobilized her at the kitchen door. Sean doubled over and struggled to turn his face toward his wife. She sat, unmoving, and watched.

He tried to stand but fell back in the chair sideways; grasping at the arms to right himself. He gave a hoarse call for help as he started to slide down toward the floor, grabbed at the end table, knocked over his wine glass and put a foot out to stop the slide. Connie got up and walked over to him. With her foot behind his supporting knee, she gave a little push. Sean crumpled onto the floor, now toppling the end table as he grabbed at anything he could.

Linda stood at the entrance of the living room, her hands covering her mouth. Connie thought she saw tears on the woman's cheeks. She pointed to the kitchen and Linda retreated.

Sean looked up at Connie, his face twisted. He tried to speak, but only guttural sounds came from his throat. His wife regarded him with an impassive, calculating stare. He tried to raise his arms but his hands only fell to touch her slacks. As he clutched feebly at the material, she stepped back and his hands slid weakly to the expensive carpet. Sweat broke out on his forehead and his skin became red and blotchy. Convulsions struck; his eyes rolled and he thrashed like a caged animal in its death throes.

Finally his body relaxed and he lay motionless, except for the rapid rising and falling of his chest as he worked to breathe. He stared at the ceiling now, his eyes no longer asking for help. A drop of sweat rolled off his forehead, down his temple, and off the ends of his hair. His breathing became shallower.

Connie knelt and bent over him slowly. She looked straight into his unblinking eyes and whispered, "Good night, Don Quixote."

The grandfather clock struck 6 p.m.

Chapter 23

The evening shift had been slow for Dianne. Beyond a few minor traffic violations, she hadn't seen too much. She was in a pretty good mood and let the three drivers she had stopped get away with a warning. She thought she would go by the elementary school, even though it was well past school hours; it would give her some mental comfort to see that it was locked up and all right. The past few weeks were making her wonder about the wisdom of the Fernandina Beach Police Department continuing its pursuit of the Leopard. She'd started to bring up the subject with her husband several times, to strongly suggest that the department let the FBI handle it. Every person on the force was doing everything they could, but Dianne was well aware that the Leopard they hunted was like its wild counterpart—smart and able to stay out of sight.

When she got home for her supper break, Wilson had fixed his secret recipe spaghetti. He was good at cooking and liked it, and he wasn't afraid to try something different, sometimes to the chagrin of the girls. His more spectacular failures had been added to the family lore, such as chicken thighs simmered in applesauce with raisins. Upon more disastrous occasions, he would shrug in good-natured defeat and spring for having dinner out

On her way back to patrol, she saw Shorty Livingstone walking along Sadler Road at the old Ron Anderson auto dealership. Dianne pulled into the vacant lot and called to him.

"Hi, Dianne, what's happening? I shoulda said, Officer Wilson," he responded

"That's okay; not much. Pretty quiet night. I'm not going to have to come get you later, am I?"

"No, I hope not. Just a few beers, then back to my room."

"How are things going for you? I heard Wilson pushed you a little."

"Oh that. He's just doin' his job. I don't know nothin' about any drug runners." He looked over his shoulder before continuing, "Some of the Carolina guys come in sometimes, you can smell their boat a mile away. The guys here...if any of them run the stuff, they don't bring it back to this port. They don't want to get caught at their home port."

"Sounds reasonable." Dianne looked at him closer. "What happened to your eye? Looks a little puffy and red." Before he could answer, a car drove by and the passenger checked them over thoroughly. "Shorty, do you know that car?" She pointed as it continued down Sadler.

"Justa' couple guys I know...an' this, I ran into a door. Ya know, I get a little tipsy sometimes."

"Uh-huh. Be careful tonight; I have to go now." She started the car and shook her head over his story about the eye.

"Right, see ya 'round." He went on, heading toward his favorite bar.

By now it was 10:30 and the night was winding down for Dianne. Her shift would be over at 11. She pulled through various fast-food parking lots to make sure the teens of Fernandina Beach were behaving. She went through the McDonald's drive-through for a cup of coffee, then parked in the Wachovia Bank parking lot facing 8th Street.

Radio chatter was light tonight, but still she was interrupted before she finished the coffee; "373, HQ."

"373."

"Signal 63 at the Flounder's Gig."

"Roger; is Shorty involved?"

"I think so. Do you want backup?"

"I'll call on my mobile when I get there." She pulled out of the lot and sped towards the beachfront bar where Livingstone often caused a ruckus. Three minutes later she drove into the parking lot and heard loud music from inside. As a couple of patrons came out, she asked, "Is a short guy the problem in there?"

They nodded and she went in. Shorty was in the corner again with his weapon of choice, a pool cue. His lip was puffed up and a trace of blood decorated the corner of his lip.

"Shorty, what am I going to do with you?" She put her hands on her hips and turned to the barmaid. "What was it this time?"

"I'm not sure. Better ask that guy there." She pointed at a man sitting with a woman at one of the tables.

Dianne went over to them, noticing that someone had killed the music when she'd come in. She asked the dark-haired man with his overweight companion, "What happened?"

He rolled his head back and growled, "That little twit made some remarks about this lady and I didn't like it—"

The woman broke in, "If he wasn't so little, I'da kicked his ass."

"Yeah, you and who, that big sumbitch you got with you?" Shorty's reply came from the corner.

Dianne raised her eyebrows, waiting to hear more. Then she lifted her open hand to silence the man as she heard her backup call. He said he was a few minutes away.

The woman spoke as the man with her finished his mug of beer. "We were sitting at the bar, having a drink when Short Stuff came over an' and sat next to Ben." She jerked a thumb at her nearly drunk companion. "They must've known each other from back aways. Anyways," she took a big gulp of her own beer, "anyways, Ben said something about Shorty mouthing off too much to the wrong people." She let out a belch. "Oops." She giggled.

"What did you mean by that, Ben?"

His bleary eyes had a difficult time focusing on her. "Oh, nothin'. You know how he is, runnin' offa the mouth alla time. It jus' upset me, what he said about Betty Ann." He let out a big burp. "'Scuse me."

"Beth Ann," the woman corrected him.

Dianne looked at her. "*You* are driving tonight, right?"

His date looked at Ben. "Looks like it, if I can get him to the car. Anyway, the little asshole got nasty when Ben told him to go away or get his ass beat." Dianne looked over at Shorty while the woman continued her monologue. "When Ben said that, the runt asked how old I was and Ben looked at me and told him 'bout thirty."

"And?" Dianne was rapidly running out of patience, yet she realized when you're trying to get information out of drunks, you need patience.

"Anyway, when Ben says thirty, the little twit asked, 'Whas 'at... in dog years?' That's when Ben hit him." The bottle blonde refilled her mug and Ben's from the pitcher on the table, and Ben gave a chuckle. Opening his eyes, he tried to focus on his surroundings, but Dianne could tell it was a lost cause.

She motioned for Shorty to come with her. After they walked past the soused couple, Shorty turned around and called loudly, "Next time I'll bring you some dog biscuits."

In a flash, Beth Ann up-ended the table and lunged

forward. Dianne wasn't ready for the quick reflexes of the woman or what happened next. A big guy collared Shorty and pushed him toward the angry woman charging toward them. Dianne's sweeping arm missed Shorty. Now that Beth Ann was on her feet, Dianne saw how tall she was and that the woman outweighed her by at least a hundred pounds and six inches in height. She needed her backup and needed him now.

If she hadn't been in the middle of this, she would have had to laugh. Shorty charged and disappeared into the huge arms of Beth Ann; he seemed to figure the best place to be was as hard up against her as he could be. She back-pedaled and screamed, trying to get enough distance between them so she could land a good punch. As she went backwards, Shorty kept pumping his short legs and pushing forward, his head buried between her enormous breasts. He was yelling something but no one could hear it above the laughter.

The bystanders were cheering them on, and Dianne wouldn't have been surprised if money had changed hands. Her own mental wager was on Shorty; the woman may have had him outmatched, but he fought dirty. His head twisted from side to side and the woman's windmilling arms tried to peel him off her. He had his teeth clamped onto her bra with the grip of a tenacious Georgia bulldog. Dianne couldn't help herself any longer and laughed with the rest of the crowd.

She ordered Beth Ann to stop, but it was much too late. Her intake of beer and Shorty's animal charge was more than gravity could withstand. The woman crashed to the floor, landing on her butt with a thump—and with Shorty still attached. When she fell flat on her back, he followed, landing on top of her. This unlikely couple brought a cheer from the raucous crowd. The crash landing and ensuing trampoline-like action propelled Shorty into the air, only to land again face to face with his assailant. Beth Ann was stunned but the ever-quick Shorty grabbed her by the ears and planted a sloppy kiss on her lips. He wiggled off of her as fast as he could, while she was still sputtering and trying to regain her composure, or what was left of it.

Shorty ran to Dianne. "Let's get the hell out of here before she gets up." He took her hand and tugged her toward the door. Their exit was accompanied by cheers and clapping hands. Dianne caught a brief glimpse of Ben's silly grin, indicating he was vaguely aware of what happened.

Shorty hustled over to the police cruiser and dived into the back seat, closing the door with a slam. The backup arrived with blue lights flashing. Beth Ann reeled out of the bar and over to the cruiser where she pressed her nose to the window. Pounding on the window, she threatened to give Shorty a knuckle sandwich, until Dianne eased her away. A Fire/Rescue vehicle heading south on Fletcher drowned out her warning to Beth Ann about public intoxication. In the car, Shorty grinned and blew kisses at the woman. Dianne told her to go get her boyfriend, take him home and go home herself.

Beth Ann seemed to resign herself to the end of her evening. She leaned over to look at Shorty and yelled, "Call me, okay?"

———————— •■• ————————

"I took a chance that you were on duty." Shorty sat in the cruiser's back seat waving to people they passed. He didn't have to know them, he just waved. They headed north on Fletcher Avenue to the blinking light at Jasmine and turned left.

"What do you mean? We just talked earlier."

He didn't answer, which startled Dianne—she'd never seen him hesitate before. She looked up at him in her rearview mirror. Finally, he turned to meet her eyes in the mirror. "I know. I hate to admit it, I'm a little scared." He hesitated again. Then, in a voice so low she could barely hear, he confided, "I know who the Leopard is."

She stopped the car in the middle of Jasmine and turned around to look back at him. Then she stared ahead, wondering what to do.

Five minutes later she was pulling into her driveway. Wilson came out and opened the back door. He motioned for Shorty to get out. "What do you know about the Leopard?"

"I heard some of the guys talking and listened in. They didn't know I was there until later; that's when they gave me this reminder to keep quiet." Shorty touched his black eye.

"Names. Of these guys and who they said the Leopard is." Wilson leaned against the car. "Henderson and a guy they call Smiley. That's all I know about them. They said this Leopard guy lives down on South Fletcher and the Leopard was pissed because they showed up at the place."

"Anyway, they said the Leopard was always going to South America and to Mexico as a front, then they laughed about it."

"And the name?" Wilson's eyes narrowed.

Shorty looked up at him. "They only referred to him as the Leopard, no names."

"How do you know he lives on South Fletcher?"

"They said the trip to South Fletcher was as close to getting killed as they wanted. The Leopard threatened them with extinction if they ever showed up near there again."

Wilson motioned for Livingstone to get back in the car. "Dianne, take him to town and book him on disorderly conduct, and we'll try to keep him alive. I'll call the Sheriff in the morning to keep him isolated at the lockup."

She drove to the station, and when the paperwork, and Shorty's booking were done, so was her shift. Later, when she and Wilson were in bed, he asked, "Who do you think it could be?"

"The Leopard? Sounds like Sean O'Brien to me. He's got contacts throughout that area where the drugs come from. What a good front," she mused, "using your wife's interest in Pre-Columbian art as a cover."

"Yes, that's what I was thinking. Remember the first time we went there? He was speaking Spanish on the phone, talking about a shipment he expected. He had buyers here ready and waiting. He sounded irritated that it wasn't here."

"How do you know it was Spanish?"

"Miami, honey. You learn it or suffer. So, how do we gather the evidence we'll need to capture this big cat? I'll have to work on that. We can't go hunting without some bait. I'll call Greg Dalton in the morning, and we'll have to work out a plan."

He kissed her good night and rolled over. He fell asleep immediately, but his wife stared at the ceiling for too long. There were disadvantages to sharing an occupation: she knew exactly what danger her husband was about to place himself in. *Please, keep him safe for me* was her last conscious thought.

Chapter 24

Monday morning Wilson called Greg Dalton, who agreed to come up to Fernandina Beach the following day to discuss strategy. Next, he called the Nassau County Sheriff's office and spoke to an investigator he knew there, spending ten minutes to explain the situation. His contact said things were tight at the moment and it would be afternoon before he could guarantee them a spot. It most definitely would be after the morning court visits by the inmates.

Wilson hung up and looked over the cases the other detectives were working on, to see where he could help. He was glad to see that all of them were on top of their own investigations.

He walked over to Al Newman, who was concentrating on his computer screen. Newman looked up and remarked, "I had a heart attack victim from last night. Patrol called me in because he wanted to be sure about not calling in the Medical Examiner, but I've seen heart attack vics before; this didn't look different from them. In fact, the wife had all his heart medications out for the Rescue guys."

"Where was it?" Wilson tried to make out the address from the screen.

"Down on South Fletcher. Name's O'Brien."

"Damn. Sean O'Brien?"

"Yeah, why?"

"He's our number one suspect as the Leopard." Wilson leaned closer to the screen. "What time was this?"

"The 911 came in around 10:30 p.m., and I was called out not long after; I was up next on the list."

"Thanks for the info." He returned to this desk and called Dianne to tell her the news and that he'd be by to get her. They were ringing the doorbell on South Fletcher less than fifteen minutes later. Wilson wasn't sure they were making this call as friends or cops, but they were there, anyway.

Linda opened the door; her eyes were red and downcast. She ushered them to the living room, where Connie sat, holding a handkerchief in one hand while a woman Wilson didn't know held the other. She got up when the couple came in.

"Oh, thank you for coming." She gave them each a hug. "This is Frances Mallory, a tennis friend who's come over." Mrs. Mallory excused herself and left, telling the bereaved widow that she was as close as a phone call.

Connie returned to the sofa, and the Wilsons with her.

"It was so quick," she said in a quavering voice. "We were watching the evening news around 6 and he was drinking a glass of wine. Two minutes later he slumped over, and that was it." She dabbed her eyes.

Wilson and Dianne looked at each other. Silently, Linda brought Connie a glass of water and offered the Wilsons a drink.

"No, thank you. Connie, was Sean having trouble lately with his heart medicine or any other medication?"

"Well, he did say that the next time he went to the doctor he was going to have some dosage increased. He finally admitted that he was getting a few chest pains but, being Sean, he didn't put much stock in them."

"May I use the phone?"

"Yes; Linda, show Wilson to the office phone." Connie took a sip of water.

A few minutes later he rejoined them on the sofa and asked, "Is there anything we can do to help? Is there other family we need to contact…any arrangements we can help you with?"

"No, his sister has been notified and will be here tomorrow."

"What about business associates? Can we contact any of them for you?" He looked up to see Linda standing at the door of the kitchen.

"No, we've called them too. He was retired from the company, you know."

"He mentioned to me once that he had contacts somewhere in South America, and that he was working on a project," Wilson remarked.

"Oh, that. He loved the food business, and he got together with some broker in Colombia on one of our trips down there to get me some artifacts. This broker has a new coffee strain." Connie looked drawn. "Sean said he wanted to corner the U.S. market on this new coffee. I don't know that much about it, but he said it would make us wealthy beyond reason."

Wilson saw Linda step quietly from the kitchen doorway. He told Connie, "I'm sorry, but Dianne has to get ready for duty so I'm afraid we'll have to go now."

Connie walked them to the door and gave them each a farewell hug. "This has meant so much to me; we've only known each other for a short time, but you've been so thoughtful."

Dianne held her hand a moment. "We enjoyed the company of you both and are truly sorry about Sean. Let us know if we can help in any way." The Wilsons turned and took several steps toward their car.

As if she had a last thought, Connie said, "You know there is one thing you might be able to help...help Sean more than me, actually. He was always terrified of having heart surgery and even getting something as minor as a shot. He always told me that he didn't want to have an autopsy because some stranger would cut him into pieces. I know it sounds silly, but, Wilson, could you see that they don't do that?"

He looked at Dianne and then back to Connie. "I'll stop over at the hospital and see what I can do."

"It would mean so much to him. Thank you, Wilson." The widow stood in the doorway and watched them drive away.

Deep in thought as he drove north on Fletcher, Wilson wondered about the reason behind the odd request for no autopsy. "I'm going to stop at the hospital and see the doctor who was on duty last night, if he's still there." He explained where he was going with his train of thought.

Dianne went in with him and they identified themselves to the Charge Nurse. Holly Williamson, who had been on duty the night before, had doubled back–pulling another shift–because nurses had called in sick. She showed the Wilsons to the Family Counseling Room. "Working twenty-four hours with about four hours of sleep between shifts isn't my idea of having fun." She shook her head, as if trying to shake off the numbness caused by lack of sleep, "But what the heck, what can I do for you?" She gave them a tired smile.

"We can relate to that. There was a DOA last night that came in around 11 p.m. Sean O'Brien. What did the doctor put on the death certificate as the cause of death?"

Holly thought for a minute. "Last night was crazy. We had two DOAs and one heart attack, along with the usual stuff. Let me get my supervisor; she'll be able to get you that information." Holly left the room and a few minutes later came back with Brenda Ward, the Nursing Supervisor. After the Wilsons identified themselves, Brenda went to the records and returned with O'Brien's file in her hands.

"The doctor didn't sign off on a cause of death. If there is *any* doubt, we have to do an autopsy."

Holly spoke up. "I remember now, he said he didn't feel right about it, the body had an unusual odor or something like that."

"Did he say why?" Dianne asked.

Holly shrugged. "No. He kinda frowned and said 'let the M.E. Office in Jacksonville sign off on it.'"

"Then the body has been sent to the Medical Examiner in Jacksonville?"

"That's right."

"That's all I need to know. Thank you for your help. I realize you didn't have to do this but it saves us time."

"You're welcome."

"If we can help you again just let us know." Wilson thanked Holly before leaving.

He held Dianne's car door open for her. He paused for a moment before suggesting they go to Slider's for a quick late lunch.

When they were seated, he looked across at Dianne. "You know, at first, I thought Sean might be the one we were after, but now it looks more like it's his missus."

Staring down at her menu, Dianne wondered how her newfound friend could be the target of such a lengthy hunt by so many law enforcement agencies. "Are you going to call Greg in on this?" They were sitting at one of the outside tables, with no one nearby to eavesdrop. "It's so hard to believe that she could be a killer, too."

"We don't know she is, honey. I have to call John Hershey down at the Medical Examiner's office when I go back to the office." He began talking about what they should order, and when the meals came, they hardly noticed the scenic ocean view in front of them, as they ate quickly, each thinking about the mysterious case. Then he drove Dianne home and headed for the police station.

———————•—•—•———————

Wilson dialed Hershey direct. "John, Wilson in Fernandina Beach. How are you today?"

"Hey, Wilson; doin' just fine. How's the fishing up yonder in the Nassau Sound these days?"

"I hate to admit it John, I haven't been lately. I've been trying for weeks now to take the girls out on the old bridge and wet a line."

"I went up there a lot when I was a kid and we hauled in some nice drum." They both paused to ponder yesterday's pastimes. "I guess you didn't call me to talk fish, so what can I do for you?"

"You got a Sean O'Brien last night or early this morning. The cause of death is of real interest to us–and the FBI, I might add. Can you move him up the line for us?"

"Hold on a sec." John whistled—off key—some old Beatles tunes. "Yeah, here it is, came in around 4 a.m. Some of the work, as you know, has to be sent to FDLE in Tallahassee. I'll put a rush on it, police investigation and all that."

"Once again, you're a master. I thank you. This may very well be the biggest thing that's hit our little town in years. We just need to confirm some of our suspicions and this will be a big help."

"We're here to please, Wilson."

"As ever, thanks, John…catch ya later."

"I'll call when it's ready and you can come pick it up." They both hung up, and Wilson leaned back in his chair to close his eyes and try to piece together the puzzle.

Already tired, Wilson found himself getting sleepy after the big lunch. Pieces of his puzzle slowly moved around in a random pattern on his eyelids. He rocked slowly in his chair as the forms began to take shape in the faint image of Connie O'Brien. *How am I going to trap her and gather evidence enough to get a conviction? Judges are tough to convince when it came to wiretaps and electronic snooping.* He opened his eyes and realized that he had dozed for a few seconds.

He rubbed his eyes, then finished up the day by helping Newman interview a suspect in a New York murder, who had been stopped on the island for an invalid license tag. The suspect's car had been impounded and given a once over by the K-9 officer and his dog. Wilson hoped that this guy was tied, even remotely, to the Leopard.

He was going to have to delay the release of O'Brien's body to the funeral home until he was able to get some test results. He would have to go back to the South Fletcher home and see if he could draw any more out of Connie. This would mean an extra day of delay.

After work, he and Dianne went to the O'Brien home and tried to explain to Connie why an autopsy had been ordered despite her objection. They tried to allay her fears that there was a suspicion of foul play.

"I can assure you, he had a heart attack," Connie tearfully insisted. "Both Linda and I were trying to revive him right after he slumped over in the chair." She alternated between waving her hands and wringing them together. "I just don't know what more I can say." Her voice was shaking. "I mean, Sean did not want this…this butchery." She sat on the sofa, looking small and beleaguered. Linda brought in what looked suspiciously like a mixed drink; nobody offered anything to the Wilsons.

"No one suspects anything but a heart attack, but doctors just wanted to be sure," Dianne said. "Connie, I hate to ask these questions now, but we need to close out our files."

Connie raised an eyebrow in question.

"Was Sean taking any new medicines? Sometimes a new medicine will react with others the patient is taking."

"Nothing new that I know of. We both knew that alcohol reduces the effectiveness of certain drugs, but he never drank for eight hours, or more, after taking the pills." Her face looked stern, and she sat back on the sofa, folding her arms in a defensive posture.

"Would he have neglected to take the medicine?" Wilson asked.

"Never." She turned her head toward her display cabinet.

Wilson looked at Dianne, knowing she too sensed the tension. He spoke softly, "Connie, we aren't looking for blame, even though it may appear that way. We're asking these questions rather than someone from the department who doesn't know you. We're just wrapping up a report, that's all."

The widow's demeanor softened a little. "He's on heart medication...or was." She wiped away a tear.

"I've called Oxley-Heard Funeral Home, and they assured me that Sean will look natural and at peace. I told them he was a friend of ours and asked they take special care." said Dianne.

Wilson added, "As soon as the coroner lets me know the results, we'll get Sean back here." Connie looked at them almost as if they were strangers. Dianne and Wilson exchanged a glance and then stood at the same time. After expressing their sympathy again, they left.

Once the visitors were safely out of earshot, Linda came into the room. "I don't think they'll find anything, do you?"

Connie dabbed her eyes. "Well, let's hope not."

"I barely put in enough to do the job; that's one reason it took so long to act."

"Sean had told me over and over again that he was thinking about going to the police. I should have gotten rid of him long ago." Connie stared past the flowering plants, tossing in the heavy winds, to the wide gray-blue ocean. A late-in-the-season nor'easter sent waves crashing on the shoreline. The sea foam, pushed by the winds across the sand toward the house, looked like a creeping horde of giant one-celled sea creatures.

Chapter 25

F our days later, Sean Albion O'Brien's family, friends, and former business associates gathered in Oxley-Heard's Burgess Chapel for his memorial service. Constance O'Brien, wife of the deceased, and Elizabeth O'Brien Kelley, sister of the deceased, sat at opposite ends of the long oak pew. The grieving in-laws wore black, as did Linda, who sat directly behind Connie. The overly-sweet smell of floral shop arrangements permeated the air. The hum of quiet conversation subsided as the minister stood, signaled for the music to stop and began the service.

The Wilsons offered what little consolation they could to Sean's sister after the service and told Connie that they would stop in to see her later. She forced a smile and said she would like that. On the way to their car, Dianne mentioned how cold Connie's hands had been.

"Tension maybe, who knows." He held the car door for her. They sat for a few minutes in silence, watching people leave the chapel. Smartly dressed men and women, executives who'd flown in on the Amherst Food Company's private jet, stood aside involved in small talk; they ignored—and were ignored by—other people leaving.

"Aren't we going?" asked Dianne.

"Not just yet. I want to wait a while and watch. By the

way, did you ever hear what Linda's last name is?"

"No." Then Dianne nodded. "Speak of the devil."

Linda walked to the edge of the porch and stopped, scanning people and cars as mourners brushed by her going down the steps. When she saw the Wilsons parked across the street, she immediately stepped back inside. A few minutes later she reappeared with Connie, whose first look was at the Wilson car. She graciously acknowledged the few people who were still there; most had left, including the Amherst contingent in their rented limousines.

"Don't you think it odd that after all the pleading about maintaining the dignity of his body, that Connie would suddenly have Sean cremated?" Dianne said looking into the sun visor's mirror to add a touch of lipstick.

"Exactly. You'll make a detective yet." He grinned.

"Well, it just seems that if he didn't want to be cut up, he surely wouldn't want to get burned up."

Wilson knew the answer to the question he was about to ask. "What would be gained from cremation? Think for a minute." He added, "Take your time."

Shooting him a look, Dianne said, "It would destroy any body evidence, plus there's no tissue left for exhumation or examination once the autopsy results are in."

Wilson smiled at her as she pushed the visor up and closed her small handbag. She looked at him, raising her eyebrows. "What?"

"You're so lovely, and I do love you." They leaned toward each other and lightly kissed.

Her finger wiped his lips. "You have lipstick on, and it's not your shade." She giggled. He grinned back and started the car. They waited for their chance to turn onto Atlantic.

Wilson eased in behind Connie's Mercedes, which Linda was driving. "We need to check on Linda and see what we can find. Call over there later and let's try to ask more questions—like, why weren't the Blackmoores here today?"

She nodded and made a mental note to add it to an already long list she'd compiled. She watched changing views of their pretty little town roll by, and then turned to her husband. "You're off tomorrow, right?"

He turned the radio's volume down. "Yes, I'm off until Thursday. About the Blackmoores... Connie didn't especially like them. She said once that she thought that they were crude and they were more Sean's friends than hers — *and* I think I know how to contact them...him anyway."

The next day, when Dianne called home from work, she found Wilson changing the oil in his personal car on his day off. Connie had called her at the station and had begged off of their getting together that day–she had "paperwork to take care of." Dianne had assured her that the following day would be just fine.

Dianne's call reminded Wilson of one he wanted to make. He was able to track down Wilbur and tell him to check out Blackmoore's business number. He quickly set up a meeting. *Darn, now I've got to shave today anyway.*

Blackmoore Electronics was upstairs in the Shaw Building on Centre Street. Wilson hadn't realized there was an electronics company in Fernandina, but he knew well about Books Plus that occupied the street level space. Dianne had introduced him to the bookstore on one of their lunch walks when the police department was downtown. She went there often to buy the latest books by her favorite mystery writers.

Wilson was ushered into the business owner's office. In the conversation, he soon discovered there was no love lost between Blackmoore and Connie. It became more evident when Blackmoore commented on how he and his wife weren't notified of Sean's death. "We read about it in the *News-Leader*. We were stunned and, honestly, a little hurt. We've known them for nearly thirty-five years."

"I've seen people do strange things when a spouse dies. Have you been in contact with Connie?"

"No, I was going to call her later today." Blackmoore crossed the room and poured two cups of coffee from the coffee maker beside the window. A swamp wren landed on the brick window ledge and pecked at unseen bugs, then flew off. "Connie *is* a strange person."

"How so?" Wilson took the offered coffee.

"Strange might not be the right word. She has her own agenda and Sean has...had...his." Blackmoore tested the coffee, then sipped it twice before he leaned back in his chair.

"Do you know if Sean was involved in any illegal activity of any kind?" Wilson probed.

"None that I know of. He was secretive about his latest pet project, but he was always that way. He mentioned something about a coffee deal to me once, but he'd tease you with bits of information to keep you interested in what he was doing. He'd keep the *real* secret on any deal until it was sealed. He'd do that on even the smallest contract."

"Did he have any girlfriends?"

"No, and if he were here, he'd shake your hand for thinking that." Blackmoore laughed.

"If there's anything illegal going on, I'd put my money on Connie and her shenanigans."

"How so?" Wilson's ears perked up.

"Always going to Mexico and South America. She claims it's for those clay pots, but I bet she's smuggling in illegal drugs for that domestic of hers."

"Yeah, what is it about her, anyway?"

"Connie's maiden name is Grajalva, not exactly Irish. Linda is her cousin. Connie is third-generation American, while Linda is an émigré, directly from Venezuela. Connie's grandfather was rich; he made a ton of money in the coffee business and emigrated to the U.S. He sent all of his grandchildren—including Connie—to the best schools."

"That doesn't make her a bad person, Mr. Blackmoore. I still don't get it." Wilson was scribbling notes as fast as he could.

"Apples don't fall that far from the tree. Her father was under investigation for illegal drug trafficking when he and his yacht exploded in the Gulf of Mexico."

"How do you know all of this?"

"Believe it or not, once she was my wife."

"What?" Wilson almost shouted.

"Yes, she and I were married for four years, back in the early '60s."

"So this is how you know so much about her background?"

"Yes. Her father, who was always up to no good and taught her everything he knew, died before we were divorced. She eventually found Sean and conned him into marrying her."

Blackmoore sighed and poured more coffee into both cups. "That was long ago and in a land far away; it seems so, anyway." He looked at Wilson and gave a sad smile. "We all got over the trauma and on with our lives." He fiddled with his spoon. "Sean and I got along great." He tossed the spoon on his desk. "Always did."

"Was Connie involved in her father's drug trafficking?"

"She told me that she wasn't, but her father's legitimate business was a good front for a multitude of opportunities to become involved. She is fluent in Spanish and often traveled with him to Central and South America." He looked out the window at two doves that landed on the sill. "She joked one time about how easy it would be to smuggle some contraband into the States."

"Do you know if she did?"

"She was an art major in college and knew about Pre-

Columbian art. She became fascinated with it for a while; and on one of her trips, discovered an operation that made fakes then sold them as genuine. She even went so far as to have them make a so-called artifact and put regular old grass inside to see if Customs would X-ray it."

"Did they?"

"No, it passed, and she broke it open to show me. On the next trip, she emptied a can of baby powder into the center cavity and it passed through too. She enjoyed living on the edge"

Blackmoore paused, while Wilson flipped his page over and continued to write. "After we were married, she continued to travel with her father. I didn't mind, it was his money they were spending, and I didn't make enough to support that lifestyle."

"After her father died, did she still travel there?" Wilson leaned back in the leather chair.

"Not as much at first. Her uncles got the coffee business. She joined a country club. Tennis and spa stuff."

"What led to your divorce?"

"We just drifted apart, I suppose would be a good answer. Connie took up with two other women she met at the spa and they'd travel to Central America together."

Wilson raised his eyebrows and thought for a moment. "Was everything okay in your home life? I know that's not delicate, but it may shed some light on things."

"Hell, that's all right. Yes, as far as I knew. She was always ready for sex."

Wilson moved on to another line of questions. "When her father was being investigated, did the authorities question her, especially about trips with him to South America?"

"Not that I know of. I had to travel a lot during those times, and if she was questioned, I didn't know about it."

"I still don't understand why you think she is involved

in drug trafficking now." Wilson's pencil broke and he scrambled to get another.

"I guess it's a gut feeling. When you're married to someone, you get to know the person pretty well. Occasionally I'd have a doubt, and later Sean confided that he suspected for a long time that she was up to something. He first thought she was having an affair, but dismissed the idea after he hired someone to follow her down to Central America. That's about all I know."

"How was your relationship with her overall?"

"In the early days of our marriage, it was great. After a few years, she spent a lot of time with her girl friends. She'd use her inheritance for going on cruises, shopping and such, while I was busy working with Sean in the food brokerage business. As I said, we drifted apart, and the divorce was pretty much amicable. You know, no shouting matches or gritty stuff, she just wanted out." He stared out the window again.

"Sean just let her do whatever she wanted, so they got along better than she and I ever had. Of course, Sean had women on the side. Connie knew it but accepted it as long as she could keep her lifestyle intact, including her own little adventures. Anyway, I have found a wonderful woman to spend the rest of my life with. But it's damn odd; I'd have thought that Connie would've called us when he died."

———— •■• ————

Dianne gave Connie a hug as soon as she opened the door. Wilson followed her into the living room, and they sat on the large couch. "We don't want to intrude, Connie. We know Sean's death has been so devastating. What can we do to help?"

"I don't know, dear; it's awfully kind for both of you to come. I met the lawyer yesterday, and he's handling the legal side. Sean had everything in order, ever since his first heart attack a few years ago. He always told me that if he dropped dead, everything would 'go into automatic.' I guess it did; the lawyer has everything all tidied up."

"I hate to ask, but did Sean have any problems with his health, I mean other than his heart?" Wilson worked hard to put concern in his voice.

"Yes," she lied, "I guess he had all of the ills of aging, but no one escapes that. He'd forget to take his pills and would get angry when I mentioned he'd forgotten. It's funny; he was so meticulous about every aspect of his life, but when it came to taking his medicine, he was terribly lax about it."

Wilson nodded. "My mother forgets her pills, too; I've tried many times to get her into a routine so she'll remember. I know it's hard to get someone to accept the fact that their health depends on the importance of taking them at the right time and in the right dosage."

"Well, Sean liked his cocktail, and that's a no-no with his prescriptions. No reflection, Wilson, but it seems to me that men have a hard head about medications." Connie relaxed back in her comfortable chair. They were in her territory and she intended to direct the conversation. "I had to remind Sean morning and night about his medications." She lit a cigarette and put an ashtray in her lap.

"How many did he have to take?" Dianne leaned back in her chair. Glancing at her, Wilson followed suit.

"Four tablets in the morning and three at night. I tried to have dinner early and discourage a lot of heavy drinking after dinner. The doctor warned that too much alcohol would diminish the effectiveness of the pills." She blew cigarette smoke toward the ceiling.

"Is there anything you need, now that you've had a few days to think?" Dianne wanted to get a level of trust going again.

"I can't think of anything. People have been so nice.

Believe it or not, the car we have is a company car and the vice president who was here for the funeral said to keep it; they'll transfer the title in a week or so."

"It's nice to have a company car," said Wilson. "We're able to use our car at all times. It helps with the crime rate."

"By the way, how is your investigation of this notorious Leopard coming along?" Connie tilted her head to one side. Her diamond jaguar broach sparkled in the light. Linda came in with a carafe of coffee and Lemoges cups.

Wilson intended Connie to believe that the investigation was stumbling. "All leads so far have led to a dead end. I talked to the FBI the other day and they have something that could lead us to the Tampa area."

"Us?" Connie raised an eyebrow. Linda poured the coffee and left.

"You know, law enforcement. By the way, how long has Linda had been with you? I understand she moved here with you; that's kinda rare, isn't it?" He sipped his coffee.

"Let's see. I think she's from someplace in Central America; we got her through an agency in Philadelphia about twelve years ago. Why do you ask?"

That's interesting. Blackmoore said they were cousins; I'll have to check with INS. "In today's mobile society, it is rare for domestic help to stay so long." He shrugged his shoulders.

"I hate to bring this up," Dianne put in, "but I was wondering how the paramedics were when they came to help Sean." She took a breath and silently asked all the Fire/Rescue people for forgiveness. "I mean, a woman complained to me the other day that the EMTs didn't know what they were doing."

Connie took a sip of coffee while she formulated an answer. "Well, like I said, after dinner, we sat in here to watch the evening news. About 7 o'clock, Sean began to rub his chest and complain about pain. I went to get his nitro, and when I came back in, he was slumped in the chair. Neither Linda nor I know this CPR thing, so I called 911. When the paramedics arrived, they did everything they could to revive Sean, but it was way too late by then." She gazed down at her cup. "As far as I'm concerned, they were great."

Dianne leaned forward. "I shouldn't have brought it up, really. I thought this woman was a little hysterical, anyway, and it was the first time I've ever heard anyone complain about our Fire/Rescue folks. I've worked with them often enough to know they're wonderful and dedicated."

"That's okay."

"Wilson's mother is taking medicine for her heart too, and when the girls and I were over there the other day, she said her arm tingled sometimes. Did Sean ever complain of that?"

"No, we knew the symptoms of a heart attack. The doctor gave us literature on it and I monitored how he felt, more so than he did. How are your girls, by the way?" Connie was clearly eager to steer this conversation in another direction.

"Causing premature grayness, I'm afraid." Wilson ran his hand through his hair. "I saw a few the other day."

"Oh," Dianne said with a laugh, "he's not used to girls becoming young ladies." She nudged Wilson. "They're fine."

Connie smiled. "I imagine it's tough to keep track of them all the time, since they're so active."

"They are a handful." After that the conversation wobbled around until finally Dianne turned to her husband. "Honey, I've got to get ready for work, and I have to stop at Publix on the way home." He took his cue and they stood to leave. "Connie, I hope you'll be staying here in Fernandina?" Dianne turned it into a question.

"Yes, I can't stand most of my relatives, anyway." She laughed. "I've got too many friends here and I'm involved in a lot of island activities that will keep me busy. Besides, I wouldn't trust anyone to move my collection."

When they were back in the car, Dianne suggested, "How about pizza at Moon River for lunch?"

Wilson agreed, but on the way, he turned onto Citrona Street. "I have to run by the station for a second." After he made a quick note there of John Hershey's phone number, they went on to the small pizza place that was a favorite with the locals.

They ordered at the counter and then found a table. Dianne looked at the pictures on the wall and remarked that she'd like to have something like one of those hanging in the family room.

"They're good for here, but the family room?"

"Well," she said, "I want some art work on the walls. I might head to one of the galleries in town next week to look for something."

Wilson didn't say anything for a few seconds while she turned in her chair and studied the pictures. "Get some prints, at least until we can afford an honest-to-goodness painting." As he lifted his soft drink, he muttered, "I've got to quit taking you out."

"What? I heard that, smarty." She playfully slapped his arm.

She let her eyes wander over the unique, modern pictures while Wilson placed a call to Hershey to see if any lab results had come in from Tallahassee.

"Yes, as a matter of fact. I left a message on your voice mail. I have to come up to your place later today, so I'll drop in around 3 o'clock or so. Some interesting information."

"What do you have?" Wilson took out a pen and note pad.

He listened to "Hey Jude" whistled off key as Hershey shuffled papers. "You may have a murder on your hands, my man. Anyway, the tox scan looks pretty strange. It's convoluted—I'll have to explain some things; it gets deep and probably over your head, no insult intended. I'll be there later."

"None taken, okay, thanks." *I think he's still in the '60s.* Wilson's experience with the Duval County Medical Examiner had been a good one; but Hershey, at times, would go into intricate detail and lose him. He closed his cell phone and whispered to Dianne, "I think we have us a murder on our hands." She started to speak but Wilson held up his hand and said, "Sorry," as he dialed the phone again. "Greg, this is Wilson, Fernandina Beach Police...Hi, not much. Listen, I've got some information and I'm going to need the power behind your push to get something done." He stood and walked outside where he could avoid eavesdroppers. "Yeah, it's about the Leopard. I need an emergency wire-tap order...yesterday...I know...but I think the bird's going to fly...okay, I'll be back in my office in forty-five minutes...Thanks, it'll sure help. Talk to you later."

He went back inside and whispered to Dianne, "I'll fill you in later. I think we're getting close." Wilson took a bite of the hot, meaty pizza slice and turned his head toward the pictures on the wall, but he wasn't focused on them.

"I see the wheels turning. What is it?" She leaned over and wiggled a finger at him.

"I'll talk to Tim and see if I can borrow you tomorrow afternoon. How would you like to have a pre-Columbian artifact?"

"For real?" Her eyes lit up. "Wait a minute, what are you up to?"

"Yes, for real." He ignored her second question.

Once he was in his office, Wilson called the supervisor of the Traffic Division and got permission to have Dianne work with him the next day. He called Sarah and Al over to his desk and carefully went over his plan with them. Then he explained what he wanted Dianne to do.

Chapter 26

Hershey had been with the Medical Examiner's Office in Jacksonville for years. His office had to support many of the counties in northeast Florida. He'd once told Wilson, "Be thankful that you don't have enough high-profile crime to require your own M.E."

Hershey had dropped his wife off at their condo on South Fletcher Avenue and reached Wilson's office by exactly 3 o'clock. With cups of coffee before them, the two settled down to review the autopsy report.

"Well, it wasn't a heart attack," John began. "Initial results indicate some form of tetrodotoxin."

"Wait a minute." Wilson put his pencil down. "You aren't going to get too far over my head, are you?"

"No, I'll explain things as we go. Tetrodotoxin is a neurotoxin that shuts down signals in nerve cells. There's a voltage gated *door,* if you will, in the sodium channel proteins of the nerve cells. This neurotoxin disrupts the flow of information in and out of the nerve cells, the ones in the fingertips, nose 'n toes, all that. The disruption leads to a shutdown of the nerve functions in the body, but not necessarily in the brain. It's a product of bacteria, like Pseudoalteromonas tetraodonis."

"John, I think you're telling me more than I want to know.

Hershey shrugged. "But it's the ingestion of a member of the family of Tetraodontiformes bacteria that causes the problem: an excruciating, painful death. And what puzzles me is how the victim ingested it."

"How so?"

"You get it from eating a select group of fish, most often a puffer fish, which is not the everyday catch in our oceans and rivers."

Wilson looked at the ceiling and tapped the pencil against the desk. Hershey drank his coffee, giving him time for his mind to catch up.

"Consuming something like the California newt, a starfish or even a certain specie of crab, the xanthid, can cause the same kind of death," Hershey continued. "But my guess is that he was fed parts of the puffer fish. He must have ingested some of the fish's liver; it's mostly the liver, as well as the viscera, where the toxins are found."

"Okay." Wilson rocked back and forth in his chair. "Exactly where are these fish found?"

"Warm waters like the coastal mid-Atlantic, Gulf of Mexico and the Gulf of California."

"And the symptoms? Like a heart attack?"

"Probably, at first, but more ghastly as time goes on." Hershey took a moment to collect his own thoughts. "Numbness, lightheadedness, shortness of breath. If O'Brien did ingest puffer fish, the first symptom he would have had was a numbness of the lips and tongue about twenty minutes after eating. Then he'd have progressed to a raging headache, maybe followed by nausea and paralysis of the face. The paralysis would proceed to his extremities. By this time his speech would be gone, and his walking wobbly or nonexistent. Finally, there comes the onset of respiratory distress and cardiac arrhythmia." Hershey looked up to see Wilson's pained expression. "Ultimately, O'Brien suffocated because his breathing mechanism stopped. Not a pretty picture."

Wilson heaved a sigh. "No, I think not. How long would this have taken?"

"Thirty minutes to several hours, depending on the amount of toxin someone fed him. If he was lucky, he'd have died quickly, because he would have been conscious the whole time his body's nervous system was slowly dissolving." Hershey tapped one finger against another. "See, it attacks the nervous system at the opposite end from the brain- at the nerve endings in the extremities like the fingertips. The toxin then goes to involuntary muscles, respiration first, and eventually the heart; but you die of respiratory failure before cardiac failure."

"Time of death?"

"Between 6 and 8 in the evening."

Wilson looked away and tapped his pencil on the pad of paper. "Emergency Services didn't get the call until a little after 10, around 10:30, I think."

"Dead bodies don't lie."

"What were the stomach contents?" He scribbled more notes.

"Small meal. And there was a lot of wine in the stomach."

Wilson looked up. "Did you find the puffer fish liver?"

"We emptied the stomach contents, sorted it out and put it in the freezer. When the tox report came back we went through the contents again and found what might be a little piece that the acid hadn't completely digested."

"*Hmm.*" Wilson made more notes while Hershey finished his coffee and whistled "Yellow Submarine" off-key again and nearly unrecognizable. "Okay, we know how he died and we know when; now the question is where did it come from?"

"It's illegal to import this puffer fish in the U.S., but it's a rare delicacy in Japan, although only specially-trained, licensed cooks can prepare it. They have about four deaths a year there from improperly prepared fish. I'd say O'Brien's puffer came from this side of the country or perhaps the Gulf of Mexico."

Wilson tossed the note pad onto the desk. "That seems like a strange way to poison someone."

"It's tough to detect, but after your call, I asked they run an analysis for some form of toxin. Blowfish toxins are almost never heard of here, but some South American Indians use those as well as scorpions' venom to kill enemies."

"Well, now all I have to do is prove someone fed it to him on purpose, and not by mistake. I can get a search warrant with this information you've given me. Come to think of it, I believe O'Brien had a saltwater fish tank in his dining room, and maybe another elsewhere in the house.

He stood and held out his hand. "John, thanks a lot. This has really helped us. If we can't get them on drug running, we'll go after murder...and murder carries a heavier penalty."

"You betcha. I have to be going, too. Glad to be of help. Let me know if you need anything else." John left, whistling a bad version of "Michelle" as he walked to his car.

———— •■• ————

The following day, Wilson and Detective Al Newman sat in a van parked on South Fletcher two houses away from the O'Brien home. Their van had bogus lettering on the side but the sophisticated equipment inside was genuine. The radio receiver monitored whoever was wired with a small transmitter. Sarah and Wilbur would be their backup, parked two blocks further south. The plan was for Dianne to go visit Connie under the guise of buying an artifact from her. Dianne, well briefed on the medical examiner's report, would try to ask question that would either back up or refute the report. She would also try to get more background information about Connie and Linda without stirring up suspicion.

Ten minutes after the two surveillance teams were in place, Dianne approached them in her little civilian car. "Hit the brake light if you hear me," she said into the tiny microphone of her transmitter. Sarah tapped the brakes. "Good. Wilson, hit the brake lights." Nothing happened. Dianne slowed to a near stop several hundred feet behind Wilson's van. The lights came on as she neared it. "Don't keep me in suspense like that," she scolded as she sped up and pulled into Connie's driveway.

She fidgeted as she walked up to the door. She'd worn loose clothes to hide the microphone and transmitter, but she still felt uncomfortable. Linda opened the door before the doorbell finished chiming.

"Hello, Mrs. Wilson, come in, please. Mrs. O'Brien is waiting for you." Linda was a little friendlier this morning, even adding, "You look very nice today."

"Thank you." In the living room, Connie greeted her with a hug. Today, the widow wore black ankle-length pants topped with a sheer, bright orange blouse, accented with the diamond-encrusted jaguar. Dianne heard Afro-Cuban music coming from down the hallway, and turned to ask her hostess about her new upbeat clothing and music. Connie had the grace to look a little embarrassed, but explained that she was tired of drab clothing and a silent house.

"I love the Pan-American colors and dress and music. I think they're helping me though is difficult time," she said as she waved a hand toward the sofa. They sat and chatted for a few minutes while Linda disappeared down the hallway; the music soon stopped. Dianne became aware of how large and quiet this house was. They eventually wandered over to the display cabinets where Connie asked what she had in mind to buy.

"I'd really like something from the Classic Period. I'm afraid I can't afford the earlier material, but I'd just like to be able to say that I have a piece of the real thing."

Connie showed her several pieces and quoted prices ranging from several hundred to several thousand dollars. While they were examining the artifacts, Linda slipped into the dining room and sat at the table watching them. When Connie noticed her, she asked Linda to get them a couple of glasses of iced tea to enjoy on the patio while Dianne made up her mind about her purchase. Glancing into the kitchen on the way to the patio, Dianne saw a chicken on the drain board, with its head still on. The coppery smell of fresh kill drifted by as they went through to the french doors.

The patio was raised, with steps leading to the lower level, where the garage was tucked under the kitchen and office. The ocean breeze played with the palm trees and the rustling sounds briefly muffled the bantering sea gulls. The array of tropical plants the O'Briens had chosen for their landscape gave a refreshing atmosphere to the patio, and beyond was a magnificent view of the ocean.

The two women sat at a table covered with bright-hued Mexican tiles in the shade of large overhanging eaves. A nearby fountain burbled softly. As they took their seats, Dianne looked down toward the corner of the garage and saw an overturned washtub with feathers next to it. A quick glance assured her that Connie hadn't noticed her peeking. Linda brought out the tall glasses of tea with a plate of cookies on the silver serving tray. Heading back to the house, she had just reached the door when Connie spoke in Spanish. Dianne had no idea of what was said but Linda paused, and then returned to join them. She pulled a chair next to Connie's, and across the table, Dianne could barely hear Linda's comment in Spanish.

"You must forgive Linda," Connie explained. "She is still more comfortable with her native tongue. But she paid you a compliment. She said you are very beautiful."

Dianne nodded. "Thank you, Linda, you are a lovely lady, too. Where are you from?" She spoke a little more slowly than usual, to allow the woman time to process the English.

"A little town not far from Caracas, Venezuela. I came here hoping to work and save enough to send a little money back home."

"You still have family there?"

"Yes, madre and padre, eh…mother and father and several brothers and sisters."

"It's good of you to want to help them." She watched as Connie measured Linda's words. "You will be staying with Señora Connie?"

Connie broke in, "Yes, she has moved into the house from the little apartment over the garage. She is a comfort to me now. Even though I have a million things going on, plus all the people who've dropped by, this big place does get quiet and lonely at times. Linda is a great help." Linda looked down at her hands clasped in her lap, as if embarrassed at this praise.

Dianne leaned forward. "Connie, can I ask a rather personal question?" She wanted to get this over with soon.

"Sure."

"We met the Blackmoores here before, but I didn't see them at the funeral." She improvised an excuse when she saw Connie frown. "I wanted to tell Sylvia something—I ran into her at Publix, and she felt hurt that they didn't know in time for the funeral."

Connie smoothed her frown into an impassive politeness. "I tried to call several times and when I finally got them, they were on their way to a son's wedding in California. Of course, they were devastated, but I understood they just had to go to California."

"That was a shame. They seemed like nice people."

"Yes, they have been good friends for years. I think I

told you he and Sean worked together for a long time."

Dianne looked her in the eye and hoped she could pull off this act. "I'm not here as police or some investigator, Connie. I'm here because I think we can be friends and I'm a person who's concerned for my friends." She leaned forward and put her hands on the cool tile table. "How long did Sean have that heart problem?"

Connie gazed out at the ocean. "*Hmm*...six years ago he had the first heart attack."

"He had more than one?"

"Yes, he had three. He was so obstinate about taking his medicine. He said the drug industry was a bunch of blood suckers."

Dianne glanced at Linda, who had a slight frown on her face. "I was talking to a cardiologist friend of ours; and he said heart attacks often come right after someone has eaten a big meal, making the stomach press against the heart, thereby causing it distress. Did Sean have a large dinner that night?"

Connie was relaxed, in control of the answers. "Yes, we had quite a large meal. He liked a full meal in the early evening before he settled down to watch the news." She looked away and gave a short laugh. "He used to talk back to the television, like someone was going to listen to him."

Dianne remembered that the medical examiner had said Sean had eaten a small meal. "I know I'm sounding nosy; my husband is the forever detective and was curious—have you had any exotic food lately?" She smiled and added, "He read somewhere that if Sean had eaten something out of the ordinary, it would have put stress on the heart and caused his heart attack."

Connie gave a forced smile. "Like...?"

"I don't know. I think he's stretching things." She wanted to come across as doubting Wilson's motives and she gave a little laugh. "Men's egos and detectives' egos can be so far out. I get frustrated with him sometimes, he tries to make something out of nothing."

"Let me assure you, Dianne," said Connie, shifting in her chair, "Sean and I were doing fine and I wouldn't have poisoned him. Divorce would have been easier, but that wouldn't have happened either."

Her smile was tight. Her steel gray eyes stared directly into Dianne's. "You probably haven't been married long enough to realize that every marriage hits lows and highs, and some eventually flatten out into a noncommittal relationship. Sean had his life of golf and dabbling in the pursuit of a coffee import deal, and I have my circle of friends." She lit a cigarette and glanced at Linda before continuing, "Sean wasn't heavily insured, so his death wasn't a monetary benefit to me."

"I don't mean to inquire…" Dianne spoke softly.

Connie's face suddenly looked as if it'd turned to stone. "My dear, Sean had a girlfriend, and I told him to be careful. If he ever wanted to divorce me, he'd walk out of here as a pauper." She turned her head toward Linda and patted her hand. "I've got friends that are true."

"Connie…I…" Dianne took the role of the embarrassed guest.

"Oh, don't worry, it doesn't rub off." The widow laughed and relaxed a little. "You'd be surprised how many of my friends are in the same boat." A gust of wind from the ocean made the palm fronds dance and rustle. The cooling breeze brought in the fresh salt smell. They were all silent for several minutes. Dianne watched the wind toss Linda's shiny black hair about and Connie reached out a hand to brush it behind Linda's ear. Linda stole a glance at the visitor and lowered her head.

Dianne hoped Wilson had enough information that would help. "I really didn't mean to get this personal, Connie."

"Hey, if we're going to be friends, you may as well know the dirt." She laughed. "Have you decided on what you'd like to buy?"

"Yes, I remember now." Dianne started to get up. "I think I have made a decision about the piece I want."

"Good. Let's go see what it is."

After wrapping the small tripod cup in several layers of bubble wrap, Connie slashed the price in half for her. At her protest, Connie said to call it a gift for being such a good friend. They said their goodbyes at the door; Linda, standing behind Connie, shook Dianne's hand while telling her how much she'd enjoyed talking to her. Dianne felt a slight tug from the woman's grasp.

She drove away with her four-hundred-dollar purchase sitting in the passenger seat. She checked the rearview mirror as Wilson, then Sarah and Wilbur, joined her to make a three-car parade up South Fletcher Avenue.

Chapter 27

D ianne, Wilson and the Chief sat in Evan's office and listened to the tape made while Dianne was visiting Connie. They played it several times before Evans sat back and looked at them. "I don't hear anything that gives us faintest excuse to go in. The guy is fed something that is strange. They went to South America all the time. Who's to say he didn't eat some exotic food down there and it didn't work until now?"

"Hershey said that neurotoxin acts within four hours max. It can start a lot sooner and usually kills its victim in a matter of minutes. We found a bit of something that might be the poisoned liver. And to top it off, they're practicing voodoo or something."

"No proof."

"You heard the music in the background and I told you about the freshly killed chicken," Dianne said. "Maybe they were getting ready for some sort of ritual? And the conversation on the patio?"

"Again I say, no proof." The Chief leaned forward. "Look, I want to nab this woman as much as you do, but we need something in the way of solid evidence—and so far, you ain't got it. Go dig some more. See if you can connect her with the murder on the river. You have the wiretap order;

see what that does for you." Evans got up, adjusted his belt. This meeting was over. He shook his head. "Then there's nothing we can do until they trip up."

They left the Chief's office and went to Wilson's, where they sat in silence for several minutes. "Who's on the wiretap?" asked Dianne.

"I got Henderson and Stone from Traffic right now. Sarah will take over later. Why?"

"You have to be sure whoever's listening speaks Spanish."

"Stone and Sarah do; I'll have to check the other shifts. What do you have in mind?"

"I think we can lean on Linda. Or drop a hint that we think Sean's death might be suspicious, and she will most likely tell Connie. Connie is in control of her emotions, but I think Linda might crack." Thinking hard, she stared at the minimal wall decorations. "Connie has something on her. Call it woman's intuition, but it's just the way Linda acted. She's afraid of something."

Dianne tapped her fingernails on his desk, then dropped her hand and slid a look at her husband. "Oh, there's something I was embarrassed to say in front of the Chief."

"Oh?" Wilson took out his note pad and made some scribbles.

"When Connie and I started to look at the artifacts, she held my hand. Women sometimes do that, but she intertwined her fingers through mine. I thought that was strange." She gave an embarrassed laugh. "She saw Linda come from the kitchen and let go quickly. It wasn't a casual thing, Wilson, she held my hand tight, like she meant it."

"So Connie hit on you. You think she and Linda are more than employer and domestic?"

"That's my guess. But we can't arrest them based on that." She looked at the clock.

"No, but if Linda sees you as a threat, you might become her target."

"But if I play up to Linda and come between them?"

"Absolutely not, that's too dangerous." He sat back and let his pencil fall on the desk.

Over the next hour, they discussed the relative merits of Dianne's idea. Sarah stopped by and tossed out a few ideas before heading out to interview a suspect. Dianne pressed Wilson hard until he finally compromised with her; the only way he'd go along with it was if she came up with a solid plan and was wired again. Dianne knew she'd pushed him as far as she could. She'd just have to come up with a killer idea. She winced at her choice of words.

For three days the wiretap came up empty, and the eavesdroppers nearly died of boredom. Dianne was desperately working to formulate a plan Wilson would approve. She saw Linda out and about frequently and tried to establish a pattern of her behavior and movements. Their break came on the fourth day when Dianne spotted her driving into the Sadler Square parking lot. Dianne's pulse quickened as she stopped at the other end and waited to see what Linda was going to do. Despite not being wired, she did want to discover if there was any possibility of a friendly contact. She drove up beside Linda's car and rolled down the window.

"Hi, Linda, how are you?"

"Oh, you startled me. Hello, Mrs. Wilson."

"Call me Dianne. That's what my friends call me."

"Okay." She paused, "Dianne. Did I do something wrong?"

"No, I just saw you and wanted to stop by and say hello."

Screeching seagulls soared around the parking lot, distracting them for a moment. Linda looked up at them and smiled. "Oh, I try to drive good."

"Listen, Linda, I was thinking, maybe we could get a

cup of coffee over at the Krystal?"

Linda looked surprised, but she nodded and smiled. Dianne pulled her car into Krystal's parking area. Inside the restaurant, she found a table in a nearly deserted section and waited for Linda to come in.

Sitting away from anyone else, she felt she could talk more openly, and maybe Linda would open up a little. Dianne began gently, "How is Connie getting along?"

"Fine. She is involved with her friends. She isn't home much."

"That leaves you with a lot of free time. What do you do? Do you have any hobbies?"

Linda glanced at Dianne, then out the window. "No hobbies. I read and study."

"I guess you both miss Sean a lot." Dianne watched for a reaction and wasn't disappointed.

Linda frowned, and her shoulders drooped. "Yes, I do." She put her hands in her lap and sucked in her lower lip a little.

It hit Dianne between the eyes. She realized that there wasn't anything between Connie and Linda other than employer and employee, and she made a mental note to tell Wilson. Then she directed the conversation to other topics and didn't press any particular issue. Before she could assemble another gentle probe, Dianne got a call on her lapel radio and had to leave. She put her hand on Linda's arm and said, "If you ever need me, Linda, I'll be there."

She waved goodbye and jumped in her cruiser to see what new adventure awaited her in paradise. Linda watched her until she was out of sight.

Chapter 28

Linda set the small grocery bag on the kitchen counter and stared out the window. In tune with her mood, a storm cloud hung offshore with its dark rain lashing the ocean. She stood for many minutes watching the storm and listening to the thunder.

"What's wrong?" She jumped at Connie's voice. "You were lost in thought. What were you thinking?" Connie came closer, passing through the dining room.

"Nothing. I didn't know you were here. I just stopped at the grocery to get a few things we needed. I mailed the items as you asked."

"Did you see anyone?"

Linda turned to her. "Only Dianne, the lady policeman. We had a cup of coffee." She turned back to the thunderstorm crashing outside.

Connie came over to put her hand on Linda's shoulder. "You must be careful who you talk to and what you say. Dianne is not to be trusted."

"She seems like a nice lady."

The fingers tightened, sending pain through Linda's shoulder. "As I've told you before, if anything happens, I only know that you are the cook; I know nothing about what you do or that screwy religion of yours. They'll believe me before they would believe some peasant who sacrifices chickens."

She softened her voice to soothe the younger woman. "Think about the other offer I made to you, too." She relaxed her fingers and massaged Linda's shoulder. When her hand moved to gently pinch Linda's earlobe, she flinched. "You never know until you try." Connie gave the earlobe a playful tug and strolled off.

"She said you wouldn't believe me if I told you."

Linda hid her shaking hands in her lap. She kept her eyes directed at the tabletop in front of her. Dianne sat across from her in the room Wilson and his detectives used for interrogations. He perched in a chair to the side, since Linda was opening up to Dianne. He'd briefed Dianne on questions he wanted answered. The only other person in the small room was a secretary recording on paper all that was said.

Dianne began by gently telling her, "Linda, what you are saying could cost you your life, and it's very possible that you will spend a long time in prison. What will your family do?"

"My brother has become a doctor and can provide for them. He is coming to the United States and will eventually bring the rest of our family over. You must understand; my family has nothing. My father works at a fish market. My mother washes dishes in a hotel in Caracas. The poor people still hold onto old beliefs and traditions.

"That's where I learned of the poison that comes from the fish. My people still use it to take care of enemies." Linda went on to describe the plot Connie devised and they both carried out.

Wilson looked at the secretary, who nodded that she had the statement down. Someone knocked at the door and handed Wilson a slip of paper. He read it, then folded it. "Linda, is

Mrs. O'Brien called El Leopardo by anyone you know?"

"Si. She sometimes calls herself that."

"It's time to move. Let's go see the Chief."

He started for the door, but turned back to Linda, saying, "We're going to wait awhile before we do anything about what you have told us. I want you to go back and act like everything is normal." When Linda's eyes grew large at this proposal, he patted her reassuringly. "When you can, tell us of anything unusual that is happening. If you help us, we will do our best to help you when the time comes." When the woman continued to look doubtful, he squeezed her shoulder gently and inclined his head toward her. "You must learn to trust us."

Dianne walked Linda to her car. "Wilson and the Chief will help you, believe me."

"I am so sorry for what I did." She began to cry. "I was forced into it. She would have torn up my green card and had me sent back home." Tears rolled down her cheeks. "I loved Sean with all my heart and he loved me. I know it to be true; he swore it to me."

———— • ■ • ————

"So, that's how we came to find out our source is solid." Wilson sat at the conference table in Chief Evans' office. "I think it's time we got the warrant to go have a look. This is a complicated operation; surely she has records somewhere of her transactions. And, according to Linda, we should find another puffer fish in the tank in the basement. So, Connie blackmailed Linda to prepare a seafood chowder and then add the raw diced puffer fish liver." Taking a deep breath, he felt the excitement building and adrenaline beginning to flow.

"And the kicker is, Connie has booked a one-way flight to Colombia, leaving tomorrow. Linda said Mrs. O'Brien moves her money around and mostly buys investment diamonds, which she keeps in a safe in her bedroom. After Sean died, Dianne and I went over to the O'Brien house and while there I phoned Newman, questioning the time that Rescue was called. Their log didn't match the time that Connie said she called. Newman said the call came in about 10:30, but Connie said she made the call about 7." He tapped his pencil on the desktop.

"Oh, and another thing; remember that black box hooked up to the telephone in Sean's office? It's a voice scrambler. According to Blackmoore, it can be controlled manually or automatically. He sold Sean and Connie five units. Makes you wonder where the other four are located, doesn't it?"

Chief Evans made a quick call to the Nassau County Courthouse in Yulee. In a few minutes he said, "The warrant's being faxed right now. You can pick it up at Susan's desk." He turned to Dianne. "You say that there's duress on the cook?"

"Yes, at first I thought Connie and Linda had something going, but when I left Linda at the Krystal, I put my hand on hers to see if there was any reaction. She snatched her hand back like she'd been shocked with electricity. She also told me that Connie threatened to destroy her green card and turn her in for being illegal."

"Did you call the FBI to let them know we're moving in on the person we suspect to be the Leopard?" Evans looked at Wilson.

"Yeah, but we need to move soon. Connie may bolt any minute." He looked at his watch. "It's 3:20. I can go over and have Sarah and Al follow me. I'll have Wilbur call the Jacksonville people; FDLE will want in on this, too, and there's a few others I need to contact." Wilson sighed, revealing some fatigue that the adrenaline hadn't suppressed. This was like planning some precision drill team performance. Like all detectives, he had hoped it would be simple... just "go out and arrest the bad guys."

"I think you should have someone go with you." Evans tapped his desk for emphasis.

"I'll go!" Dianne spoke up quickly. Wilson shot her a look and she knew what it meant and added, "Or not."

"Who'd take care of the girls?" he said just above a whisper. Then he turned to Evans, although knowing it would be faster to travel alone. "I'll take someone from the office." He stood up. "This has been a long one; if we can't get murder one in Sean's death, we'll at least get more drug trafficking information."

Dianne went back on patrol and Wilson went to his office to see the status board. Everybody was out. He used his Nextel and told them to get back to the office. While he was waiting for his troops to arrive, he made all the necessary phone calls.

He'd just finished talking to an excited Greg Dalton at the FBI, when his phone rang. He lifted the receiver as he looked at his watch. 3:45. "Investigations, Wilson."

"Detective Wilson, I wish you would come over here. Irma wants to talk to you about the unfortunate incident in Oklahoma." Mrs. Boxer was on the line. Wilson covered the receiver and groaned.

"Mrs. Boxer, this is not the best time. We're right in the middle of something very sensitive." He was going to try his best to get her off the line while still being civil. "Can I call you tomorrow?"

"That's fine with me, but Irma said that sensitive thing is about the Panther or something like that."

Wilson hugged the receiver to his chest and closed his eyes in exasperation. *God save me from little old ladies who read the newspaper.* He took a deep calming breath. "Yes, Ma'am, something like that."

"Well, Irma knows about that, too. She knows where the Panther is. She has done some investigive work. I know there's going to be another killin'. Irma says it may be here in Fernandina Beach."

Wilson listened to Mrs. Boxer ramble on for another ten minutes, only because he was waiting for the other detectives to get back to the office. Finally he had to say, "Mrs. Boxer, I'll have a patrolman come over and see if he can't talk to Irma. Okay? I really have to go…Yes, ma'am. I'll get them over very soon."

He hung up and called the dispatcher to send a patrol car over to Mrs. Boxer's place. It should take an hour or so for that low-priority call to work its way up the list. Wilson looked at the time again. 4:05. *Where are those guys? We've got to get going.*

He went to the front desk. The secretary looked up from behind the glass enclosure and smiled. He waved and walked over to the window of the Shift Sergeant. *Nothing happening here.* As Wilson returned to his office, his phone was ringing, but he heard it transfer to voice mail just as he reached for it. He waited a few seconds and tried to retrieve the call, but it was too late. He sat down and looked at the clock again. 4:18.

I'm going on over. I'll call the guys on the Nextel to meet me over there. Wilson walked through the reception area. He told the secretary he was heading for Mrs. O'Brien's and if any of his people came in, they were to join him there.

Dianne wondered how Wilson and the rest of the detectives were doing, as she stopped for the light at 14th and Beech streets. She wanted to be in on the action that Wilson was headed to, and she decided to drive by and see if his car was still in the station's lot. She was glad that Wilson had taken her into his confidence about this case. Sometimes, after the girls were in bed, they would sit at the kitchen table and go over the case. Wilson knew she had learned the basics of investigative work at the Police Academy, but they couldn't teach the nuances you learn in the field. He was patient in showing her the whys and hows of his business.

Dianne walked into the reception area. "You're about a minute behind him; he just left for the takedown," the secretary told her. She flew to her car after the secretary said he'd gone alone. *No backup. That was stupid, what was he thinking?*

———————— •■• ————————

Connie stopped at the sink and looked at the chicken that Linda had killed. Her distrust of the other woman had grown because of Linda's increasing involvement with Santeria. Connie had heard whispers of this syncretistic religious group when she was a child. Linda's family was Catholic, but the other religion, especially among the impoverished in the Caribbean, had made inroads, when people had become more mobile. Although far from being a religious person, Connie found these strange practices were beginning to wear on her.

This movement, with roots in the Bantu people of Southern Nigeria, had long ago been unknowingly spread by slave traders who did business in all countries of the Americas, including the United States.

Connie was afraid that her employee was delving more into the religion than was wise. She felt as though her world was beginning to come unraveled; there were too many people around her and she was losing control of people and events. She had decided it was time to leave.

She was going to have to cover her tracks; if Linda didn't want to become a partner with her, then she must be dealt with. She looked at the wall clock. 4:19. Linda's hypnotic music quietly undulated its way through the house. Connie took a large chef's knife from the drain board, walked silently into the dining room and laid it beside the fish tank. She covered the knife with a linen napkin from the table.

"Linda, ven aqui uno momento, por favor." She moved to a position behind a chair at the dining room table.

Linda turned the music down in her room before she joined her employer. "Si, ma'am." She hesitated for a few seconds at the room's entrance.

"I'm going away for a few days. I've already packed. Come in here and sit down a minute." She indicated the chair in front of her. Linda hesitated again. "Come on, I need to talk to you for a second. It won't take long," she wheedled.

Linda finally sat where she was told, folding her hands in her lap. "Yes, ma'am?" She craned her neck to look at Connie, who was standing behind her.

Connie put her hands on Linda's shoulders and felt them tense up. "Relax, Linda. While I'm gone," she began to massage her shoulders, "I want you to please think about not doing those Santeria things anymore." Her fingers dug deeper into one shoulder. "Understand what I mean?"

"Yes, ma'am. You're hurting my shoulder."

"Sorry, I don't want to hurt you," she whispered, and began to rub Linda's shoulders with a lighter touch. Slowly she removed her right hand to slide the knife from under the napkin and hold it low at her side. She leaned over and kissed the top of Linda's head and drew in the scent of clean hair, mingling with the incense that Linda often burned during her rituals. It was intoxicating to Connie.

As she rubbed one shoulder with her left hand, she could feel Linda begin to shake from fear. Connie bent down to whisper, "Relax." Standing upright again, she slid her left hand down to Linda's breast and said, "I'm going to miss you."

Linda felt the hand tighten around her breast and looked up to see the descending blade.

Chapter 29

Wilson sped over the familiar route to the O'Brien house. He looked at his watch again and wondered why he didn't see any of his team waiting outside. 4:32. He had to wait for oncoming traffic to pass before he turned into the driveway. In his rearview mirror he saw a patrol car several blocks behind him coming his way. He went to the door and saw someone coming toward him. Connie moved a curtain aside and smiled at him. Wilson heard her say she had to get the keys, and she disappeared.

Suddenly the door opened and she beamed at him. "Well, Wilson this is a surprise. Do come in."

"Connie, I have a search warrant." He saw the stunned look on her face. "I have several more people right behind me. Right now, I need you to sit on the sofa and stay there." He stepped inside the doorway as Connie moved back to let him in. She turned and quickly moved to pick up her purse on the coffee table. Wilson started to object, but he was distracted when heard a car door shut. He looked back to see Dianne coming around the front of her car.

Turning his attention back inside, he took several steps further into the room. He saw Linda in a chair at the dining room table. The same table he and Dianne had eaten at on several occasions. Linda's head was tilted back, a knife protruded from her heart.

A movement glimpsed from the corner of his eye had him turning, reaching for his Glock. Too late. Connie was standing at the end of the sofa with a small-caliber pistol pointed at him.

"Sorry, Wilson, you came too soon." She pulled the trigger.

Chapter 30

Dianne heard the shot. She unholstered her Glock as she ran to the door and flung it open to see Wilson fall to the floor. Connie stood there, too, and watched him go down. It was only with her peripheral vision that Dianne could see Linda over at the table. Connie raised her pistol a second time, but Dianne's reactions were fueled by fear and anger. She raised her Glock, firing one shot.

The bullet's impact snapped Connie's head back and she fell, knocking over the coffee table on her way to the floor. Her purse had been open on the table, and when it fell, the purse went with it, spilling its contents. Nearly a hundred carats of flawless diamonds danced from their black velvet bag to come to rest near Connie's head. Her empty eyes were aimed at the ceiling, separated by a small hole between the eyebrows.

Dianne rushed to turn Wilson over. She keyed her lapel radio and screamed, "Officer down! Officer down! Need medical help now!" She was barely conscious of the answering squawks coming from her radio; she never heard the screech of tires as the other detectives pulled in, nor did she hear the grandfather clock strike 5 o'clock.

A growing dark red spot stained Wilson's shirt on the left shoulder. She ripped it open and saw a small entry hole two inches below his collarbone. She removed her clean handkerchief from her pocket and applied it to the seeping wound, then leaned on it to stop or, at least, slow the bleeding. She closed her eyes and realized she was chanting over and over, *Please, God. Please, God. Please, God.*

Dianne heard voices and looked up to see Sarah, Al and two uniformed officers rush in. Looking at her unconscious husband, she told him, "Come on, baby, hang in there. Help's on the way." Blood oozed between her fingers. He hands shook as she pressed harder. She suddenly realized that Sarah was kneeling beside her.

"What happened?" Sarah's voice trembled.

"Wilson walked in to that," she nodded toward Linda's body, "and Connie shot him. I was twenty steps behind him and when she raised the gun at me, I shot her." Dianne hung her head, trying not to cry. *Please, God. Please, God. Please, God.*

Sarah gently squeezed her shoulder. "Was there only one shot?"

"Yes, I saw him go in as I got out of the car. I heard only the one shot when I was halfway up the walk." Dianne rocked a little back and forth. "Where's Rescue?" She looked around.

"I hear them coming, they're almost here."

Newman and the uniform made a quick search to clear the house. The Advanced Life Support wagon screeched to a stop and killed its siren, and Lt. Simmons led the run to the house. He barked orders on the move "Get your vehicles out of the drive–now!" Two uniforms ran to do his bidding. The street was a mess; the call of an officer down had attracted half the law enforcement vehicles in the county. Traffic was backing up for blocks in both directions.

Sarah got out of the EMTs' way and walked to the front door, where she saw that the traffic jam was going to slow down the Fire/Rescue units when they left. She ran to the street and told some of the younger, nervous officers to clear a path for the ALS unit. As she turned to the house, Sarah saw two Nassau County Sheriff cars stop at the roadside and a Florida Highway Patrol join in.

Sarah watched as the EMTs worked on Wilson. She looked at her watch: 5:17, but she had no idea why the time was suddenly so important to her.

Chapter 31

4:52 p.m. - Holly Williamson set a cup of cold coffee down at her work station in the Emergency Room of Baptist Medical Center on Lime Street. The evening shift had been at it for two hours, treating an overdose of childhood maladies: bad sprains from skateboard accidents, broken arms from falling out of trees, a busted lip caused by a spirited soccer game. And these were just the new cases; they already had one suspected heart attack, a construction worker with a severe gash on his head delivered by a falling concrete block, a mother-to-be who couldn't speak English very well, but managed to convey that she was in some sort of prenatal distress, and at last, a baby running a high fever who needed a good scrubbing to remove the dirt from its body.

Holly was ER Charge Nurse on the 7-to-7 PM shift, and she fervently hoped that the evening would go better than last night. She gave a sigh of relief when she checked the triage list and peeked into the waiting room. Only three patients were there; it was their many family members who were in attendance that made the place look like Grand Central Station.

As soon as Holly opened the door, one woman gave a quick jerk of her head and loudly demanded, "How much longer do we got to wait? My daughter an' I been here twenty minutes already."

"Your name?" Holly smiled, but experience told her that manners weren't this woman's long suit.

"Leonard."

"I'll check and have someone get back to you." She let the door close, but not before she heard the woman's shrill complaint. She returned to the triage list again and found the entry, Leonard—possible sprain of left wrist. "Fine. That's all we need now," she mumbled to no one in particular, and then said, "Paulette, go tell Mrs. Leonard that it could be about another half hour but we'll try to get her darling in here earlier."

The nurse's aide laughed and said, "You chicken?"

"I've already had the honor." Holly went to her station and sipped her cold coffee.

5:00 p.m. — In the Fernandina Beach Fire Rescue Station on 14th Street, the unwatched television news was starting. Three of the men sat around a table discussing the relative merits of the Jacksonville Jaguars' new quarterback, while another firefighter studied lessons for an upcoming test. Other team members were scattered throughout the building, ready for when the alarm sounded.

5: 02 p.m. -- In the Emergency Room, Holly stopped by Betty Cannon, who sat at the ER secretary's desk, to check on the status of several patients. Though referred to as a secretary, Betty filled a more important job of monitoring all telemetry in the ER. A tone came over the Fire/Rescue radio speaker. Betty paled as she wrote down the information. Holly heard the dispatcher's message: "Police officer down on South Fletcher. Gunshot wound to the chest. ALS unit 101 dispatched at five oh two."

"Damn. Where's Dr. Burgess?" Holly looked at the ER cubicles.

At the Fire Station, Lt. Randy Simmons, an eighteen-year veteran with Fire/Rescue, sat in a comfortable lounge chair, reading the new issue of *Sports Illustrated*. The tones came over the station speaker system followed by instructions from a calm female voice. "Rescue 101, police officer down, gunshot victim at 4078 South Fletcher."

5:03 p.m. -- The years of training immediately kicked in and the crew of Station 101 moved to action. Forty-one seconds after the call came in, Fire/Rescue was rolling with siren and claxon sending the sparrows outside the station into frantic flight. Both the fire truck and Advanced Life Support vehicle raced south on 14th Street.

As he made the turn onto Sadler, the ALS unit's driver, Richard Guest, reflected that one of the more dangerous phases of Fire/Rescue calls is the trip to the scene. Motorists swerve in all directions to make room for the huge, loud trucks coming their way. And about once a week, someone makes a turn in front of the speeding ALS.

Guest shook his head as civilian vehicles moved erratically to get out of his way. The urgency of this call was compounded by the fact that the Fire/Rescue crews take special interest when a police officer or rescue personnel are injured.

Adrenalin immediately began to work on Holly. She raced to find the ER doctor in a cubicle with the mother-to-be. "We have a Code Blue coming in. Gunshot in left upper chest. It's a police officer."

Dr. Patricia Burgess gave the very pregnant lady a pat on the arm and left the cubicle. "What do we have so far?" She took the note pad from the secretary at the desk. "Okay, call the Code." She turned to Holly. "Get the room ready."

Holly fired orders to her nurses, sending them running to make sure the trauma room was ready for the wounded officer. She followed them into the room just left of the two large double doors of the Ambulance Entrance Only sign.

Dr. Burgess stood at the door leading to the outside, waiting for Rescue 101 to arrive before she went to check the trauma room herself. She knew this ER staff was on top of the situation and would be ready. At the call of the code, nurses came running from other areas of the hospital.

5:05 p.m. — Lt. Simmons sat in the front of the Rescue 101 truck and made the radio call for TraumaOne's helicopter to be on standby. The Shands Hospital-based helicopter could be here in twelve minutes. Unit 101 slowed as it approached the traffic light at Courson Street. A tractor-trailer rig had turned onto Courson Street and stopped, blocking the southbound lanes of 14th Street. 101's driver moved over into the oncoming traffic lane and went around the obstacle with siren blaring. Guest thought this was a setup for an accident to happen, but fortune fell in their favor and they sped on southward.

Lt. Simmons heard a jumble of radio traffic on the police channel. Up ahead at the intersection of 14th and Sadler Road, a police car had all traffic stopped, for which Guest silently thanked him. This allowed 101 to make a fast turn onto Sadler and head east toward the beach road. Simmons was making a call to the Baptist Nassau Hospital Emergency Room as they cleared the roundabout and headed south for the 4000 block of South Fletcher.

5:10 p.m. -- Simmons called the police dispatcher. "HQ, Rescue 101, is it safe to enter the scene?"

"Roger, there are no other threats." Suddenly, Simmons saw the flashing lights about a mile ahead. Guest followed the directions of the Fernandina Beach police officer at the scene.

5:13 p.m. -- The paramedics ran into the house and saw a uniform kneeling over a man lying in the foyer. "He's been shot in the chest and there's bubbling coming from the wound." The uniform was Dianne and her voice shook.

"Yes, ma'am. Let's have a look." The paramedic eased her back as he put the stethoscope around his neck; his partner opened the medical case and started placing monitor pads on Wilson. "How long has he been like this?"

Dianne looked puzzled. He explained, "I mean, how long has he been unconscious?"

"About fifteen minutes. I was right behind him when he was shot and fell down here. He was unconscious then. I immediately called in to HQ." She stood and hugged herself as if she were cold. *Please, God. Please, God. Please, God.*

Simmons looked over at Connie O'Brien, lying nearby, then at the body at the dining room table. Dianne shivered. "Don't worry about them. They're both dead."

She nodded toward Connie's body. "She's the one who shot him, then I got her." Her voice was tinged with ice.

The scene grew more chaotic, with three uniforms in the living room, their radios competing with each other. No one had secured the crime scene yet, but two officers were outside, keeping the neighbors at bay. Someone called Chief Evans and told him that Wilson would be transported as soon as he was stable enough to move.

5:14 p.m. -- The paramedics rolled Wilson over to check for an exit wound in his back. They found none, then called Baptist Nassau Medical Center.

"Officer down with gunshot in left upper quadrant of shoulder. BP, 105 over 65. Heart rate, 38. Pulse irregular. We're getting a twelve-lead hook-up." They were nearly finished hooking up the monitor pads.

Lt. Simmons touched Dianne on the elbow. "Ma'am, do you know about the officer's medical history?"

"Most of it; I'm his wife."

Simmons sucked in air through his teeth at that bit of news. "Okay, let's go over here for a moment so I can get some information from you, so we can take care of your husband."

Dianne followed him but didn't take her eyes off her husband, still sprawled on the foyer floor. Simmons asked about Wilson's medications, allergic reactions and any conditions that might be affected by medications. It was all surreal to her. She'd been sent to a traffic accident where people horrendous injuries, but she had been able to detach herself from the injured. Here, her emotions were at the forefront. The answers to Simmons' questions seemed to come from someone else.

5:18 p.m. — "What do you think?" Fear made Dianne blunt.

"Ma'am?" Simmons was taken aback for a second.

"Is he going to make it?"

The lieutenant was cautious with his answer; it was still early. "He looks to be in good health, and I don't want to give you false hope, but initially, I'd say he'll get through it."

They watched a paramedic insert a needle into Wilson's arm and tape down the tube, sending a saline drip into him. Another paramedic slid the needle containing epinephrine into the IV branch and pushed the plunger. The first paramedic unwrapped a vent tube and inserted it into Wilson's mouth so the airway would not be obstructed. His chest began to move a little easier with each breath. The oxygen was hooked up and one of the team started to squeeze the bag in a steady rhythm to assist his breathing.

5:21 p.m. -- Lt. Simmons knelt beside the radio, calling the 911 dispatcher to send the ATU, TraumaOne's Air Transport Unit. The reply was one he didn't want to hear.

"The ATU will be there in twenty-five minutes. They are on the way to Shands and will restock, then be out."

"Roger. Pickup will be at the hospital helo pad."

Simmons passed on the word to the team, and then went back to Dianne. The room was quiet as the paramedics continued to stabilize Wilson. A uniform ventured in to tell Simmons that they had called for Oxley-Heard Funeral Home to pick up the bodies of Mrs. O'Brien and the domestic worker and keep them for the Medical Examiner.

5:25 p.m. — He's stabilized now," a paramedic said to Dianne. "We're going to send him to Shands Jacksonville. You can ride with us in the ambulance over to the hospital if you want. We're about to pull out now."

Dianne nodded and watched Wilson as they slid a backboard under him. They looped nylon straps over him to restrict his movements, before moving him to the gurney. The team moved in a carefully choreographed ballet, one they'd clearly performed many times. She could hear them talking, but their words were a blur. Simmons took her by the elbow and walked outside with her, noting that she was pale.

5:28 p.m. — Dianne sat in the ambulance front seat next to the driver; the paramedics and Simmons were in the back with her husband. The ALS raced over familiar streets with flashing lights and blaring sirens. They laid small sandbags on the right side of Wilson's chest to ease the stress on that lung.

5:29 p.m. — The call came in on the Telemetry Station's radio. "Baptist Nassau, Rescue 101."

"Baptist Nassau, go ahead."

"We're inbound with the wounded officer... Seven minutes out. Male. Age thirty-three. Wound in upper left chest. No exit hole visible. Twelve-lead hook-up. Pressure dressing applied to wound. Stabilized patient with one amp of epinephrine, will administer another in two minutes. Junctional rhythm, BP 85 over 45, pulse thready at 110. Two IV's in place with saline drip. Intubated. No sound from left lung, suspect collapse. Spouse on board. Over."

"Roger, we're ready to receive."

5:35 p.m. -- The ambulance entrance pneumatic doors

rushed open. Three paramedics pushed the gurney into the hospital and made a left turn into the trauma room. With Simmons at her side, Dianne hurried inside, her husband's blood still on her hands.

Other hands came to move Wilson's unconscious body from the ALS gurney to the hospital gurney. "One, two, three lift."

Many voices came alive at once, but the sounds and movements reflected hours of study and practice.

"One amp of epi given…two minutes ago," came from a paramedic.

The staff transferred hook-ups from the ALS unit's equipment to the hospital's monitors. The doctor's stethoscope funneled Wilson's chest sounds to her ears. His ruined shirt had disappeared, and would never be seen again.

5:37 p.m. — "Nothing from the left lung. X-ray, stat." Dr. Burgess moved to Wilson's other side. The X-ray technician rolled her machine into place. They all stood back and heard the buzz of the image being taken. Within seconds the technician was on her way to the Radiology Department. Burgess glanced at the two IVs on each arm and saw that they were placed properly. She continued her rapid exam of the man, moving methodically down his body. Holly helped the doctor roll Wilson over, first to his right and then to his left side, looking for an exit wound. They saw none. The doctor palpated Wilson's lower abdomen for swelling. "Okay; so far, we're lucky that there doesn't seem to be any blood pooling. Let's hope the lung's not full. Cut the rest of his clothes off."

Monitors continued to record and beep while the ER team removed Wilson's clothes. "BP 85 over 45, oxygen at 96, heart rate 60, rhythm still junctional."

The doctor looked at Dianne, "What's his weight?"

"About two hundred pounds."

"Ninety-five kilos.   Hang Dopamine, five mics per."
Burgess took his wrist and felt his pulse. Nurses moved to
hang the bag of drugs to raise his blood pressure and to
stabilize his heart rhythm. Dianne leaned against the wall,
her legs barely able to keep her up. She knew enough to stay
out of the way. A nurse looked over and gave her a reassuring
smile.

5:38 p.m. — Dianne felt, rather than saw, Chief Evans
standing next to her. Unable to maintain her composure any
longer, she fell against him, sobbing. He enveloped her with
his big, muscular arms. She'd never been so glad to see anyone
in her whole life. The last forty minutes had put her life onto
a rollercoaster speeding from adrenaline overdose to
numbness and back.

"He'll be okay. He's young and healthy, and these people
are great." The Chief got a glance from Dr. Burgess, who
gave a little nod to tell him to take Dianne out of the room.
"Listen Dianne, we're sorta in the way, let's step outside.
Jacqueline will be here in a second."

5:39 p.m. — Following her boss out the door, Dianne
stepped aside as the technician returned to shoot more X-
rays. She could only hear a mixture of voices and couldn't
tell who was talking, inside or outside of the trauma room.
She wiped tears away. *Get hold of yourself; he needs you to
be strong now.*

The hospital parking lot was filling up quickly with blue
lights and officers moving in and out of the ER, unnecessarily
adding to the traffic congestion. An officer led Jacqueline
Evans over to where her husband and Dianne stood. The Fire/
Rescue 101 team returned to their truck. Civilians began
milling around the rescue truck, asking questions about what
happened.

5:41 p.m. — Detective Sarah Grant's quick strides
brought her to the chief; her face wore a questioning look.

Evans frowned slightly and shook his head. He gave a small shrug and Sarah took his place beside Dianne. She and Jacqueline held Dianne's hands and tried to comfort her.

"Reynolds," Chief Evans called to a patrolman, "get everyone out of here and back on the street. We'll keep them informed. Do it now. I don't want to see anything but your car out in that lot." Evans was trying not to raise his voice. "When you get rid of them, come back here and stand guard at this door. Don't let any curiosity seekers in."

He nodded toward the gawkers on the other side of the glass doors. "And get those people out of here, Rescue can't even move."

Reynolds spun on his heels, and in short order police cars began driving out of the parking lot. Evans looked out the large doors to the ambulance bay to see the dissipating crowd that had spilled out of the waiting room.

Dianne was suddenly aware of the relative quiet in the room. Only muffled voices came from the ER room where no unnecessary words were spoken; only information and orders were relayed. Betty whispered something in Evans' ear and he took Dianne's arm, gently suggesting that they go to the Family Consolation Room, "...just around the corner."

5:43 p.m. — "Keep the bag in him until we get the I.T. in. Keep an eye on the numbers," Dr. Burgess spoke softly.

"BP 80 over 40, rate 68." Nurses gave reports of information they were receiving from the monitors.

"O_2 is 95."

5:44 p.m. – "75 over 40."

"Increase Dopamine 20 mics."

The X-ray technician shoved the film up on the lightbox, then moved to the side. She had more film at the ready.

The doctor took a quick look at the X-ray and paused, then said, "Damn, where's the bullet? Holly, step over here and see if you can find it."

Holly stepped close to the X-ray. "Here it is, Doctor."

Burgess squinted at the image. "Okay, I see it. It must have ricocheted off the clavicle, then stopped in the lung. Thanks"

The doctor swabbed a spot between ribs five and six, then quickly made a small incision. She raised the flesh away from the ribs using a curved clamp and inserted into the chest cavity a hard plastic tube, slightly larger than a pencil. It was attached to a flexible tube that ran into a liter bag to catch any fluids that might have built up in the lung. As the tube pushed through the chest wall there was a sudden *whoosh* of air, accompanied by a fine spray of blood. Only a small trickle of blood made its way into the bag. The doctor looked at the amount. "Good, not enough to worry about now."

5:46 p.m. — As the doctor stopped to look at the monitor, she asked; "Was that woman his wife? The police officer?"

"Yes, I think so," said a voice from the back of the room.

"How'd she get the blood on her?"

Someone else volunteered, "I heard her tell the police chief she got to her husband about fifteen seconds after the gunshot dropped him. She's one cool lady. She fired the shot that killed the shooter as the gun was turned on her, and then administered first aid to her husband. She held that chest wound closed and called for help on her radio."

5:47 p.m. – Dr. Burgess kept her voice quiet. "BP and heart rate are acceptable now. Betty, TraumaOne helo is coming here, right?" The telemetry technician/secretary nodded an affirmative. The doctor continued without missing a beat, "Where's the shooter?"

"A paramedic said she was DOA, and there's another DOA at the scene."

"I think Lt. Wilson's stable for now. Let's hope so." Dr. Burgess took a deep breath and let it out slowly. She looked at the many bags hanging from the end of the gurney, then nodded to a nurse. "Go see if we can get a history from his wife. I know ALS got one, but see if we can add to it." She looked at another nurse and asked, "Did you draw blood for type and cross?" The other woman nodded. "I didn't even see you do that, thanks," the doctor said. "Call the bank and get four units O-positive up here for standby."

5:50 p.m. — Everyone paused for a deep breath. Short beeps from the monitors and a quiet hiss from the respirator were the only sounds. The staff looked at each other and waited for the TraumaOne helo.

5:54 p.m. – Dr. Burgess stepped away from the table and motioned for the X-ray technician to shoot another film. Once that was done the technician raced to process it. "He should be stable enough now to get him on the helo. It should be here in a few minutes," she said to the room full of people.

"BP 80 over 45. O_2 is 98. Rhythm…stabilizing also."

5:56 p.m. — The breathless X-ray tech returned with yet another set of images. All eyes looked up at the lightbox. "He's a good looking guy," said Dr. Burgess. She looked at the secretary who stood guard at the door. "Tell the missus that we're about to send him to Shands and that she needs to get a ride down to Jacksonville."

In the Family Room, Jacqueline Evans and Sarah Grant sat on either side of Dianne, who had been staring at the blank wall in front of her for several minutes. Sarah bit her lip to keep from crying. The secretary came in and knelt in front of Dianne. "I hate to do this now, but we need some more medical history."

"That's okay."

Dianne calmly answered all her questions and when she was done, the secretary said, "We're going to transport him to Shands when the helicopter gets here. We'll come and get you before he leaves. Right now he's stable and doing very well. To help him breathe and so he won't expend energy breathing, we've sedated him, only until he's able to breathe better on his own. Don't worry; it's a normal procedure. Dr. Burgess is doing all she can and she won't let him out of here if there is any danger of things getting worse."

Dianne wiped away a tear. "Thank you."

6:02 p.m. — She turned to the chief and said, "You know, I left my car down at the O'Briens' and I've got to get the girls, somehow and then his mother will want to be there. Oh God, this is the first time I've even thought of her."

"We'll get your car. Sarah will get the girls and Mrs. Wilson. Where are they?"

"The children are at our house. I called a neighbor before I left and she came over."

Sarah stood and Dianne took her hand. "Sarah, just tell them that their daddy's been in an accident and has to go to the hospital in Jacksonville. Be careful with Mrs. Wilson, she had a stroke a few years ago and we can't afford to get her too upset. What the hell am I saying? What's more upsetting than having your son shot?"

Chief Evans crouched in front of Dianne. "Listen, Wilson is going to be okay. You let us take care of the small things and you concentrate on being where he needs you. We'll take care of all the logistical stuff. Jacqueline will drive you down to Shands. I'll be along about ten minutes later. Okay?"

She gave a quick sob, nodded, leaned forward and hugged Evans. "Okay."

6:05 p.m. – Dr. Burgess looked at the monitor and the X-ray images on the panel, while she listened for the helicopter's approach. A technician from the blood lab came through the door and a nurse immediately hooked a bag to a waiting IV line.

"Get me Shands."

A nurse dialed the Trauma Center at Shands Hospital in Jacksonville and Dr. Burgess relayed what they had. She read the monitors and gave them the latest information about the patient. "I hear the helo landing now; be good to him, he's a cop here on the island."

"Sinus rhythm. 75 over 45. O_2 back at 100."

6:07 p.m. – The medical crew from the helicopter burst through the doors into the Trauma Room. Several nurses left to give the helicopter team room to work.

Dr. Burgess recognized the nurse and paramedic, since she worked at Shands on her days off from the local hospital. "He's stabilizing now."

The T-1 crew began their own evaluation of the patient's condition. They were unsnapping the hospital's monitor leads as they put theirs in place. They had their own portable system under the gurney they brought in with them. Whatever the hospital had, the helicopter carried a portable version of it. They switched over the oxygen feed line. The doctor told them what occurred since Wilson's arrival and stood back as they checked their monitors. An assistant brought an envelope containing the records of this case, and laid it across Wilson's thighs.

6:11 p.m. — "Okay, I want to wait another five minutes, just to be sure. We don't want a patient to crash en route." The nurse's name tag read *Kathleen*; she looked down at Wilson. "What happened?"

"He's a police officer and a suspect shot him while he was trying to arrest her."

"And the suspect?"

"Dead. His wife is also a police officer and was only a few steps behind him when he went down. She killed the suspect, with one shot."

"Go, girl." Kathleen grinned.

"We'll be ready in a few minutes," Kathleen's partner, Brad, announced.

6:13 p.m. – Charles and Jacqueline Evans escorted

Dianne to the Trauma Room, but stopped at the door as she went in. She put her hands to her mouth as she saw her husband draped with a sheet.

"We had to cut his clothes off. We'll get everything to you." Dr. Burgess put her hand at Dianne's elbow. "He's a tough guy."

Dianne tried to say something, but nothing came out. She took Wilson's left hand and held it against her cheek. Silent tears rolled off her cheek and fell on his arm. *Please, God, Please.*

"It's time. He's stable enough now." Kathleen went to the head of their gurney. All their portable life-sustaining equipment was on the platform under Wilson.

Dianne gently laid his arm down and kissed him on the forehead. "I'll be nearby, sweetheart."

"Go on ahead with your ride, ma'am." Dr. Burgess stood beside her. "He'll be there before you, but we'll tell them you're on your way; they'll take care of you." The doctor gave her a hug and said, "Don't worry, he'll be fine."

6:18 p.m. -- Jacqueline took Dianne's arm and led her to the car. Evans leaned over and gave his wife a quick kiss; his admonition to drive carefully was nearly drowned out by the *whomp, whomp, whomp* of the helicopter lifting off.

Chapter 32

6:18 p.m. — As soon as the helicopter gained enough altitude, the pilot pushed the cyclic forward and the rotor blades propelled the TraumaOne craft in a straight line toward Shands and its landing pad on top of the parking garage. The pilot, a Viet Nam veteran, called Jacksonville Tower to let them know he was airborne and flying to Shands at one thousand feet. The paramedic and nurse in the rear monitored Wilson all the way. The Shands Trauma Center was notified of the inbound flight and was ready to receive the patient.

Chief Evans had detailed Officer Reynolds to escort his wife and Dianne to the hospital in Jacksonville; the blue light run was going to take about forty minutes. Evans had dispatch call Shands, alerting them that the patient's wife was on her way to the center.

6:30 p.m. — Twelve minutes after lifting off from Baptist Nassau Hospital, the pilot gently set the copter down on the pad. Brad threw open the clamshell doors. Kathleen and Brad rolled the gurney out and headed for the elevator at a dead run. The Trauma Center was seven floors down. The center's crew made way for Wilson's unconscious body as it was wheeled into an examination room. Here the process reversed itself; the hospital's life support equipment was connected as the helicopter team's equipment was disconnected

6:38 p.m. — In the Trauma Center, the surgeon made a quick evaluation and ordered a CT scan. He reviewed Wilson's history and gave the nurses orders for medications. He flipped the X-rays onto the lightbox. As soon as the CT scan came in, he'd order Wilson to surgery.

6:56 p.m. — Jacqueline stopped the car in front of the *Emergency Room Parking Only* sign. Dianne threw open the door and stepped out; she never heard Jacqueline tell her that she was going to park the car. A nurse recognized her the moment she stepped inside. After pinning a badge on her, the nurse led her to a special waiting room. "We'll have someone in here in a moment to help you. Is there anyone else coming?"

"Our daughters and his mother," Dianne said. "Oh, the lady that drove me here, the police chief's wife."

"Okay, we'll get them back here as soon as they come in." A blonde woman in her early forties entered the room and sat down next to Dianne. The nurse said, "I have to go now, but I'll be back periodically to update you. And before we take him to surgery, we'll come get you so you can see him."

Dianne whispered her thanks. She was too frightened to say much more.

7:03 p.m. — Leaning over, Dianne put her elbows on her knees and her face in her hands.

"Mrs. Wilson," the blonde woman began, "I'm Beverly Williams and if you want anything, you ask and I'll get it for you."

Dianne looked straight ahead and was surprised that some of her senses were coming back when she smelled the light perfume that Beverly wore. "Thank you. I'm worried now about his mother and the girls. This is going to be so hard for them."

"Like I said, if there is anything we can do…"

"His mother had a stroke about five years ago and we'll

need to watch her." Dianne looked up as Jacqueline came in. She sat down and laid a comforting hand on Dianne's shoulder.

"Mrs. Wilson, should we have a nurse in here when his mother arrives?"

For the first time Dianne looked at the woman here to help her. "Yes, that's kind of you. Thank you."

Beverly went out for a moment to let the floor nurses know. Then they sat in a silence interrupted only by calls over the P.A. system.

7:15 p.m. — Dianne looked up at the sound of footsteps. Michelle and Lisa ran into her arms and they all hugged fiercely. Sarah followed them in with Wilson's mother holding her arm.

"What's happened to Daddy?" Lisa said through her sobs. Mrs. Wilson hugged Dianne, who explained that their guy was going to be fine; he'd been shot, but they were taking him to surgery real soon to fix him up. His mother fell back against the cushion and let out a small cry of relief mixed with anguish. Both girls began to cry harder. Beverly stood and closed the door.

"Listen, girls, we all have to be brave for Daddy." Dianne held them close.

"Mrs. Wilson." The nurse had returned. "He's going to surgery in about two minutes. You can come back until they take him."

Dianne followed the nurse through the large double doors.

7:18 p.m. — Wilson was on yet another hospital gurney, now draped in green sheets. Dianne took his hand and was dismayed to discover it was limp. She looked at him closely, looking for the vibrancy that so characterized him. The doctor quickly explained the surgical procedure and urged her to try to rest over the coming hours. "At best, it will take two hours." Looking at Wilson, he added, "He's strong; I don't expect any problems."

Dianne nodded, still numb from the trauma that had descended on her. She leaned over and whispered in Wilson's ear. "You're going to make it, darling. I know it. You're a strong man and we'll be here when you wake up. Besides, Horace Leitrim Wilson, we're going to have a son." Her lips gently brushed his cheek.

"Mrs. Wilson, it's time." She relaxed her hand and felt a quick squeeze from Wilson. She held onto him as far as the operating area, where they stopped and she laid his hand down.

7:20 p.m. — In the waiting room, tear-stained faces greeted her, searching for an answer. "He's in surgery, and they'll let us know when he's out." She sat down. Michelle came over, put her arms around her neck and sat in her lap.

"Mommy, don't let him die." Michelle held tightly onto her.

"Baby, he's not going to die. They are doing everything they can to make him well. They just want to see inside him and fix anything wrong. He'll be okay." *Please, God. Please, God. Please, God.*

Chapter 33

S ix weeks later, Dianne sat in a chair in the bedroom and looked at all of the clothing spread out on the bed. Volunteers from St. Michael's Catholic Church had stopped by with boxes, and several of them offered to help with the project that faced her. She had thanked them and said she wanted to do it.

She could hear the girls in the living room watching television with the volume turned down. She took a moment to remember all the wonderful times she had with the person whose clothes were going to the Barnabas Center.

Now that she was pregnant, she wanted to take it a little easier, so she sat for several moments longer. Tears blurred her vision.

Dianne didn't hear the footsteps come near, but felt a hand on her shoulder. She looked up and said, "You try not to think that this day will come, but you know it will. The shock of your being shot was too much for your mother, I think. She was on a downhill slide since then." She laid her head on her husband's hand.

"I think so, too." Wilson knelt at her feet, looked into her eyes and whispered, "Let's go make a nice pot of decaf coffee; we can always do this later."

They walked arm in arm toward the kitchen. She smiled and said, "It was awfully nice of Shorty to come to the funeral. I wouldn't have guessed he even owned a tie."